Devastation

A Beastly Tale
Part 3

M.J. Haag

D1707720

Devastation
Copyright: Melissa Haag
Published: August 25, 2015
ISBN: 978-1-515064-15-2
Cover Design: Melissa Haag

One

The tattered remnants of the world I'd held so dear drifted from my mind. Anger and hate clouded my thoughts.

I shook fiercely but refused to give in to the tears that so desperately wanted release. My stomach cramped from the recent abuse and the restraint to contain myself, and my face ached from the blows Tennen and the baker had delivered. Yet, the pain did not distract from the lingering feel of that grotesque, vile man as the carriage rumbled toward the Water. My skin crawled, and my lungs refused to work properly.

I remained so lost in the violent experience that I barely noticed when the carriage pulled up before my father's house.

The driver hopped down from his perch and offered a hand to help me down. I needed the help. The shaking in my legs had only grown worse.

Once I was on my feet, the driver turned to Father's home and knocked on the door. Trembling in Mrs. Medunge's cloak and my nightgown, I stood behind the man.

Father opened the door, took one look at me, and ushered me in.

"Benella, what's happened?" he said, wrapping an arm around me to steady me.

I could only shake my head. He tried quizzing the driver, but the man bowed and said to expect to hear from his master soon.

That penetrated my clouded mind. My stomach dropped. The returned Lord of the estate. The image of him standing so calmly burned my eyes; still, no moisture gathered.

As soon as the door closed, Father led me to a chair then quickly left to pull water from the well. When he returned, he dipped a cloth into the pail, wrung it out, and held it to my cheek. I flinched from the pain and the reminder of what had happened.

"I'll fetch the physician," he said, already turning away.

"No." I caught his hand to stop him.

I wasn't hurt so badly that I could justify what a physician would cost. I would recover. Yet, as Father faced me with concern, I knew he would insist unless I explained my abused appearance.

I averted my gaze as words spilled forth.

"I interrupted an attempted thievery at the beast's estate," I said, staring at the table. "The beast was...elsewhere. The thief carried me to the baker. The baker attempted to rape me. His grotesque belly saved me," I said in a broken whisper. "I'm shaken and bruised. Nothing that won't heal."

"Oh, my girl." Father knelt beside me and wrapped me in his arms. His compassion almost released the tears I struggled to withhold.

"I don't want to go back," I said in a tight, pained voice. "They all play cruel games. I thought Aryana a friend, but she's the enchantress who has held the beast this whole time. They were both there at the baker's." I lifted my head and met my father's agonized gaze. "Their presence stopped the baker, but they otherwise stood by indifferently."

"I'm so sorry, Bini," my father whispered with tears in his eyes. "I wish I knew how to fix this."

I knew he meant more than the attack I'd suffered. He pulled me back into a comforting hug, trying to protect me as he had from Tennen's bullying when he'd moved us to the Water. Yet, instead of Father making the sacrifice he'd intended, I'd been tricked into staying with the beast who I had thought would protect me as zealously as he'd protected his estate. Sadly, I had wrongly assumed his level of affection for me. The ache in my chest continued to grow, but for Father's sake, I withheld my tears.

Father pulled away and offered me the use of his room, along with some of his clothes. After I dressed, I sat on his bed with my elbows on my knees and stared at my folded hands.

All the advice Aryana had given or not given made more sense. She'd used me in her game with the beast. As Rose, she'd tried to dissuade me, thus steeling my determination to help. As Aryana, she'd given me the knowledge I'd needed to navigate a world I'd not understood. I recalled all the times she had said she worried about me. She had been sincere; I didn't doubt it. Yet, it hadn't been enough to stop her game.

Finally, tears fell hard and fast. With a muffled sob, I curled up on my father's bed. I cried until I felt empty and numb. Then I just lay there, remembering not the attack but my last days with the beast and his caring attentiveness. It made the pain I already bore twist bitterly. How could I miss someone who so easily watched my abuse and just as easily sent me away?

A knock sounded at the cottage door more than an hour later, jarring me from my thoughts. I recalled the driver's promise, and I felt a stab of pain through my chest. A small part of me wanted Alec to rush through the door. Yet, if he did enter, which Alec would it be? The mercurial beast or the cold lord?

A shiver ran through me a moment before Aryana strode into my father's room without knocking. Though her unannounced appearance shocked me, I didn't sit up or acknowledge her. Instead, I continued to stare at the space the door had once occupied.

My heart continued to break as I realized Alec wouldn't come because there was nothing left to say. Bitterness began to eat the pain. He'd gotten what he'd wanted. His freedom. And by mere seconds, he'd made sure I'd left with the last piece of myself for my husband. I almost snorted. Husband. There would be no husband for me.

"Fifty years ago," Aryana said, pulling me from my musings, "Alec's mother came south looking for a way to help her son. She found me just before she died. Her story and love for her son moved me enough that I gave her my word I would help him become a better man, a man of whom she could be proud.

"When I came to the North, I could not believe the depravity. It was simple to open the Whispering Sisters. We serviced men, and I gained power from their lust. I used that power to shift the balance. I cursed the beast and drove out the dregs he had let in. Those of his servants who had stood by and let their Liege sink lower and lower without attempting to reason with him joined him in his enchantment.

"To give him hope, I set the price of his freedom on one night of pleasure. His earliest attempts fueled me so much that some of the energy seeped into the estate, making it possible for him to control some of the enchantments when I allowed it."

When she allowed it. The phrase struck me cold. She had been the one to control the vines, then. She'd allowed Tennen to take me, even after witnessing his past crimes against me. She'd sacrificed me so the Lord of the North might be free. Whatever friendship I'd thought we'd shared had only existed in my mind. The knowledge hurt me more than Tennen's fist had.

"When I saw you, time and again, bravely walk the mist surrounding the estate and boldly confront the local boys, I knew you were the one to help him." She paused for a moment. "I'm sorry for the lies and all you have suffered to free Alec. Yet, if he had been warned about your danger before dawn broke, he would not be free now."

I could feel her expectant stare but didn't meet her gaze.

After several long moments of silence, she stood. Did she think her story would justify how she'd used me? Anger and disbelief clawed at my insides.

"I'm sure his mother would be pleased with the result," I said in a raw whisper.

She looked down at me for a moment, her expression closed, before sweeping from the room.

Father came to look in on me, but said nothing as I continued to lay there and sort through my thoughts.

When Tennen and Splane had started chasing me, I hadn't hated them. I understood their angry reaction to my knowledge of what their mother had done with the baker. However, I struggled to see any possible explanation to excuse Alec and Rose from my burning resentment. The way she'd gone about trying to help him was a mockery. And, how could he have held me and listened to me read the night before, then make no move to help me when I needed him most?

When my father checked on me a second time, wringing his hands with worry, I decided I'd given those who'd hurt me enough thought. To think of them further would only allow them to harm me more. So I closed off my heart, sealing in the pain, and sat up and gave my father a small, reassuring smile.

"Is there anything to eat?"

He nodded and went to the kitchen to fix us a modest meal.

His attempt, boiled oats that looked more like paste, made me smile. We ate while laughing about it. The laughter didn't touch me inside. I doubted anything would ever again.

* * * *

For the next several days, I stayed indoors, and Father remained my constant companion. When I asked about his teaching, he declared he'd educated the sisters as much as he thought possible for the time being.

I wondered if that meant we would be moving soon. The thought stopped me. Would I be moving with him? I was of an age where I should marry. However, where once I thought marriage something to look forward to, I no longer did. The memory of the baker pinning me to the lounge as he thrust down on me gave me shudders.

For how long could I ask Father to keep me as his dependent? I cringed, thinking of how he'd struggled to provide for his grown daughters so far. Yet, what other options did I have?

I contemplated the possibilities for my future often; there wasn't much else to do with my time.

Father left one morning and came back a short while later with a package. Inside, lay a plain, coarsely spun dress. Nothing fancy, but entirely suitable for leaving the house, unlike my shirt and pants. I knew my seclusion needed to end for his sake; so, I smiled my thanks and went to his room to change.

When I emerged, he offered to walk with me to the market street, but I declined. Content to keep my solitude, I left the house alone.

Memories continued to haunt me and not just of the baker. As much as I'd tried to lock away my thoughts of him, the beast dwelled in my mind. I'd always known he would forget me, but hadn't realized how quickly, and I missed his mercurial presence.

Needing a distraction, I walked to Bryn's new home to see how she fared as a bride. When I stepped in the storefront, I was surprised to see her wearing an apron and assisting customers. She looked tired, though it was still early morning. I moved to the counter to see if she would have time later to talk.

Bryn caught sight of me and marched over.

"Your kind is not welcome here," she said with a malevolent hiss to her words.

A woman next to me gasped and took a step back as if I were in quarantine again.

"My kind?" I asked, puzzled by my sister's hostile attitude.

"Whore," she spat. "We heard what happened in Konrall. How could you refuse the baker's offer after lying with him? Get out." She thrust out a finger, pointing toward the door.

I stared at her, my temper spiked and spiteful. She called me a whore? She had another man's babe growing in her belly. My gaze flicked there, and she paled. Her hand trembled.

"Have care with the titles you bestow me," I said, then turned to leave. Only the babe's future held my tongue. The innocent child she carried need not feel the sting of her parent's misjudgments and cruelties.

Word of the incident quickly followed me home. Father said nothing when I closed myself in his room once more to sit on his bed and consider my fate. I had no skills other than my education; and with my new reputation as a whore, no one respectable would want me teaching their children. The only unrespectable place to teach—the Whispering

Sisters—was out of the question because of Aryana's betrayal. Discounting a teaching post, I reflected on my other skills. I could hunt and fish, but not well enough to make a profit to pay for a home. Enough to eat, though.

I shouldn't have shunned the occupations that my sisters had learned. Skills such as cleaning and cooking would have been useful to gain employment as a maid; yet, the effort I'd put into restoring the beast's estate made my incompetence at those skills painfully obvious. What did my future hold for me now?

After bundling my shirt and pants in a pack, I left the room. Father looked up at me with a slight frown of worry.

"You need to go back to teaching, and I need to figure out what I will do with my life," I said with determination.

He nodded slowly, opened his mouth as if he would say something, and paused.

"What is it?" I asked.

"I want you to be happy," he said with a sigh. "Would returning..." He cleared his throat. "Did he make you happy?" he asked tentatively.

A sad smile curved my lips. He had. While he was the beast.

"He made life interesting, but there was more danger there than I'd realized."

I left through the back door before he could say more.

Skirting around town, I headed south, wandering aimlessly through the woods until I felt I'd hiked far enough from town to set traps. I walked a long circuit twice, gathering as I went.

Time had passed quickly while at the manor, changing the seasons, so the forest provided several herbs and berries that I used in the traps. Three rabbits found their ends in my snares before I returned to an empty house.

Dressing the game brought back memories of my attempts at cooking with the beast. I smiled as I started a fire and brought out a kettle. I set two of the skinny hares in the pot and filled it with water. Then, determined, I wrapped the other and walked to the market street again.

Everywhere I went, I met censuring eyes. No respectable business would trade with me. Giving up, I turned from the market street and walked toward the less respectable trade district, taverns where women served men in several ways.

Houses of those working that area lined the next street over. I approached the door of one that had a small garden. The woman who answered greeted me with a smile when she heard my offer—the hare for two carrots and a small onion. She assuredly received the better part of the deal. When she hugged me in thanks, I saw two small children behind her. Their large eyes followed the game.

Happy that someone had welcomed the trade, I returned home and added the carrots and onion to the stew and left it to simmer. When the carrots were tender, I placed a portion in a much smaller kettle with a lid and walked to the seamstress where Blye worked. Living in a tiny room above the shop, I couldn't imagine she ate well.

A bell tinkled above my head when I opened the door. Blye knelt at the feet of a woman, pinning the woman's hem. When Blye looked up and saw me, her polite expression closed. She murmured to the woman, begging for a moment, before she stood and strode toward me.

"You can't come in here," she whispered. With a firm hold on my elbow, she turned me around.

"I just wanted to bring you some stew," I said as I offered the little kettle.

Her eyes shifted to the woman who watched us with disapproval.

"I can't accept anything from you. Just go, Benella," she said in a low, urgent tone. "Associating with you will ruin everything for me."

Disbelief coursed through me. I turned stiffly and walked out, hiding how her words hurt me. The lure of accomplishment and status had robbed my sisters of basic kindness.

My feet carried me to the houses close to where I'd traded for the vegetables. A thin child played in the dirt outside one of the homes. Inside I could hear moaning and knew her mother's work. I waved the child over and offered her the food. She nodded eagerly. Since there was no spoon, I wiped her dirty hands on my skirt and watched her use her fingers. After she finished, I showed her how to write her name in the dirt. She smiled brightly as I left her practicing.

I watched the faces of the people I passed and realized something. The pursuit of success and respectability hadn't just led my sisters astray, but many others as well. It shouldn't be that way.

* * * *

While I fetched water from the well out back that evening, a knock sounded at the door. I didn't move to see who it was. No one I knew wanted to speak to me, besides my father. Inside, I heard him move to answer the door. The quiet exchange as I hauled up the bucket had me wondering. When Father called for me to join him, I became even more curious.

Carrying the water inside, I found a young woman standing just inside the door. Dressed in a demure gown, with her dark hair pulled back, she watched me with an unsure smile.

"Hello, Benella," she said quietly.

She seemed to know me, but I could not recall her.

"Hello." I looked to my father, but he excused himself and walked out the front door, leaving me alone with her.

"Please, come in," I said, unsure what else to do.

She smiled once more and stepped in further, so I could close the door. She didn't move to sit, however. She lingered near the table, her hands tightly clasped before her.

"I wanted to thank you," she said. "We all wanted to, but we decided I would be the best to speak to you."

"We?"

"My name is Egrit. I understand if you want me to leave."

Egrit. The familiar name brought a bittersweet tingle to my nose. I blinked twice to ease the sensation then moved forward and wrapped her in a firm hug. She returned it with a sniffle.

"We weren't sure if you would be angry with us," she said, pulling back.

I looked into her bright hazel eyes and saw the nymph still there.

"Not at all. You all tried to help me when you could. I understand that."

"No," she said, shaking her head. "Not that." She looked down at her hands. "We are part of the reason the master was cursed." She sighed and uncomfortably looked around the room. "As a child he was a handsome handful, I was told. His teachers and nurses spoiled him as his parents ran the estate. His father passed away before the master's fifth birthday. His mother took over the estate responsibilities until he turned sixteen. I came to the estate before his fifteenth year."

I motioned for her to sit, and she did.

"As maids, we were told by the butler to give the master anything he wanted." She met my eyes steadily. "The older ones introduced him to women for his birthday. After that, all he needed to do was crook a finger. We all ran to please him, instilling in him an attitude toward women that caused many so much grief later."

She looked down at the table. "After the last time he was with me, he carried me to Rose. He knelt beside me and begged my forgiveness as she began to clean me. I told him there was nothing to forgive. I didn't blame him. I could have run. I could have solidified; he couldn't truly hurt me in that state. But I hadn't run. I'd stayed because, when he'd come for me, part of me had burst with excitement that someone like him would want me again. How could I expect him to value me when I valued myself so little?

"We all needed to learn what you had to teach us, and now we want to thank you and to beg your forgiveness for everything you suffered."

I listened to her tale with a heavy heart, seeing the beast in my mind.

"Egrit, his rough use of you, whether with your consent or not, was unspeakably horrible. You cannot forgive him. Your forgiveness is only for you. Your hate and pain are released with it, healing you, not him." She nodded slowly, a new light of understanding in her eyes. "And you can't take the blame for the choices he made, absolving him of all responsibility. That's what caused the curse. Hold him responsible. If you truly do feel no hardship toward him, give him the chance to make amends. Don't be easy on him." Only after I finished speaking did I realize the beast I knew, the one I spoke of, no longer existed.

Egrit smiled widely and stood.

"I have other errands to run. Do you know the name of the best dressmaker?"

Though I remained angry with my sister, I still wanted her happy. So, I gave her name. Egrit's smile changed slightly, but she nodded and took her leave.

* * * *

Less than a week later, another knock sounded at the door. The man who stood outside looked slightly familiar, yet I could not place his name. He noticed my uncertainty and gave me a genuine smile.

"Egrit mentioned speaking to you. I wanted to stop and give my thanks as well."

He continued to grin at me. Could this be Egrit's man?

"Do I know you?"

"Swiftly, at your service." He bowed slightly, keeping his eyes on me.

I grinned and did the unexpected. Pulling him into a quick hug, I brushed his cheek with a kiss.

"I owe you my thanks for all the times you carried me to and fro and kept me out of the baker's hands."

His smile faded.

"Except the last time."

Suddenly, I placed why he seemed familiar. He had been the one to help me into the carriage and drive me to my father's home.

"Don't fret, Swiftly. The odious man's own fat saved me from the worst of his eager attentions."

"He no longer dwells in Konrall," Swiftly said of the baker. "His mother and sister have taken him south."

"That is good for Konrall."

Over Swiftly's shoulder, I caught the unexpected sight of a man turning toward our house.

"Henick," I said with surprised delight.

"Excuse me, madam," Swiftly mumbled.

With a bow, he quickly left. I thought to call him back, but Henick claimed my attention with a friendly wave. Henick nodded to Swiftly as they passed each other.

"Benella, I heard about the baker and wanted to tell you how sorry I am for it. And I wanted to remind you I am still here, hoping for your consideration...as are my younger brothers."

His words touched my heart.

"I haven't forgotten," I said with a kind smile, "but I'm not sure I'm still suitable for marriage."

"Don't," he said. "Your worth has not diminished because of a man's crime against you. Don't ever believe otherwise."

"I swear to you, I do not devalue myself. I only meant, I cannot submit to marriage as I once thought I could. Certain aspects would be infinitely distasteful to me."

Understanding lit his features, and a blush stole across his face.

"What if a husband promised not to touch you until you thought his touch no longer distasteful?"

"Henick..." I struggled with the words to explain myself. "When I see you, I feel light and happy because you are one of the kindest people I know. When you marry, it will be to someone who carries sunshine in her hair and rainbows in her eyes just for you. Anything less wouldn't be good enough." I glanced at the floor for a moment. He waited patiently.

"The clouds of my life have planted seeds of bitterness in me. I find myself looking at people with," my voice dropped to a whisper, "hate. It's burning me slowly from the inside, eating at me, and stealing the color from my life." I met his gaze and took his hands in both of mine.

"Do you see why I must say no? I would not have what I carry poison you, too. I would not poison anyone with what now dwells in my heart."

"What will you do?" he asked.

"Find a way to live," I said. I stood on my toes to kiss his cheek once more. "Perhaps I will see you at the stream sometime."

He nodded and left. I watched him walk away, and my chest swelled with pity. Twice rejected. The second time for his own sake. I hoped he would find someone worthy of him.

Closing the door, I turned back to stir the thin stew I'd made. Not long after, the door opened again, and Father strode in with a frown on his face.

"Benella, the Sisters have let me go," he said without preamble.

I felt a surge of relief. I'd worried that Aryana might try to manipulate my father in some way.

"We have a few options open to us that I wanted to discuss with you. We could move south, but because of your sister's wedding feast, I have very little coin. We would only be able to take what we can carry," his eyes flicked to his remaining books.

I didn't turn to eye the meager display.

"Is there another option?" I asked.

"Moving south would give us both a fresh start," he said, still trying to speak for the first option.

"Yes, but I've learned the baker has moved south. The North with all its snobbery and deceit no longer seems so bad."

Father's lips twitched for a moment before he grew serious and withdrew a letter from his coat. I recognized it immediately as the letter I'd delivered so long ago. He handed it to me and watched me unfold it.

For a moment, I could only stare at the beast's script. A pang of loss pierced me before I read the words.

> *Whether I return to my rightful form or not, the North still needs a lord to carry out certain responsibilities. During my youth, I ignored many of my lessons, especially those in mathematics, and need someone I can trust to help account the estate's expenses and so forth. Please consider my invitation for employment.*
> *Regards,*
> *Alec Ruhall, Lord of the North*

"Why didn't you come?" I asked, meeting my father's gaze.

"I asked myself why he would invite me for employment when he had you, a person well able to account the estate's expenses. I thought that he perhaps sought to use me to coerce you as he'd done once before. Do you think this a serious offer for honest employment?"

I read the lines again and slowly nodded. "I do. But I wonder if the offer still holds."

"As did I. I went to see him," he said.

"What? Why didn't you tell me?" I paced the room, too restless to sit. I'd not spoken to the beast since...memories swamped me. Reading to him in the library, feeling his fingers in my hair. Then, running from Tennen and the baker's weight pressing the air from my lungs. It had been almost two weeks since I'd last seen the beast.

"I wanted to be sure before we discussed it as an option. He well knows my circumstance and that we come as a pair. He assured me of a place for you and a more than fair wage for my work."

My mind raced. I could see him again. Excitement surged for only a moment before I killed it. No, I couldn't see *him*. I would never see the beast again. He was gone. Lord Ruhall, the man who had watched with dispassionate eyes as the baker tried to force himself on me, had taken the beast's place.

"Is this why you asked if I wanted to return?"

"Yes. When I visited, people were coming and going through the gates at will. I don't think there would be any danger."

I considered the letter once more and didn't see that Father had much choice but to accept. The idea of returning made my stomach churn with anger. Yet, unlike my sisters, I would not make Father sacrifice any more of his books when there was a viable option to save them. His books meant so much to him. Books...I stopped my pacing and smiled at him excitedly.

"We most certainly should go, then. You will love the library, Father. There are more books than you can imagine." Of the beast and the Liege Lord, I forced myself to give little thought. One was dead and the other a cold stranger.

Father smiled and patted my hand, and we agreed to travel to the manor the next morning with the hope that we might return with a carriage for our belongings.

Two

The gates stood open as Father had said. Around the iron, vines curled, green, yet lifeless; the vitality the enchantment had imbued, gone. A man with a scythe hacked at the growth that crowded the drive. Another man worked not far from there, pulling out roots and picking up the cut remains the first man left in his wake.

Father and I walked the drive, each of us carrying a single bag. With the sun shining and the lane mostly cleared, the estate lacked the feeling I'd previously associated with it. A forbidden safety. Now, it seemed only a rundown estate.

When we reached the door, the man who swept the steps looked us over. There was no recognition in his eyes when he glanced at me, and I knew he was new to the Liege Lord's service. He directed us to the kitchen door. Familiar with the grounds, I nodded and led the way along the newly-made, narrow path. As I walked, I wondered how many of the original staff had remained after the enchantment had broken.

The kitchen door stood open, the hearth overheating the room as the three cooks set about making the morning meal. This room appeared much the same, yet with so many present, very different. Those differences gave me hope that the memories of my time spent here would remain buried and that I might be comfortable here once more.

"Good morning," my father said to the kitchen staff.

One of the cooks looked up with a slightly disgruntled expression.

"We've hired the staff we can. Come back next fall. There might be more work then."

Father didn't even blink at her less than welcoming tone.

"I am his Lord's man of estate. Mr. Benard Hovtel."

The cook glanced at us once more then dusted her hands on her apron.

"I'm Mrs. Wimbly, Lord Ruhall's head cook. I'll have the maid inform him of your arrival." She moved toward the hall and yelled for Egrit.

The familiar name almost made me smile. So, a few had stayed.

"Have a seat," the cook said with a nod toward the table. "I'll feed you while you wait."

We'd barely seated ourselves when she set a coddled egg before each of us and moved away.

Behind us, someone strode into the room. Thinking it Egrit, I glanced over my shoulder. It wasn't Egrit, but still a face I recognized. And the sight of it killed my appetite.

The events that had unfolded at the bakery had overshadowed my glimpse of Lord Ruhall. Now, however, I saw him clearly. He was young and handsome with a strong jaw and a regal nose. His dark hair and thick brows made him appear a bit imposing while his blue eyes lent an air of cool detachment. He was dressed in fine clothes, his hair was neatly combed, and he appeared quite well.

Resentment clouded my thinking. How could he look so well when I felt so ill?

The Lord of the estate looked around for someone, presumably the cook, and froze when he saw me. Surprise colored his face as his gaze swept over me then moved to my father.

"I would speak to your daughter, with your permission, sir," he said to Father, not even looking at me again.

"It is not my permission that matters, but hers," my father said, looking at me in question.

"It is yours that matters at the moment," the Liege Lord said.

My eyebrows rose, and my hand instinctively closed over my coddled egg. Suddenly the egg sailed through the air and hit the returned Lord of the North in the chest. I couldn't remember throwing it. Yet, I didn't regret it.

"I think my permission matters most, sir," I said, standing. Despite his apparent disregard for me, I mattered.

His shocked gaze swung to me. Yolk dripped from his neckcloth onto his coat.

Several of the servants looked at me with rounded eyes as well. Of course, I'd shocked them. One of our rank did not disobey the Lord of the North or, at least, didn't lob an egg at him. The assistant cook moved forward to offer him a cloth to clean up. He accepted the rag.

"Sit," he said in an authoritative voice that rang in the kitchen.

While he looked down at the mess I'd made of his shirt, I ignored his command and marched from the kitchen toward the hall. I was wrong to think I could reside here. Wrong to think I could avoid my feelings of resentment and mistrust for him or that I might avoid him entirely.

"Benella!"

Anger laced his voice, sending a chill through me. My pulse leapt, and I instinctively lifted my skirts and ran. Egrit barely twisted out of my way near the laundry room.

Behind me, he yelled, asking which way I'd gone. I needed to leave. Quickly.

I slid into the entry where a weathered butler stood beside the door.

"Open the door," I said as I raced toward the man. His black eyes widened, and I immediately knew him. "Mr. Crow, open the damn door."

He hurriedly tugged it open. Just a few hand spans, but it was enough for me to squeeze through before the Liege Lord raced into the room.

"Why did you let her out?" I heard him demand as he pulled the door open.

"Because she was trying to escape you, sir."

I kept running but almost laughed. The servants who'd been enchanted had learned well.

Without warning, an arm encircled my waist, and I found myself tumbling forward. Something pressed against my back, and I turned in midair.

Facing the sky, I landed on something soft. Him.

I scrambled off and backed away a few steps as he slowly climbed to his feet. Poised to run, I glared at him.

"Why are you always throwing food at me?" he asked, his face red.

"You deserved it," I said, my temper freeing my tongue. He deserved far more than a lobbed egg.

His eyes flashed, and he took a step toward me. I backed up a step. He stopped his advance and threw his hands in the air.

"Why are you acting as if you fear me now?"

I almost snorted. When had I ever let fear rule me?

"How should I act?"

His expression softened.

"The same as you always have."

This time I did snort. "I thought you didn't like me throwing food."

He relaxed his stance. "You are correct. Act the same as you always have with the exception of the food throwing. Stop that."

"I cannot act the same. I am not the same person and neither are you. I thought I knew you, but I do not."

He frowned at me. "What do you mean?"

Bitterly, I eyed him. "The beast I'd grown fond of growled at me, ranted at me, and clawed through doors to get to me. He fed me. Cared for me. The Liege Lord stood in the doorway of the bakery and did nothing when that pig of a man rutted over me."

He paled and reached for me. I pulled back, and he dropped his hand.

"I am still that beast. Only Rose's restraining hand kept me from—" He closed his eyes briefly. "Benella, I wanted to kill him for touching you."

I struggled not to scoff.

He studied my unforgiving expression for a moment then took a slow breath.

"I need you here," he said. "I'm barely in control. Rose is watching me. She doubts I can be a lord in truth."

He needed my help, just as the beast had, but the pity I'd felt for the lonely beast didn't pertain to the man before me. I didn't want to help the Liege Lord. Yet, I knew I could give only one answer. For my father's sake and to avoid destitution, I had to agree.

"Of course I will help you, my Lord."

He stepped close again, and I quickly backed away several steps.

"Why do you keep doing that?" he asked, anger flashing in his eyes.

"It is not proper to stand too close to a servant. Haven't you learned anything?" I glanced at the lower windows of the manor, glad for the several faces that peeked out at us.

He followed my gaze and growled but kept his distance.

"We have more to discuss. Come to my study when you've finished your meal." Then, he stomped back inside.

I chose to walk around to the kitchen door. My heavy heart dragged my feet and slowed my progress. Seeing him had shocked me. And I realized my affection for the beast hadn't disappeared with the dear creature. Yet, it didn't extend to the man, either.

When I returned to the table, Father looked up from his eggs and studied me with a slight smile on his lips.

"How did your talk go?"

"Well, I'm not sure we ever got to the point of his request. He wants me to go to his study after I've finished eating."

"You have egg in your hair," Egrit said as she passed me.

* * * *

After washing in the laundry, I made my way to the library. Lord Ruhall paced in his study. As soon as I entered, he turned toward me. Some of his agitation faded as I approached.

"Sit," he said.

"Do you ever tire of giving commands?" I asked as I sat. Behind me, he closed the study doors.

"No."

He walked around my chair to stand in front of me. He still moved with the grace I'd grown accustomed to, walking with more of a prowl than a stride.

"Is it different? As a man?" I asked before I could stop myself.

"Yes. Uncomfortable, truthfully. I had more freedom before. Everything feels so restrained now. Not just my clothes, or how I move, but my own skin."

"How old were you when you were enchanted?"

"No more than twenty-three," he said.

"You are over seventy years old. Of course you'll feel a little strained." He grunted, but I caught the amused twinkle in his eyes so like the twinkle the beast had in his eyes in the weeks before I was taken. I felt an ache in my middle at the sight.

"Of what did you wish to speak?" I asked, not wanting to spend more time than necessary with him.

He leaned back against his desk and studied me for several long moments. I fought to remain still under his scrutiny. Finally, he sighed.

"I think estate concerns are the safest subject for the time being. As you suggested, I read up on farming and contacted your friend, Henick, whom you shall never kiss again, by the way."

My eyebrows shot up, but he continued without pause.

"There is no hope for planting any of the overgrown fields this year, but there are many ways to prepare them for next year. I need you to listen to my plans and point out any flaws."

He explained that he'd harvested several bags of primrose from the lands and contracted with the local candle maker for scented candles. He also contacted the traveling merchant to establish a permanent trade route, though he didn't state what he planned to trade.

For the candles that the candle maker had created from the flowers, the merchant paid the estate half of what was owed in gold and half in goats. The twenty goats now grazed in the overgrown fields, helping to prepare the ground for spring.

The remaining gold had been used to hire three cooks, two housemaids, five workers, a butler, a teacher, and a man of estate.

"Why three cooks?"

"I would slowly starve if I were left to feed myself."

The memory of the beast dropping eggs on the floor pressed against me, and I frowned. I didn't want reminders.

"I'm concerned with the expense. Surely one cook can handle simple meals through the summer."

"What of preparing food stores for the winter?" He tilted his head, appearing truly interested in my thoughts.

I recalled all the work Bryn did for the four of us and adjusted my thinking.

"Two cooks perhaps, but certainly not three. What are the five workers doing?"

"Two are clearing the drive so wagons with supplies can pass. Swiftly is repairing the stables. And the other two are gathering and re-sowing the seeds from the primrose to expand the field for next spring."

"How many horses do you have?"

"None yet."

"What of the one..." I couldn't finish the question. The image of Swiftly bringing me home in a horse drawn carriage also called to mind the baker. Lord Ruhall seemed to read my mind.

"Borrowed," he said quietly.

I struggled to think of something else.

"Have Swiftly help with the drive. With three there, as soon as it's passible, all five can work on the seeds. Re-sowing will give the greatest return next year. A horse, if you obtain one, can wait for stables to be repaired."

He rubbed his jaw as he listened intently.

"And having two maids seems extravagant when not much of the manor is being used," I said.

"But it will be soon. Some of the rooms haven't been touched in fifty years."

"Why a butler and a teacher?"

"Because they were enchanted with me. I owe them employment for as long as they want it."

I nodded in agreement.

"Is there anything else, then?" I asked, ready to leave.

"Yes. Konrall is missing a baker now. Going to the Water will be a hardship on many. I've contacted the bakers in the Water. Bryn and Edmund will be coming to take over the bakery. I thought you'd want to know."

Bryn's rejection still stung too deeply to feel any happiness for her opportunity. I inclined my head in acknowledgement and stood at the same time he straightened from the desk. The move brought us close. His breath fanned my face for a moment. Then, he leaned in as if to kiss me. I turned my head.

"I'm not here for that kind of help," I said. "I never was."

He sighed.

"Come back tomorrow morning to discuss more. You'll take your old room. It's the only one still ready."

I hurried away.

* * * *

The room was just as I'd left it with the exception of the wardrobe. Two dresses waited within it, obviously meant for me. Pretty, yet practical creations made by real hands. I touched the taupe material of the first dress as I tried to understand the turn my life had taken yet again.

The Liege Lord confused me. I understood he depended on me to continue helping him. I could even accept the dresses as a gift of thanks. But why place me in this room? I could easily clean and air out another one for myself. And why had he moved so close to me in the study? Did he think I could continue with the physical side of the relationship I'd had with the beast? My breast tingled at the thought while my stomach lurched in a sickening way, giving me mixed signals.

I understood my reaction. Although I'd liked everything the beast had done, I had not liked what the baker had tried. Fornication wasn't for me. Perhaps if the beast were still here, I might eventually feel differently. However, if he were still here, I wouldn't have suffered the baker's touch at all.

I sighed and moved around the room, looking for something that might distract me from my dark thoughts.

Egrit saved me from boredom by knocking on the door a few minutes later.

"I'm happy you came," she said, stepping into the room. "Your father sent me with a message that he's left to settle your home in the Water."

I nodded, and she hesitated.

"Do you need anything?" she asked.

"No. Wait, yes. A way to occupy my time."

She grinned at me.

"I'm to clean the top floor and attic. Would you like to help?"

The thought of staying in my room for hours with nothing to do had me quickly agreeing. We walked to a dark and dusty section of a seldom used inner hall on the other side of the manor.

"Anything not of practical use or of sentimental value, we're to place in the main hall for trade," she said as she led me to a staircase I'd never discovered. Our skirts cleaned the cobwebs from the steps as we ascended.

"Most of the rooms up here are guest rooms and are seldom used, so very little should have sentimental value."

Dust danced in a beam of light that pierced the dirty pane of the nearest window. I sneezed twice and followed Egrit into the first room. We tried not to disturb anything until we had a window open. With the breeze, we started cleaning and sorting.

We finished two rooms by dinner. I grabbed a quick bite to eat from the kitchen, washed up in the laundry, then eagerly sought my bed before the sun fully set.

During the night, a sound woke me, sending me into a panic; I'd never learned of Tennen's fate.

"Shhh," a familiar voice whispered. The bed dipped, and a strong arm curved around me.

I froze for a moment then relaxed at the feel of fingers gently working my braid free. I kept my eyes closed and imagined the beast next to me.

Comforted, I drifted back to sleep.

* * * *

A knock woke me a second before Egrit opened my door. I sat up quickly, remembering the beast's visit, and turned to view the empty bed next to me. Not the beast, I thought. Alec. No, the Liege Lord. I wondered what it meant that he'd come to me at all. Did he still have trouble sleeping, even after the removal of the enchantment? If not that, then what? If he sought to use me again, he would be disappointed.

"Are you all right?" Egrit asked.

"Yes. It's just odd being here again," I said, slipping from the bed.

My dress from the day before waited draped over a chair. Dust streaked it, but I wasn't about to dirty another dress when we would be cleaning more rooms today.

"I'll leave you to dress," she said, walking to the bed. She set a napkin on the cover. "I brought you something to eat." She left the room and closed the door.

I quickly tossed aside my nightgown and slipped the dress over my head. Straightening the bedcover, I eyed the honeyed biscuit and wished for the magical trays the beast used to leave me. But, not one to spurn food in any form, I grabbed the biscuit as soon as the bed was made and took a bite on my way out the door.

When I located Egrit, she was already busy in a new room. I found cleaning a tedious chore best avoided under normal conditions. That we cleaned rooms untouched these last fifty years turned tedium into an exercise of willful perseverance.

Egrit and I had managed to complete two rooms before Father found me.

"Would you have time to meet in his Lordship's study for the midday meal?"

I had no wish to see his Lordship; yet, the need for air not clouded with dust had me glancing at Egrit.

"Go," she said. "I'll find my own food and meet with you here when we're both finished."

I nodded and left the room with Father.

"You seem to have found a way to keep yourself busy," he said.

"Yes. I can see now why two maids are needed."

Father made a noise between agreement and amusement.

"Lord Ruhall dismissed the other this morning."

Poor Egrit, I thought. Then realized I should have thought poor me for I certainly would not leave Egrit alone to deal with those rooms.

"Are you happy here?" Father asked as we descended to the second floor. "I could still seek employment elsewhere."

I loved him so much for the offer.

"I am content," I said, though I wasn't.

I followed Father toward the library. My nerves wound tightly as we neared. I swallowed hard as we entered the library and crossed the rugs to the study. Inside, a tray waited on a small table. Lord Ruhall sat behind his desk, reading something. He didn't look up at our arrival.

His dark head of hair was so dissimilar to the shaggy coat of the beast. Yet, I found similarity in the position in which he held himself in as he read. The connection brought an ache to my middle, and I had to look away.

"Sit, Benella," my father said. "I'd prefer you didn't touch the food." He winked at me and brought me my plate.

I sat and listened as Father and Lord Ruhall began to discuss estate accounts over our meal. Besides the maid, he'd let go one of the cooks as I'd suggested. The benign conversation and Father's presence eased my mind over the possible reasons Lord Ruhall had asked for my attendance. I remained quiet, enjoying the break and the food, and as soon as I swallowed my last bite, I excused myself.

Egrit had already returned to cleaning on the third floor when I arrived.

We finished four rooms that day, and my back ached when I made my way to my room. Dust coated my skin, and my stomach begged for dinner, but I didn't care. I barred both doors, stripped from my gown, ran the washrag over my face and arms, then crawled into bed.

Sleep claimed me quickly.

Again a noise woke me, the slight rattle of the door and a soft curse followed by silence. I smiled sadly and closed my eyes against the tears that wanted to run down my cheeks. I missed the beast.

* * * *

My days settled into a routine. Egrit and I continued to clear four rooms a day, I ate an amiable meal with Father and Lord Ruhall midday, and Lord Ruhall quietly tried my doors each night.

The pile in the main hall grew and shrunk as carts came and hauled away things for trade. Spare chairs from already over furnished rooms, a few mirrors where there were duplicates, scented candles—many, many scented candles—rugs from rooms where they overlapped; I even placed a few questionable portraits depicting women in various nude positions on the pile. Egrit said nothing as I rid the manor of them.

The first week expired with little notice as everyone worked from dawn to dusk. On the following day, I went to join Lord Ruhall and Father for the midday meal and arrived before Father. Lord Ruhall sat behind his desk as usual but set his book aside as soon as I entered. He didn't mention my locked doors and kept the conversation strictly estate related as we waited for my father to join us.

Thankfully, Father didn't leave us waiting long.

"The third cart just left. The estate now has three hundred twenty-three gold, sir," Father said as he came into the room. "There were some portraits of value that the merchant was too eager to take. Egrit bargained the price higher than I would have thought to go."

"Family portraits?" Lord Ruhall asked, concerned.

A choked noise escaped me.

"I should hope not," I said.

"Ah." He changed the subject. "Now, what to do with that amount?" he said, looking at me. It was the first time in a week he'd directed a question to me.

I took a moment to gather my thoughts.

"The primrose seeds have been harvested and re-sown, and the drive has been cleared," I said. "I suggest bringing one hand inside. Egrit and I could use someone to carry the heavier items down the stairs. Then, set the other four to haying. There is enough time to put up a good supply for winter to allow for a horse or two, which we will need for tilling fields in spring."

"The estate records did show a savings by planting our own crops. Do you have a different suggestion, Benard?" he asked, turning to my father.

"I think Benella's suggestion the wisest choice and can offer nothing better than the purchase of a horse or two with that amount." My father glanced at me with a smile.

Lord Ruhall agreed to my plan with one exception. All five workers would attend the fields, and he would help clear the top floor. My back didn't care who helped so long as Egrit and I didn't have to carry anything more down the stairs.

However, my easy agreement to his assistance came back to haunt me the following day. Often, when I looked up from whatever task occupied me, I found him watching with a nearly indecipherable expression. At times, it hinted at anger and expectation. At others, remorse. He was courteous and respectful toward Egrit and cautiously cool around me.

I could find no fault in his behavior, yet it angered me. My conversation with Henick echoed in my ears. Inside, I had changed. A bitterness existed where none had before, and I had no idea what to do with it. So I sought jobs that would keep me away from his company as he walked to and fro, bringing items to the main entry.

Egrit and I were working together in one of the smaller guest rooms to hang a rug out the window to shake the dust from it.

"We might be better off rolling them up and taking them all outside for a thorough airing," Egrit said, eyeing the rug. Dust still stuck to it.

I nodded. I didn't want to carry the thing down the stairs, but holding that much weight out the window strained my back fiercely.

Behind us, I heard footsteps on the wood floor.

"It's time to eat," Lord Ruhall said.

"A moment, please," I said, helping Egrit pull the rug back in.

He waited by the door as she and I worked together to roll the rug. When I stepped toward him, he motioned for me to lead. We remained silent as we walked the halls.

In the study, Father waited for us. Lord Ruhall sat behind his desk as Father said there was nothing new to report. Our polite meal felt strained without estate affairs to discuss.

"Perhaps we don't need to meet as often?" I said after swallowing a bite of stew.

Lord Ruhall flushed noticeably. Father looked down, keeping busy with his meal as the Lord of the manor shot me a disapproving look.

"We will continue to meet as we have."

I nodded and concentrated on my own food, and as soon as I finished, excused myself.

*   *   *   *

Another two weeks saw the top floor cleared, the purchase of two horses, and the estate coffers steady at three hundred gold. The men worked to repair the stables with a few leaving to hunt. Stag, boar, and fowl occasionally lay on the butcher block in the kitchen as the two cooks put away stores for winter. Per Lord Ruhall's orders, they kept meals simple as their days filled with storage preparations.

With the top floor cleared, I convinced Egrit that we needed a day of rest. Before the house woke, she met me in the laundry where I had two fishing poles waiting; the same poles the beast and I had used so long ago.

"Are you certain he won't mind?" Egrit asked, doubt lacing her voice.

"I'm certain." We'd made significant progress, and we deserved a day of rest after the weeks we'd worked.

Egrit and I left through the laundry door. The light breeze teased stray strands of hair back from my face. Not a cloud decorated the sky. It was the perfect day to be outdoors. I stretched my stride, enjoying the walk. Egrit talked of her man, Tam, and the money they were saving to purchase a home off the estate once they wed.

"How old are you?" I asked. She seemed so young to be thinking of marriage.

"I was seventeen when I was enchanted. So, I must be sixty-seven now," she said with a laugh.

I smiled but said nothing. Even if she hadn't been enchanted, she wasn't too young. And neither was I. My seventeenth birthday was not far away. So much had happened so quickly that I felt much older in many ways. Still, marriage...I wasn't sure I would ever be ready for that. Yet, most girls my age were already planning weddings. If a girl saw eighteen unwed, it usually meant she had no hope of marrying. Out of love, my father had held on to us far past when he should have. I wondered what my life would have been like if he'd wed us off sooner.

Egrit didn't say anything as the silence stretched. We passed the newly planted fields and crossed many more that still needed attention.

When we reached the wall, I looked up at the tree.

"Can you climb?"

Egrit snorted. "I was a tree, living among trees for fifty years. I can climb."

"Toss your boots over first. You'll want to put them on once we reach the other side."

We sat on the grass to unlace our boots. In no time, we were up the tree and climbing down the other side of the wall. The wind on my face and rocks under my hands steadied me and quieted some of the unrest that had been building for days.

We spent the morning by the stream in the same spot where the beast had laid me back on the banks. My mind dwelled on the memory, and Egrit, sensing my pensive mood, left me to my thoughts.

In truth, I wanted the beast to return, and it shamed me. He'd spent so many years punished for his youthful pride and arrogance. Yet, I missed the beast's unpredictable moods, zealous attention, and his comforting presence.

My feelings toward Lord Ruhall were more undecided. He said Rose watched him still, judging his actions as Lord. I watched him, too. He left the maids alone and attended to estate business. His only overture to a female had been to me when he entered my room the first night I had returned. But, he'd done nothing more than lay beside me.

During the time we had spent together clearing the guest rooms, his watchful, aloof attitude had remained consistent with the man who'd stood in the doorway and watched the baker's thankfully pathetic attempts to compromise me. Had it been the beast, I knew without a doubt he would have charged into the room and ripped the baker from me. The enchantress wouldn't have been able to hold the beast back.

Egrit's excited squeal pulled me from my musings.

"What do I do?" she cried, holding the pole tight, fighting the fish.

I wished I could ask her the same. Instead, I moved to help her. She was thrilled at her first catch and swore she would take her man fishing if I would allow them the use of the poles. We stayed on the banks until six fat fish decorated the string. Our stomachs begged for food, and we gathered our poles to head back.

We rounded the estate before the sun hit its zenith and entered an empty kitchen. The butcher block waited, clean and empty, which I found unusual; one of the men typically returned with something by now. I laid the fish out, content to let the cooks clean them.

From somewhere in the manor, I heard a familiar, raised voice. Both Egrit and I shared a worried look before we hurried down the hall.

"Then look again," Lord Ruhall roared at the staff, who stood in line before him.

He spun at the sound of our steps. His red, angry face surprised me as our gazes met.

"Where have you been?" he asked, stalking toward me.

Egrit made a move to step in front of me, but I firmly grabbed her wrist and held her back.

"You wish to speak with me, my Lord?" I emphasized his title, trying to remind him he was no longer the beast, though his current tone and the prowling steps he took did remind me of the dear creature.

"I asked where you were." Despite his very human form, he growled.

Ridiculously, I almost smiled that he thought to intimidate me.

"Thank you for asking, my Lord. I shall certainly accompany you to your study to explain."

His eyes narrowed. He cocked his head to the side and studied me for a moment before waving for me to lead the way. I gave a gracious nod and leisurely moved past him. The servants all watched me with worry and trepidation. I stopped before the head cook, giving her a calm smile.

"There are several trout on the block. They still need cleaning."

She frowned but nodded slowly before she glanced at the man who impatiently waited just a step away.

"Thank you," I said.

He followed me through the halls, the angry click of his shoes puzzling me. I sincerely doubted he minded that Egrit and I had taken a morning from cleaning when we'd dedicated so many days to the task already. What then had made him so angry?

I walked through the study door and stopped in the middle of the room, preferring not to sit just in case I needed to leave quickly. The door closed. He walked around me and stood behind his desk.

"Well?" he said.

"We went fishing. I would think that obvious after telling the cook about the trout," I said with an arched brow.

His face, which had recovered its natural color, flushed again.

"My Lord, Egrit and I have worked tirelessly since I arrived. My back needed a rest days ago. Egrit would never complain, but I'm sure hers did as well. Certainly you cannot begrudge us a morning to relax. It wasn't a completely idle activity either; we brought back fish."

He looked heavenward.

"Fish." His regard settled on me once more. "You think this is about

Devastation

you fishing?" He rubbed a hand over his face.

"I honestly have no idea what would cause you, the Liege Lord, to start yelling at the staff in a most unbecoming manner and then to turn on me as soon as I walk into the room, in front of an already shocked staff," I said with annoyance. "You said Rose is watching you. What do you think she made of such beastly behavior?"

He had the grace to cringe. "I was less concerned about her than I was about you when I woke to find you missing."

"First, how did you know I was missing unless you tried to enter my room," I said in a harsh whisper. He snarled in return. "Second, my absence should not concern you. You hired my father, not me, if I recall. I should be free to move about as I please. I am under no obligation to stay locked in my room any longer. And don't even think about taking Egrit to task for some idle time. You owe her that and much more."

He opened his mouth, no doubt to shout back at me, when the door burst open. My father stood there looking flustered and slightly embarrassed.

"You summoned me, my Lord?"

Behind him, I caught sight of Egrit leaving the library.

"Father, you are just in time," I said, calming myself. "The boorish man behind the desk has spent too many years without the counsel of his father. Perhaps you can still help him desplte his dotage."

My father's brows rose, and his gaze darted to Lord Ruhall, who watched me with a clenched jaw. I turned away from both men and stormed out the door.

"She gets her stubbornness from me and her intelligence from her mother," my father said.

His words made me pause in the library, just out of sight. I would argue that I had his intelligence.

"Books, the written word, captivate me. But I forgot them all when my wife first spoke to me. We were wed twelve years before she passed. I learned a few things in those years. When a woman leaves a room in a storm, best wait till the thunder fades before you walk out lest you risk being struck by lightning. Or worse, a frying pan."

Lord Ruhall said something too quietly for me to hear. With a smile, I left him to my father's sage advice.

Three

Just outside the library, the entire staff waited. Egrit flashed me a relieved smile.

"All is well," I assured them. "Mrs. Wimbly, the fish would be an excellent midday meal if there's time." It would also serve as a reminder to Lord Ruhall.

"Egrit, you should watch how they are cleaned if you plan on fishing again in the future."

Egrit nodded and, with a smile, left with the frowning cook. The rest of the staff seemed reluctant to leave.

"Swiftly, how are the repairs on the stables coming along?"

"I would be happy to show you," he said. Mr. Crow opened the door for us. The other men followed.

* * * *

Swiftly's explanation of the repairs claimed my attention for almost an hour. I hadn't yet read anything about building but planned to in the future. The calculations needed to brace a structure's roof correctly astounded me.

My father caught me just as I entered through the main doors.

"Stop provoking the Lord. As you reminded him, he is the Liege Lord," he said.

"Father, truly, my intent wasn't to provoke him when I left this morning. I only wanted some peace and relaxation. Even with his help carrying the heavy items, I still think I might start walking with a stoop soon."

"Daughter, for such an astute girl, your ability to observe and learn concerns me," he said with a frown.

"How so?" I tried to think of what I might have done to upset him.

"Think of the last time you disappeared from his manor, daughter.

You worried him."

My mouth popped open, and I struggled with how I felt about what Father was hinting at. Lord Ruhall, the cold man, cared if I disappeared? No, not me, but two people under his protection.

"Mrs. Wimbly announced the meal is ready. I'll fetch the tray." With a shake of his head, my father walked toward the kitchen.

That left me to face Lord Ruhall alone while we waited for Father. It sat wrong that I needed to apologize for an idle day of fishing. With slow steps, I made my way to the study. Lord Ruhall's bent head did not lift when I entered. He continued to read from the open book before him.

His hand rubbed his forehead, and his hair sprouted about in disarray. The set of his shoulders, tense and pushed back, told me enough. He was still angry with me.

Ignoring the chairs my father and I usually took, I walked around the desk and rested a hand on his jacketed shoulder to gain the attention I knew he wouldn't otherwise give. He sighed and dropped his hand. Leaning back into his chair, effectively removing my touch, he met my gaze.

"I'm sorry. We didn't mean to concern you."

He closed his eyes, not saying anything.

"We were safe. The baker's gone." To me, he and Tennen were the only ones that posed a real threat, and Tennen wouldn't have tried anything with Egrit beside me.

Alec snorted and opened his eyes to glare at me.

"Safe? You think the baker is the only man to look at you with lust?"

I refrained from naming him as one of the men to do so. But, no, it hadn't been him. It had been the beast, my sweet Alec.

"Benella," he said, leaning forward. A noise from the door stopped him from reaching for me. My father cleared his throat and moved to the desk with the tray.

"Fish," he announced.

"Of course," Lord Ruhall murmured, looking at me with a shake of his head. "Next time you'd care to fish, please take Swiftly with you and leave word."

I nodded and moved to my usual chair, ready to discuss estate affairs.

* * * *

Carrying the tray to the kitchen, I found the cooks at the table, enjoying idle conversation. The assistant cook caught sight of me and quickly stood. I smiled a greeting and set the dirty dishes on the empty butcher block.

"No game today?" I asked as the assistant cook moved around me to start wash water.

"No," Mrs. Wimbly answered. "The hands were out looking for you."

"Not my best decision," I said with a cringe.

She continued to scowl at me. So, I tried changing the subject after a moment of silence.

"Have you explored the cold storage yet?"

"When we first arrived. There's still ice in it from the winter so we've been putting the extra goat milk there."

"Is there cream?" I asked excitedly. I'd read a bit about making butter and thought the process sounded interesting. The cost of butter being too high, it wasn't something Bryn used. Lard was less expensive and easier to obtain.

After a moment, Mrs. Wimbly nodded.

"Might we make butter?"

She gave me an odd look before answering.

"If there's time. There are several buckets still in cold storage. Enough for a bit of butter."

"How long does the milk stay good?" I asked.

"We've thrown out several already that went sour."

The waste brought to mind all the times my family had dined on fresh goat's milk and nothing else while living in Konrall.

"Let's skim the cream we need and pour what's left in a large barrel to be taken to the Water. There are people there who could use the surplus instead of wasting it," I said.

Her expression grew more indignant as I spoke, and I wondered at the cause. I seemed to have acquired a knack for upsetting those around me.

"I'll need to check with Lord Ruhall," she said.

"Of course," I agreed. I didn't think he would disagree with my plan, though. "Do you know how to make cheese?" I asked.

"Of course," she said as she gave me a hard look.

"I meant no disrespect to your skills," I quickly assured her. "I was only wondering if we should do so here or perhaps trade a portion of the milk to the cheese maker in the Water for premade cheese." I tilted my head. "What do you think is the best use of your time? Storing food for winter or cheese making?"

She studied me for a moment, most likely trying to gauge if I mocked her with my question. She heaved an aggravated breath and started to explain the process of making cheese. It fascinated me, of course. Soft cheese would be easy enough for us, but hard cheese would require more ingredients, time, and space to cure.

"So it's not the preparing time we need worry about, but the items we need to make it. What do you think of making the soft cheese and trading milk for the hard cheese?"

"We won't get much in return for the milk," she said. "At least, not the goat's milk."

I nodded, thinking of cows, but decided the expense not yet worth the return given the small staff we housed.

"Please let me know what Lord Ruhall says. I'm very interested in assisting," I added.

She gave a single, curt nod.

With Lord Ruhall still annoyed with me, Egrit missing—most likely cleaning, which I wasn't eager to resume—and Swiftly and his men busy with repairs, I had nothing to do to occupy myself. I hesitated in the kitchen while Mrs. Wimbly left, presumably to speak with Lord Ruhall.

The assistant cook watched me closely.

"If anyone is looking for me, please let them know I've gone to Konrall," I said, deciding to check if Bryn had yet moved to the bakery.

The last time I'd seen her, she'd called me a whore. Yet, I refused to believe she would do so again. In her heart, she couldn't really see me as a whore. Most likely, she'd been afraid of losing her position among the merchants of the Water. But she wasn't in the Water anymore. Konrall was different, and I needed to see her again so we could mend things between us.

The assistant cook nodded and watched me leave. I decided the people at the estate an odd bunch. They didn't know what to make of me. Neither did I. I wasn't a servant, but not a guest either since my father was employed there. Yet, I slept in the Lady's quarters. Obviously, I was a nuisance. It made me smile.

Birds sang along the dirt and pebble drive. I found myself missing the vines and dark mist. Though eerie, it had felt safe, like my own place to hide with only the beast to trouble me.

A wagon rumbled in the distance. I waited on the shoulder and smiled at Henick as he neared.

"Your timing is impeccable," I said with a laugh. He smiled in return and braked.

"It looks like I'm traveling the wrong direction, though," he said. The wagon pointed north toward the Water.

"It's not the ride I'm after as much as it is the news. Has Bryn settled in Konrall, yet?"

"Yes. A few days back. The smoke's been pouring from the bakery. The new baker makes a fine tart and cake. His bread's not bad either."

"How is Bryn?"

He shrugged and looked down at his hands. "I know she thought she would have a hard life with me. But I don't think it would have been any worse than a fancy baker's wife."

My heart went out to him. "Remember to watch for rainbows, Henick. It's what you deserve."

He looked up at me and gave a small smile.

"Are you well?" he asked.

It was my turn to shrug.

"I think I'm still broken inside. Too quick to anger at times. Too scornful at other times, though I try to keep that hidden."

He looked sad for me.

"What a pair we are," I said with a small smile. My mother once told me time changed everything. In that moment, I realized what she meant. Nothing ever stayed the same.

"If you visit your sister, I hope it's pleasant," he said, nodding farewell.

I waved him off and considered his comment. I hoped, by the end, I would be able to call the visit pleasant.

But it wasn't meant to be. As soon as I walked into the bakery, Bryn's welcoming expression closed.

"Get out," she hissed, coming around the counter. "Whore," she spat. Thankfully, there were no customers to witness her clasping my arm and tugging me toward the door.

"Bryn!" Bryn froze.

"Go upstairs and calm yourself. Perhaps think on the names you choose to use."

Bryn released me, and I turned to see Edmund standing in the doorway to the bakery. He looked quite angry, and with reason. Tennen stood just behind him.

Bryn paled, and a sob escaped her. My heart broke for her, despite her name calling.

"Go," Edmund said softly.

Tennen smirked as she ran up the stairs, and a fire lit inside of me.

I stalked around the counter and pushed past Edmund as I balled up my fist. Without hesitation, I struck Tennen. Again, it wasn't hard enough to bloody him as I wanted, but his head still moved from the blow.

He growled and stepped toward me, but Edmund stopped him with a hand on his chest.

"You used her then come in here to boast about it to her husband?" I said to Tennen. "Her only fault was to believe your intentions honest."

"You're a whore just like her," Tennen said.

Edmund's hand on Tennen's chest fisted then flew to connect with Tennen's jaw. Tennen grunted as the hit drove him back a step. Edmund managed what I hadn't the first time. He made Tennen bleed.

Tennen narrowed his eyes at the baker, but he didn't move to retaliate.

"Get out," Edmund said between gritted teeth.

Tennen narrowed his eyes.

"Remember what I said. I'll tell everyone." Then he left.

"Let me guess. Bread for life or he'll tell everyone he's the father of the babe?"

Edmund nodded.

"Don't give in. As soon as you do, they have you," I said, rubbing my hand. Hitting someone hurt.

"I know. His mother was already here to see me."

I shook my head, troubled that the smith had sent his wife out again.

"The last baker was not a good man. I hope you're better." I glanced at the stairs before meeting Edmund's gaze again. "I meant what I said. Bryn's shame was in trusting Tennen. I know she's not perfect. She's selfish and lied to you about the babe, but she has some good qualities as well."

"Name one," he said flatly.

I felt badly for him. I knew what it was like to discover people weren't who you thought they were.

"She can cook well. For a baker's wife that's a good thing," I said with a small smile.

He gave a short, derisive laugh, showing just how much he was hurting.

"Everything she's been through has been hard on her," I said. "I don't think she knows who she is yet. She's been what we needed her to be. If you can forgive her, I think she'll forgive herself and maybe find out who she can be."

He studied me for a moment then looked away.

"Did you need any bread today?" he asked after a moment.

"No, I was just here for a visit. Is business doing well?"

"Not very. People here do not have the coin they did in the Water."

"I hope your fortune changes soon."

He nodded, and I left with nothing more to say. I wished Bryn would stop her whore nonsense. As her husband pointed out, we both knew I was not the whore.

Outside, I caught sight of Tennen, pacing before the smithy. I groaned. Being with the beast had made me impulsive. I shouldn't have hit Tennen. I headed to the butcher's.

"Hello, sir," I said as I walked through the door.

"Benella!" The butcher's glad smile lightened my heart. "I thought we might not see you again. I heard your father is now employed with the returned Liege Lord," he said, wiping his hands on his apron.

"He is. I'd hoped to visit with Bryn, but she holds me accountable for what happened with the old baker."

He made a sound of disapproval as Tennen walked past the butcher's door.

"And, I need your help," I said softly.

"It seems so. Why does he have such an issue with you?"

"The old baker hurt others as well, not just me," I said quietly. "I saw something I shouldn't have. Tennen knows. I think the smith knows, too."

The butcher heaved a pitying sigh.

"How can I help?"

"Speak with Tennen while I slip out the back door? I just need a head start," I said with a confident smile.

"Perhaps you should mention this to your father," he said.

I nodded with no intention of doing so. After all that Tennen had done to me, I still didn't have the heart to punish Sara by telling all. She might be sent away with her husband who would hold her accountable or, worse, make her do the same thing in another village. No, the punishment should lie solely on Mr. Coalre. As far as the son...well, perhaps he could be apprenticed to the south. Somewhere near the baker.

Slipping through the curtain that led to the butcher's kitchen, I listened to the butcher cross the store and walk outside. I waited a few moments, then I peeked out the back door. Seeing nothing, I sprinted to the trees and used my old route past the cottage toward the estate. It didn't take long for Tennen to shout my name, but thankfully it was in the distance. Then he shouted for Splane. Neither of them would have a chance.

I grinned too soon.

Splane stepped out in front of me, knocking me to the ground. He looked behind me nervously, and Tennen shouted again.

"You better have her, Splane!"

Tennen sounded closer, and I scrambled to my feet.

Splane watched me, but I could see he was torn. His gaze shifted behind me and then toward the estate. No matter what he chose, he would face either the wrath of his brother or of the beast. No, not the wrath of the beast. The beast wasn't there anymore to protect me, and Splane's brother was just behind me.

Lifting my skirts high to free my legs, I made an obvious feint to the right. Splane widened his stance to block me as we eyed each other. I kicked out, clipping him sharply between the legs.

"Thank you for the target," I said as I took off, not staying to watch his slow fall to the ground.

Tennen yelled again, much closer this time.

I kept my skirts high and ran as I hadn't in a long time. My side ached by the time I reached the gates. I flew past a very surprised Swiftly. There was only one place I felt safe.

Mr. Crow opened the door before I reached it, my pounding footfalls probably giving away my presence. I sprinted up the stairs into the dark interior and crashed into a solid chest with an "oof." Strong arms and a familiar scent wrapped around me. In that instant, I felt safe.

"What happened?" Lord Ruhall asked.

The sound of his voice ruined my illusion.

"A moment...please," I gasped, dropping my skirts and sliding from his arms. I leaned my hands on my knees as the pain in my side clawed its way into my lungs. I'd found in the past the position eased the pain.

Swiftly entered just then.

"Is she all right?" he asked.

"She's out of breath," Lord Ruhall said, still close. "What happened?" he repeated.

"I don't know, my Lord," Swiftly said. "She ran past me full out. I looked behind her but saw nothing. There was fear in her eyes, though," he added.

I struggled to force slower breaths, knowing it would win me more air than the gasps.

"I feared," I managed, "missing the meal."

"Benella," Lord Ruhall said with unmistakable warning.

Straightening with effort, I kept a bland expression.

"Did I already miss it?"

He rubbed a hand over his face and remained curiously quiet for a moment. He cleared his throat three times before he spoke in a slow, calm tone.

"Do you recall speaking with me just a few hours past?"

I nodded, wondering at his point.

"Then why did you leave the estate without taking Swiftly with you?"

"Ah! Not just for fishing then. Sorry about that," I said. I turned toward Swiftly. "I promise to take you with me next time I go to speak with my sister. We'll try not to discuss anything too embarrassing."

Swiftly looked slightly uncomfortable. His gaze darted to Lord Ruhall, whose eyes had closed. A red flush was making its way up his neck.

I took the opportunity to leave. Mr. Crow gave me a slight smile. Perhaps he was on my side after all.

* * * *

I collapsed on my bed, sweat soaking my back and face. How I wished for a magical bath to appear. I needed a long soak and to think. I'd never before felt so lost and confused.

Konrall still wasn't safe. Poor Sara was still being used by her husband. Bryn had turned her self-hatred on me. Blye wouldn't speak to me, either. The Whispering Sisters no longer offered peace and guidance. Aryana, herself, had betrayed me. And above all, I missed the beast. I still had my father, but he had been burdened too much already in his life by trying to protect his daughters. Where did that leave me? With no one to talk to. Alone with my confused thoughts. Wondering what I should do with myself.

I stood and wandered to the adjoining doors, opening them. He didn't have his side locked. The room looked the same. Smelled the same. I opened the door of his wardrobe. The same shirts hung there. I took one and left, closing the doors behind me.

Stripping from the gown, I washed with the cool water in the pitcher and changed into his shirt. With his smell wrapped around me, I crawled under the covers, ignoring the sun.

Nothing ever stayed the same. But tomorrow had to be better.

Four

The sound of my door pulled me from a light, troubled sleep where Tennen and Splane continued to chase me through the trees. Before I thought my dream reality, Alec spoke.

"Benella, are you awake?"

Had I actually slept, his soft words would not have disturbed me. Still, I pretended to sleep, hoping he would leave and wishing I had remembered to lock the door.

The mattress dipped as he sat next to me. His hands found my hair, undoing my braid, and the wood creaked as he leaned back against the headboard. His fingers combed through my long tresses and helped me forget the day's chase, the dream, and my troubles.

At some point, he stopped sitting beside me and slipped under the covers. I woke with his arm draped over my side and his hand splayed over the skin of my stomach under my shirt. His deep breathing told me he slept. Yet, I frowned. His smooth skin wasn't right. It made my skin crawl and my breathing shorten with dread.

I rolled to my stomach, seeking a more comfortable position while remembering the pleasant touch of the beast's fur on my skin and fell back to sleep.

* * * *

Egrit woke me with a chipper good morning. I burrowed deeper and refused to open my eyes. She went on, undeterred.

"You've slept long enough according to Lord Ruhall," she said with a laugh in her voice. "He's waiting for you in the study."

I groaned. Despite his warm presence, I hadn't slept well. My dreams had returned to Tennen chasing me and the beast rescuing me.

"Please extend my regrets," I said, pulling the covers higher. "I'm ill disposed." To sunlight and men, I thought.

There was a moment of silence.

"I'll leave the tray. If you feel better, you'll want to eat."

She left the room, and I remained in bed. My problem was two-fold. I missed the beast, and I missed the direction my life had while I was helping him. My father's employment by Lord Ruhall was perfect. For him. Not for me. Seeing Lord Ruhall just made me miss the beast more.

Perhaps it was time I ventured into the world on my own. The thought terrified me as much as it did excite me. Yet, I wanted to feel useful again.

With a sigh, I rolled toward the window and opened my eyes. Lying in bed wouldn't change my future.

I washed with the cool water in the basin then removed a plain gown from the wardrobe. I dressed slowly, thinking of the possibilities. They were too far and too uncertain. I needed to speak with my father. While I refused to burden him with my troubles in Konrall, I saw no reason not to seek his guidance regarding options for my future. In the past, his counsel always proved helpful.

I left my room and sought him out in the library. He had a small desk set near the fire where he liked to work. If he wasn't there, he tended to hunt the kitchen for food or monitor the progress on the barn.

When I stepped through the library doors, he looked up from his ledger and smiled at the sight of me. He stood as I approached and leaned in to kiss my cheek.

"We missed you at breakfast. Are you feeling better?"

"I feel fine, Father. It's my thoughts that plague me."

He motioned for me to take a seat then sat beside me.

"Tell me," he said.

I clasped my hands and thought for a moment.

"I've lost my purpose and am struggling to think of a new one. Bryn and Blye have both found their way. I'm old enough to find my own." I hesitated for a moment. "I'm thinking of leaving." I watched his expression, afraid what I said might have hurt him.

"Leaving?" He looked troubled and glanced at the study door, which stood open, then back at me. "Do you seek my blessing or my advice?"

"Advice."

He sat back and stared at the flames for a while. I waited patiently.

"I believe the suggestion I would offer you now, might be selfish. I don't want to lose you. May I have some time to think on this?"

"Of course." I kissed his cheek. "That's why I came to you. As much as I want to leave, I want to stay," I said, standing.

My father remained there watching the flames as I walked away. I wandered the halls for a while, letting my feet choose their own path. Eventually, I found myself back in my room. I opened the window to let in the fresh air and leaned against the sill.

A crash followed by a string of cursing came from the adjoining room. I recognized Lord Ruhall's voice and walked to the door. Something hit it with a thud and fell to the floor on the other side. I laid my hand on the door and smiled. It reminded me of the time I'd locked myself in his room. But the beast was gone, leaving behind a man I didn't understand or very much like. Straightening my shoulders, I knocked.

The room on the other side silenced then the door swung open. Lord Ruhall's disheveled appearance shocked me. He'd ripped the seam on the right shoulder of his jacket, his neckcloth hung askew, and his hair stood on end. His chest rose and fell with his rapid breathing.

"You wear my shirt to bed then tell your father you want to leave. Why?"

I blinked at him. I'd forgotten about the shirt when he'd entered the room last night.

"I wore the shirt because I miss him," I admitted, tearing my gaze from his.

"Him?" he said with a confused frown.

A brief small smile lifted my lips, a sad offering of amusement.

"The beast. The very creature chosen to be your punishment, the one you loathed...the one I want back." I kept my eyes on the ground, unable to look at him to see what he thought of me.

"Why?" He didn't sound angry or upset anymore.

"He growled, threw fits, chased me about the estate, made all manner of inappropriate demands of me, but he also did something else."

"What?"

My chest ached with the truth.

"He made me love him," I said, finally meeting his eyes.

Joy lit his face, then after meeting my sad gaze, a somber frustration crept in.

"You stubborn girl," he growled. "I am still that beast!"

"No, you are not." It hurt speaking the words aloud. My heart ached with what I'd lost. The man before me was but a poor replacement for the beast who'd stolen my heart.

"You growl and yell at servants, yet you are stuffy and detached.

The beast with all his anger and frustration didn't hold back his feelings. Well, not much," I added, recalling the many times he had in fact shown restraint.

"Are you calling me cold?" he asked, appalled.

I considered how he had stood in the doorway when he'd found me with the baker, how he'd helped Egrit and I clear the top floor, and how he'd sat through so many meals with me, speaking of nothing but estate affairs. His tantrum on the other side of the door just now wasn't his usual behavior.

"Yes, I think I am."

"I see," he said.

I expected him to walk out the door. Instead, he turned the lock.

"Sir?" I asked hesitantly.

"Alec," he corrected, removing his jacket.

"What are you doing?" I asked as he turned and stalked toward me.

"Changing your opinion of me." With a slight smile, he reached up and unknotted his neckcloth.

Panic flared in my chest as I understood his meaning, and I started to back away. He caught my wrist.

"I don't think so."

His thumb gently stroked the sensitive skin protecting my pulse, and my heart started to beat in fear.

"Please don't do this." My breaths started coming too fast. I felt the baker's weight pushing down on me again. "I won't let you do this." Panic and desperation pitched my voice.

Horror filled Alec's expression.

"Benella, no. I would never..."

Instead of stepping away, he wrapped his arms around me, pinning me to his chest.

"Never," he whispered in my ear as I shook.

He made no further move, other than to run his hand over my hair. I breathed in the smell of him and closed my eyes, imagining I had the beast back. He held me tightly until the shaking stopped.

When he pulled back, he looked as lost as I felt. He dropped his hands to his sides and stared at me.

"I don't know how to prove who I am."

"You don't need to."

"I don't need to because you think you already know." His gaze reflected the pain I'd caused him. He shook his head and left, slamming his door.

For some reason, my eyes began to water.

I hoped Father wouldn't need too long to consider my plight.

* * * *

An hour later, someone knocked, disturbing my musings. I opened the door and found my father standing just outside. Hope lit me from the inside, despite his grave expression.

"I cannot find Lord Ruhall. Do you know where he might be?"

Lord Ruhall? Keeping my disappointment hidden, I answered.

"Did you try his room?"

"Yes. Right after you left, a boy delivered this. I've been looking for him since then." Father handed me a letter.

I fully expect you to hold with tradition and open the manor for the harvest feast with invitations sent to appropriate guests only. I will be watching. ~Rose

"Harvest feast?" I said, looking up at Father.

"I don't have the details of what this means but with only three hundred gold to last until spring, I cannot see how the estate might host any feast. That she wants invitations sent..."

Invitations typically went to those of wealth. Those equal to Lord Ruhall's standing. For two heartbeats, happiness filled me. It was impossible to do, just as my father had suggested. The beast would return.

Guilt killed my brief joy. No matter how much I missed the beast, I could not condemn Alec to a fate he did not deserve. He had paid for his past sins and truly seemed to have learned from them. He didn't chase after women, drink, or gamble; and he was working hard to amend the poor affairs of his estate. He had suffered enough. Rose's game needed to end. And my father deserved steady employment without the threat of enchantment.

I tapped the letter against my palm with resolve and started to consider options. The three hundred gold currently noted in the ledgers needed to remain there for the estate to endure over winter and prosper once more in spring. Could a feast be hosted without spending estate gold?

"We need more information to know exactly what this feast entails. I'll find Mr. Crow; you keep searching for Lord Ruhall."

With purpose, I strode from the room.

* * * *

Mr. Crow proved as hard to find as Lord Ruhall. His usual post by the door was vacant as were the library and study. I left Father in the study to wait for Lord Ruhall while I continued my search. Near the kitchen, I heard voices.

"If the food preparation is complete, then use your time to polish the silver. Idle hands will not be tolerated here."

"Yes, sir," Mrs. Wimbly said with a bob of her head as I entered. Her gaze met mine, and I suspected we had the same thought. My hands, when idle, seemed tolerated well enough.

Looking away, I spotted a kettle on the block and realized I'd missed breakfast and the midday meal. My stomach rumbled hungrily but I knew I would not be welcomed to eat just then. After Mrs. Wimbly turned away to find an appropriate task for herself, I moved toward Mr. Crow.

"May I speak with you?"

"Certainly, Miss Hovtel," he said formally.

He walked me to the cook's personal room. The cookbooks that the beast and I had combed through were missing, the floor was scrubbed, and the window was open to let in the fresh air. Mr. Crow sat behind the desk.

"Is this your study now?"

"Yes. I made the mistake of ignoring the day-to-day activities of the staff in the past and will not repeat it."

I wondered how an office in the kitchen helped that, but didn't ask.

"Can you tell me about the harvest feast that used to be held here?"

"Large affairs that stopped long before Lady Ruhall left for the South, just after the current Lord Ruhall invited several...unsavory guests."

That explained Rose's note about appropriate guests.

"How many guests usually attended? Were certain families typically invited?"

"The harvest feast wasn't as formal as the winter feast. The doors opened to whichever locals Lady Ruhall saw fit to invite. Music and dancing filled the ballroom, and the tables groaned with food in the dining room." He sighed and looked out the window for a moment. "So many looked forward to the harvest feast. It was a time when the Lord and Lady did not stand above the rest. They joined them, listened to their problems, made merry with them. From Konrall to the Water, everyone looked forward to seeing an invitation delivered to their door."

I withheld my cringe. Though inviting locals meant a less grand affair, it also possibly meant a larger number of guests.

"An estimate, Mr. Crow. How many guests do you recall hosting?"

"As many as would fill the ballroom."

I sat in the chair across from his desk and set the letter before him. Sharing the information was necessary as it affected them all.

"Mr. Crow, Rose is placing a condition on the estate's continued freedom. The tradition of the harvest feast must renew. When does the feast typically take place?"

Mr. Crow paled.

"After the harvests are complete. Another three or four weeks, perhaps."

Four weeks. Three hundred coin. I bit my lip, thinking.

"How many servants did you have then? Twenty, wasn't it?" I said, answering myself.

"Yes. That included the cooks, livery men, housemaids, and myself."

The hopelessness in his tone caught my attention.

"Mr. Crow, do not give up before we start. We need an accounting of the stores. Every last thing from milk to wine, from wilted carrots to salted pork," I said, standing.

"Where will you be, Miss?"

"The ballroom."

I left the room and called for Egrit.

"I sent her to milk the goats," Mrs. Wimbly said, sounding impatient.

"Please send Swiftly or Tam to milk the goats and have Egrit meet me in the ballroom," I said as I walked toward the hall. I stopped, suddenly. "Oh, did Lord Ruhall say anything about the excess milk?"

She raised her nose a notch in the air.

"I have not yet approached him. Who are you to say—"

"Mrs. Wimbly," Mr. Crow said, walking from his study. "Afford Miss Hovtel the same respect you would afford Lord Ruhall or you will find yourself without employment."

His words surprised me. I wasn't the only one. Mrs. Wimbly looked shocked, and it took a moment for her to give the barest of nods.

Mr. Crow turned his attention to the assistant cook.

"Kara, show me the cellars. We need an accounting."

I was glad he wasn't giving up.

"Mr. Crow, have all the milk from the cellar loaded into a wagon. Let me know when it's done."

"Yes, Miss," he said.

Mrs. Wimbly still hadn't moved from the cutting board.

"Get Egrit, please," I said.

She nodded stiffly and left the room.

I strode through the halls, my heels striking the floor with determination. Rose would not win.

At the ballroom, I pushed open the doors. It wasn't as I remembered it, and I wondered if Rose's magic had enhanced it. Now, dust drifted in the thin streams of midday light that filtered in from the curtained windows. The large room echoed with my footfalls as I crossed to the windows and pulled back the drapes, one by one. Two sitting rooms opened from the ballroom, and balcony doors led to a tangle of vines. A dust rag wouldn't be enough to set the rooms aright. It would take a shovel, several scrub brushes, and an army of help to fix fifty years of neglect.

"Benella?" Egrit said from the doors.

I pulled the balcony doors closed and turned to face her.

"Egrit, Rose expects the estate to host a harvest feast within four weeks." I held out the letter to her.

Her shocked, pale expression matched Mr. Crow's as she glanced down at the brief note. I looked around, and the same hopelessness crept up my spine.

"It will take us a week just to get this cleaned and polished."

"The men are making good progress on the barn. Perhaps we could have two help in here," Egrit said.

I shook my head and rid myself of any thoughts of futility.

"I have another idea. Where did the servants stay? The room off the kitchen has only four beds."

"There's room for three pallets on the floor. There are also rooms in the attic. That's where I stay."

"Will you show me?"

She nodded and led the way to the third floor. Once there, she pushed against a panel that matched the wall, and a door swung open.

"How do I keep missing these staircases?" I asked.

Egrit laughed. "They're meant to be missed."

She led me up a narrow staircase to an equally narrow hall lined with little rooms fitted with two beds each. At the end of the hall was a locked door.

"The attic?"

She nodded. The rooms were small and dusty but otherwise serviceable. Each had a small round window for airing. I reached for a window and opened it.

"Egrit, it's time for us to visit the Water."

* * * *

The wagon rumbled past the market district. No one paid us attention until we turned onto the narrow path lined with the rundown homes of those who worked in trade. Children stood aside and watched us with wide eyes as we stopped before the house where I'd found a garden and someone willing to trade.

"Egrit, start knocking on the doors. A pail of milk for each house that wants it. Find out which homes have children between the ages of eight and twelve. Swiftly, stay by the wagon and keep an eye on Egrit." Both nodded and started working together to pour the milk. Children slowly drifted toward them.

I turned away and looked at the house I remembered. The soil in the side garden had been turned already. Nothing remained.

I knocked on the door, and it opened immediately. The woman looked a little thinner as did her children, and her eyes trailed to my hands. Her hopeful look faded when she saw them empty.

"Can I help you?" she asked, meeting my gaze.

"I think you can. May I come in?"

She nodded and held the door open. The children stood just behind her. Their neat clothes were well mended. Two rolled pallets sat near a cold hearth that was stacked with a few sticks of kindling.

"My name is Benella Hovtel. I'm here on behalf of Lord Ruhall."

Her eyes widened at the name.

"I'm Mrs. Palant."

"Pardon my question, but where is your husband?"

"We lost him last winter. He was a woodcutter." She didn't say more.

"How old are you two?" I asked, looking at the little boy and girl.

"Six and eight, Miss," the little boy said. He was the older of the two and held his sister's hand.

I looked at his mother. "The Liege Lord would offer your children an education in exchange for your work." She gave me a wary look. Many children were forced into work at an early age. Only those families with funds could see their children schooled.

"This is no trick. The children would attend private teachings at the estate six days a week from just after breakfast until just before dinner. All meals for you and your children will be provided by the estate. The children can do whatever tasks you give them to help you in your duties but will not be given work by any other member of Lord Ruhall's staff or by Lord Ruhall, himself. You would all live at the estate. There will be no other compensation for your labors," I said clearly. It was more than a fair deal while the children needed schooling.

She looked at her daughter, and I knew her thoughts. Most of the women in nearby houses traded their bodies for coin. If she stayed without a husband, it wouldn't be long before she found herself in the same position. What future could she then offer her daughter?

"There's a wagon just outside with enough room to carry what's needed. Take your time to think over the offer. I intend to return each week with the spare goat milk from the estate. It's not much, but it could help if you choose to stay," I said, standing and placing a hand on her shoulder. "I'll not play games with you. If you choose to accompany me, your children will not be ill-used and neither will you."

She nodded, still looking at her children. I let myself out.

A hand tugged my skirt, and I looked down at a girl no more than ten. Dirt dulled her pale blonde hair and streaked her left cheek. Her blue eyes darted to the wagon, then met mine.

"May I have milk?"

"Certainly. Did we miss your house?"

"I have no home."

"Where are your parents?"

She shrugged.

"Is there anyone here to care for you?"

She shook her head, and I felt a surge of pity for her.

"How old are you?"

"Eleven, Miss."

No one that age should be alone to fend for themselves.

"And your name?"

"Otta."

"Otta, I'm here to offer employment at Lord Ruhall's estate in exchange for an education. You would be required to attend school six days and work afterward. You will be fed, clothed, and given a warm place to sleep. You will be treated fairly and cared for. Does that interest you?"

"Very much, Miss."

"Then into the wagon with you. Ask Swiftly for a cup of milk while you wait," I said, pointing at the wagon.

Egrit met me by the wagon.

"There are three houses on this side with children those ages. Many more with younger."

I nodded and mentioned Otta, who already waited in the wagon.

"She will be returning to the estate with us."

Egrit nodded. I'd already shared my plan with her and Swiftly during our ride to the Water.

When she moved to the wagon to continue distributing milk, I went to the houses Egrit had indicated. To those houses, I offered the same opportunity I had Otta since the women already had a trade to support themselves. The children would be educated during the day but would be required to work before breakfast and after dinner.

Only two of the women agreed to release their children. The third woman intended to introduce her twelve-year-old daughter to her trade. When she told me the price a virgin would fetch, I thought of the baker and struggled not to hit her.

I walked away from the house, not seeing the road I trod. Egrit caught my arm and pulled me toward the wagon.

"Horrid woman, that one," she said quietly.

"Quite," I agreed.

Two children already sat in the wagon. Mrs. Palant and her two children were working together to pack their belongings.

Watching them gave me an idea, and I stopped Mrs. Palant.

"What happens to your home when you leave it?"

She looked up and down the road at the other houses.

"One of them will claim it most likely."

Her house was in much better repair. All of the wood was solid, no rot, and there were no gaps between the boards.

"With your permission, I'd like to try trading it with the woman in that house," I pointed, "in exchange for her daughter."

"Meg has had plans for her daughter since she flowered. She's just waiting for the right buyer," she said quietly.

"Do you think your home might tempt her?"

"Not when all she needs to do is wait for me to leave."

"Yes, but so is everyone else."

Determined, I walked to Meg's door and knocked again. She answered with a surly expression.

"The house for the girl," I said without preamble.

Her eyes drifted behind me, and she laughed.

"I have no chance at that place. As soon as you leave there'll be a fight for who gets it."

"Unless we help the new owner move her belongings there and make it official." She glanced at the structure, her interest plain. "The girl will only be pure once," I said, the words souring my belly. "But that home will keep you warm for more than one winter."

"Retta, come here." A young woman stepped into the light of the doorway. A little girl held her hand. "You're going with this woman. Go."

She waved her hand at me. The little girl started crying.

"Want both of them?" the woman asked, looking at the younger child with no obvious affection.

"Yes."

* * * *

While Egrit led everyone to the top floor to air the rooms and settle in before dinner, I went to find Mr. Crow.

He sat behind his desk, staring down at a piece of parchment. When he saw me, he wilted a bit and without a word handed me the paper. Scanning the list, I understood his despondency. We did not have enough to feed us for the winter, especially with the additional staff I'd brought.

Absently, I sat across from him and stared out the window. Surviving with meager supplies was familiar to me. But would that knowledge help produce an excess of food for a feast? It had to. I turned to Mr. Crow, who watched me expectantly. I gave him a reassuring smile.

"There are plenty of fish in the rivers to the northwest and southeast. On the estate land, a skilled hunter could also find more large game." We just needed the men to fish it and hunt it. "We will succeed." I stood. "I'll speak with Lord Ruhall about having three of the men hunt and fish every day for the next several weeks. It will keep the cooks busy. Meals will need to be simple. See if you can recall any of the families who may have attended in the past. We'll need to create a guest list quickly."

Leaving Mr. Crow, I went to search for Father or Lord Ruhall. As I approached the library, I heard them both.

"What good could milk possibly do?" Lord Ruhall's angry voice rang through the room.

"I'm sure her reasons are sound," my father said.

I caught a glimpse of Alec, pacing in his study. His wide shoulders were hunched and his head bent as he worked his path. I could imagine his expression. No doubt the news of Rose's letter had upset him.

"My reasons are quite sound," I said, walking into the study. His tense face swung in my direction. "Lord Ruhall, I'm sure Father's explained Rose's letter." I handed him the note I still carried. "I left with the milk and returned with several additional servants."

He studied me for a long moment, his anger fading to frustration.

"We can't afford to employ more," he said, bracing his fisted hands on his desk. "You, yourself, suggested trimming their numbers."

"Their wages will not be paid in coin. You have a teacher who is not teaching. So I brought a mother who could never afford an education for her two children and several older children who are willing to work in the morning and evenings in exchange for their education. It's a fair trade."

"Children, Benella?" my father said with shock.

"Father, here we will not ill-use them. They will have the sleep they need, a warm bed, food in their bellies, and an education in exchange for four hours of work a day. It is a far brighter future than what waited for them where they were."

Though Father continued to look troubled, he nodded.

"Benella, servants aren't enough." Lord Ruhall straightened away from the desk and began to pace behind it once more. "What she's asking is impossible for three hundred coins."

I agreed, but I kept quiet. He already looked ready to yell. He didn't need me to further his despair. He needed hope, at least until I could look at the ledgers to discover the cost of past feasts. So, I walked toward the desk and leaned in until we met eye to eye.

"As impossible as freeing a beast from a fifty year enchantment, I imagine. Allow me a chance to try."

As his gaze swept over my face, the rest of the anger faded. Another expression took hold. Tenderness. I couldn't call it anything else. My stomach flipped, and my cheeks warmed in response.

"Of course," he said. "Tell me what needs to be done."

I straightened, putting distance between us.

"Please speak with your teacher and inform him he will have students starting tomorrow. There are seven aged between four and twelve. Most cannot read. He should start teaching after they've eaten. The children are not to be given work during their schooling hours, and Mrs. Palant's children aren't to be given work by anyone other than their mother.

"Also, if possible, we need three of the five men to focus on hunting and fishing. We need a larger quantity of game to store in the next few weeks."

Unable to maintain eye contact any longer, I cleared my throat, and met my father's gaze.

"Father, I need you to work with Mr. Crow and determine a guest list from Konrall and the Water. Mr. Crow said that, in the past, they filled the ballroom. I'd like to be conservative with the invitations while still meeting Rose's requirements. Next year, we can pack the room. As soon as you have a count, please let me know."

Five

The daunting task of cleaning loomed before me. Even with the extra help, cleaning the ballroom, parlors, dining room, and main sitting rooms before the feast would be difficult. But not impossible. Since Egrit, Mrs. Palant, and the children would remain occupied with airing the attic until after dinner, I meant to make some progress in the ballroom yet that day.

In the laundry, I filled several of the large, empty vats and started a fire in the pit under the first one. Everything in the ballroom and parlors needed a dusting and a washing. Hot water would make the task easier.

Mrs. Wimbly's voice reached me as I stepped into the hall.

"Seven more mouths to feed and she influenced Lord Ruhall to dismiss one of my staff? What is that woman thinking?"

I quickly moved away. Her tasks, to keep us fed and to store enough food for the feast and the winter, would not be easy. Yet, we couldn't afford more help for her. I hoped we wouldn't find ourselves missing a head cook.

In the ballroom, I stopped to look around and plan. The room needed more light to clean it properly. I checked the parlors and found the same problem. Though I was tempted to yank the curtains open, I did not. They were filthy like everything else and needed to be removed. I stared up at the hooks that held the drapes to the runner above the window.

"Need help?" Alec's quiet voice startled me. I turned and found him just behind me, scowling up at the hooks.

"The curtains here and in the ballroom need to be removed, beaten, and washed."

"Are you sure they will survive that?" He reached around me and plucked at the dust covered fabric. His arm brushed against mine, sending a tingle of awareness through me.

I moved away and studied the material.

"I hope so." The estate couldn't afford to replace them and winter without them would be chilly.

"I'll have one of the men come in with a ladder and remove them after sundown. Perhaps you can join me for dinner, and we can discuss the details of what you plan."

"Certainly. Father can join us and share his progress on the guest list."

He gave a small sigh before he left the room.

I had an hour at least until dinner. Best to put the time to use.

* * * *

"He sent me looking for you," Egrit said from the door. Amusement laced her voice.

I straightened, and my spine made a loud cracking sound. The furniture of the first parlor now sat in the ballroom. It had taken much effort to pull the pieces out, and more effort still to roll up the large rug that dominated the space.

"I think he expects you to dine with him," she said.

"Yes. Of course." I brushed my hands on my skirts. "Are Mrs. Palant and the children settled in?"

"Yes. And fed." Amusement changed to barely contained laughter. "Are you going like that?"

Looking down at myself, I saw dust had made a muddle of my skirts. My sleeves, though rolled back, were dingy, and my bodice had finger streaks. I couldn't remember touching my bodice.

"I'm afraid I am. I plan to return here as soon as I finish meeting with Lord Ruhall. I have resolved to keep cleaning until I lose the light."

"Hmm," she said, eyeing the room.

I saw doubt in her gaze. In the time I'd spent in the room, I'd made no progress actually cleaning it, just emptying it.

I wiped away a stray strand of hair from my face as I moved toward Egrit. While I knew I'd eventually make progress on the parlor, I still wasn't sure what to do about the menu for the feast. Fish and game were only a start.

"I've been considering what foods to offer. In your jaunts around the estate, do you recall any fruit or nut trees?" I asked as we walked through the halls.

"Several actually. There is an apple grove and a couple stands of hazelnut trees."

"Perfect. Tomorrow, I want to see them. But I'll need you and Mrs. Palant to help in the sitting rooms and ballroom. Do you think Tam could show me the way?"

"I'll speak with him tonight. I'm sure he can."

At the library, she gave me a large smile then left me.

I strode through the doors and found Father's desk empty and the study door closed. The whisper of my boots across the rugs sounded loud in the silence. What could Father and Lord Ruhall be discussing that brought about such a hush? I paused to knock.

Lord Ruhall opened the door. His tense shoulders and tight jaw told me he was upset. His eyes swept over me, lingering the longest on my face.

"Benella, what happened to you?"

"I've been in the southern sitting room off the ballroom and am pleased to say I've made good progress." I didn't clarify that the progress only included furniture arrangement and not actual cleaning. His daunted expression told me he already worried enough.

He stepped back and motioned me in. Several paces into the study, I stopped short. A small table with two place settings waited before the fireplace. The room was empty, save for the two of us. Behind me, the door closed.

"Where's Father?" I said, turning to look at Lord Ruhall.

He scowled at me. There was no mistaking his surly mood.

"He has no progress to share yet and wanted me to remind you that he just started the list today."

I nodded absently and edged my way toward the table. Lord Ruhall slowly followed. Why was I feeling so wary? Perhaps it was his focused attention or perhaps the expression he wore was similar to the one he'd worn this morning after he'd thought to show me he wasn't cold. Right now, he looked anything but cold. His flushed face concerned me.

"Isn't it a bit warm for a fire already, sir?"

"Alec," he said, correcting me. "It was a little chilly in here after a day with the window open." He trailed me, making a game of slowly chasing me around the room. It reminded me too much of the way the beast had stalked me on more than one occasion.

"I believe I'm not yet hungry."

He stopped moving and narrowed his eyes.

"Benella, sit."

"I think not."

He ran a hand through his hair, looked ready to yell, but then took a deep breath.

"I made this myself," he said, gesturing at the covered plates. Though his manner hadn't changed, that he'd cooked piqued my interest.

"Really? You cooked?"

"You know the extent of my skill," he said.

My gaze met his. I realized he sought to show me that he and the beast were the same person. My heart lurched. He didn't understand.

Logically, I knew they were the same. Yet, inside, I remained torn in reconciling the two. The man who had been held back by a simple hand on his shoulder, the man who had chosen his freedom over saving me from—I felt a heaviness on my chest and stopped the direction of my thought. That man was not the beast who had scared off Tennen and Splane so many times. Neither was he the beast who had risked Rose's wrath to fetch me from her cottage. One side of him wanted me above all else, and the other sacrificed me for his own desire.

I closed my eyes against the ache in my chest. It wasn't for loss of purpose that I wanted to leave the North. It was to avoid the pain of seeing the man who didn't want me enough.

Lips brushed my cheek, and my eyes flew open.

He pulled back enough to meet my gaze.

"As a man, I can finally do the one thing I craved to do as a beast."

"What is that?"

"Kiss you." He leaned in once more to the other cheek. His touch was infinitely light. Warm lips, soft compared to the beast's, yet still firm. A little bird took flight in my breast, beating its wings against its boned cage and robbing me of air.

His lips retreated.

"Sit. Please." He pulled out a chair for me.

Sitting, I watched him walk to his place. He seemed more relaxed now. Why? Was it the kiss or that I'd agreed to dine with him?

He uncovered the plates, and I couldn't help the smile that spread across my face. The sad little egg tartlet wasn't as burnt as the last time we'd made it. He was getting better.

"It looks delicious, my Lord."

"Alec."

"How did Mrs. Wimbly react to the use of her kitchen?"

His puzzlement over the name I'd used disappeared as quickly as it had appeared.

"Ah, the cook. I sent her and her assistant away so no one would witness my attempt."

I took a bite. The flavor was there, and the texture not bad.

"Much improved," I said after I swallowed. "Where did you find the eggs?"

"Tam and I left this morning to search for the game keeper's cottage. I had recalled the estate having one. We found it."

I nibbled on the tartlet as I listened.

"The cottage is in good repair, spared perhaps by the enchantment. Beside the cottage is an overgrown, fenced pasture. The grass had grown so high we couldn't see the goats after we'd herded them in. It will help the winter hay last longer. On the other side of the pasture, we found a barn that can easily house the goats as well as several other animals. But the prize was the quail pen beside the barn. When we opened the door, Tam almost took a quail to the head. They flew out in a drove but didn't go far. No one has been out there in fifty years yet the birds seem tame. Tam is working on the netting for their side pen."

"This is wonderful news. Eggs and milk. The estate is on its way to self-sufficiency. How close is the cottage?"

"It's a distance, near the east wall. Tam and I believe we found the old path to it. We'll need to clear it again for a wagon."

"Egrit told me the estate also has apple and hazelnut trees. I've asked if Tam can take me to them tomorrow. I'm hoping we can incorporate the fruit into the feast's menu. If there's anything to harvest, we will need Swiftly and Tam to switch from the main barn to those efforts. I plan to keep our new help busy cleaning in here. I'm reluctant to pull the hunters from their task until we have a full cellar."

"A sound plan."

I took another bite of my dinner and considered how the addition of eggs and apples might help the menu.

"Do you recall the food you usually served?" I asked.

He shook his head and shame painted his face.

"My mother handled those details. The last few years, I didn't attend regularly; but when I did, I brought unsuitable company." His words grew strained. "I was such a fool. I miss her," he said.

I reached across the table and set my hand on his. I had no words to offer him. We were meant to make mistakes. We learned from them. But how did one console another for a mistake that cost him his mother? He turned his hand to hold mine. His thumb softly rubbed the back of mine for a moment before I pulled away. When he touched me like that, my heart felt too vulnerable.

We ate the rest of the meal in silence, and I was glad he didn't ask for any further details of what I had planned for I didn't yet have any.

If we had eggs, milk, apples, and nuts, we had the base for some simple fare. Father and Mr. Crow would handle the guest list, Mrs. Wimbly the cooking, and the rest of us the cleaning. Could it be that

Devastation

simple? What was I missing? I needed to look at his ledgers.

While I absently stared at the table and took a sip of my water, a missing piece fell into place, and I wrinkled my nose.

"Table linens, serving dishes, and something to drink." I groaned as I thought of another piece. "And music. What kind of music?" I looked up and met his amused gaze.

"That wonderful head of yours never stops, does it?"

"As my father recently brought to my attention, when it does, I grow bored."

The relaxed calm fled his expression as his jaw tightened.

"And boredom doesn't suit you, does it," he said softly. He straightened in his chair and, with an almost accusatory glance, continued our conversation.

"The linens we have—if time hasn't damaged them—as well as the serving dishes. If there are enough apples, Mrs. Wimbly could press them for cider."

"A perfect harvest drink," I said in agreement. I itched to wander out to the grove now to see if there were enough, but I needed to start the actual cleaning of the southern parlor.

"Thank you for cooking for me, sir—Alec," I quickly corrected myself after a hard look from him. "I want to continue working in the parlor until the sun sets. Did you want me to take the tray back to the kitchen?" I stood.

"Go," he said with an annoyed wave. "I can take care of this."

I didn't try to guess what had irritated him. It was better not to delve too deeply. I felt his gaze on me as I left the library.

In the ballroom, just outside the sitting room, I found two buckets of ash. Inside the room, I found Egrit and Mrs. Palant hard at work. Soot no longer coated the fireplace, and the smaller rugs lay rolled up in the ballroom, leaving the sitting room floor exposed to their exhaustive effort. A good half of the area was clean.

"Thank you both," I said, stepping into the room. "I didn't expect you to work on your first night, Mrs. Palant. Are your children asleep?"

"Retta offered to put them to bed. I wanted to see what work needed to be done."

"Make sure Retta and the children know they can seek you out whenever they wish. This isn't a strict household and you working here should not deprive them of their mother."

I picked up a wet rag and joined their efforts. With three of us laboring, we finished the floor just a bit after dark. As we were leaving, Tam and Swiftly entered with candles and a ladder.

"We just washed the southern parlor floor," Egrit said to both of them. "Don't dirty it with your boots or dripping wax."

"Yes, ma'am," Tam said with a wink.

Egrit shook her head at him and turned to me.

"I saw Lord Ruhall refilling the kettle when I went for the last bucket of warm water. There should be plenty for us to bathe." She handed me a pail of dirty water. "I'll run and get us something clean to change into."

Mrs. Palant and I went to wait in the laundry where we worked together to fill a large washing kettle and the wooden tub with warm water.

When Egrit returned, she insisted I take the tub while they washed from a bucket. They'd somehow avoided wearing the grime I wore. I willingly stripped and slid into the water with a sigh. Once I finished washing away the dust, I forced myself from the pleasant water and dressed in a clean nightgown and wrap before throwing my dirty dress into the bath water. Egrit and Mrs. Palant threw in the aprons they had wisely worn. At Egrit's insistence, I left them to finish the laundry since Tam planned to take me to the woods at first light.

I padded barefoot through the halls but didn't go to my room. Though I had an idea of what the feast might entail because of Mr. Crow and Lord Ruhall, I wanted specifics. I needed to read the ledgers.

In the library only a glow of coals remained in the fireplace, which didn't surprise me. Father usually left after dinner unless Lord Ruhall requested something from him. Tiptoeing across the room in the moonlight, I focused on the dim study. An unlit candle waited on the desk, along with three ledgers. The three years before Alec's enchantment. Each held a bookmark on a page with the feast's accounting. Alec had obviously wondered the same thing and sought the answers in the ledgers as well. I quickly scanned the marked pages. The feast cost the estate dearly. Even the last year Alec's mother had hosted it. Three hundred gold. An impossible amount. I would just need to find a way to spend as little as possible and keep Alec from worrying.

I left the study and quickly made my way to my room. Someone had turned down the covers. I slipped under them and closed my eyes.

* * * *

The bed moved, waking me. Alec sat back against the headboard and ran his fingers through my damp, unbound hair.

"Please," he whispered, his voice raw.

My breath caught. Did he know he had woken me? I could think of only one reason he came to me in the middle of the night with such a pretty, desperate word on his lips. Panic took flight in my chest. Yet, he didn't seem to notice the change in my breathing as his fingers continued to run through my hair.

"Please. Please don't let her leave me."

The desperation in his whispered words stopped the panic. My heart broke for him as I suddenly understood his anger in the ballroom and at dinner. He had been in the study when I had spoken to Father and knew I meant to leave him.

He truly believed he needed me. Perhaps he did. Rose's letter regarding the feast made it clear she wasn't done with him. I would need to assure him I meant to stay through the feast. But not now when his mood was so volatile. I remained still as his fingers ran through my hair until he lulled me to sleep once more.

* * * *

The next morning, I woke with a start and sat up. The bed beside me was empty. I stared at the spot for a moment, disoriented, then flopped back onto the bed. Alec thought I meant to abandon him before the feast. I'd need to tell him I meant to stay through the feast. But, how could I tell him without making him aware I'd been awake?

The door opened.

"Good morning," Egrit said in a chipper tone.

I groaned.

"You go to bed the same time I do. How do you wake before me?" I asked.

"When I set my head to my pillow, I immediately sleep. Do you?"

I used to. Lately, however, my mind raced long after I set my head to my pillow. It didn't help that Lord Ruhall interrupted my sleep as well. Egrit didn't wait for me to answer.

"Tam's waiting for you."

I didn't need further motivation to remove myself from bed. I hurried to dress.

The apples proved plentiful but not yet ripe, whereas the nuts had already ripened and most had fallen. With Tam's estimate of another two weeks for the apples to be ready, I gathered what nuts remained and took them to the kitchen. Given Mrs. Wimbly's continued surly mood, I kept the news of the apples to myself and went off to help in the ballroom once more.

While I assisted washing the large, long curtains, I pondered the menu. The unripe apples were a blessing as the kitchen could now remain focused on preparation and storage until just before the feast. Yet, would such a short timeframe be enough when they still had to cook meals?

I left Mrs. Palant and Egrit to wring and hang the material and went to the kitchen to seek Mrs. Wimbly's opinion. Hard at work with a stag on the block and several fish waiting on the table, she scowled at me when I entered. I left the room with my answer. She would not much appreciate additional work.

While the curtains dried, Egrit, Mrs. Palant, and I returned to the ballroom to move the furniture outdoors for an airing. The first piece gave us trouble as we moved it into the overgrown garden. Brambles tugged at our skirts and poked the old material covering the cushions.

"I'm going to tell Tam we need this weeded," Egrit said.

I nodded my agreement. If the ballroom became stuffy during the feast, we would need to open the doors for air. The tangle of vegetation would prevent anyone from stepping out.

The three of us stomped down what weeds we could and spent the rest of the day moving pieces outside.

After dinner, Retta and Lettie found us and explained that Otta had remained behind to watch the younger children; and Tom, the older boy, was with Mr. Crow. I'd forgotten they were to help clean but quickly found tasks for them to perform. Once we finished, they helped us move the pieces indoors. Though I knew the work they did was better than what would have waited for them, it did bother me to see the weary droop to their shoulders at the end of the day.

Yet, the children were no wearier than we were. Making the barest of efforts, I washed before bed and slid under the covers. It was only then that I recalled I hadn't spoken to Lord Ruhall about staying through until the end of the feast.

I briefly considered locking the door before I closed my eyes.

*   *   *   *

The next day Egrit, Mrs. Palant and I worked on the second parlor, and our progress moved slower than the passing hours. By dinner, the furniture and rugs were outside and beaten and the fireplace free of soot. This time Retta and Otta joined us.

"We'll take turns watching the little ones," Retta said. "If that's all right."

"It is. Did you two eat already?" They shook their heads. "Let's all stop for dinner."

We walked together to the kitchen and found the other children already at the table. They quietly watched Kara, the assistant cook, scoop a portion of dinner into their bowls.

Mrs. Wimbly stood at the block, scrubbing the surface clean. As she worked, she mumbled. I couldn't catch everything but enough to know that she didn't like that the children had come in for dinner. She moved a polished tray to the clean block then started to set it precisely.

She'd just set the food upon it when one of the men came in with a string of fish. She heaved a sigh.

"Set them in the basin. I'll deal with them in a bit."

"Is there somewhere the tray needs to be, Mrs. Wimbly? I'd be happy to deliver it so you can address the fish."

"It's a tray for Lord Ruhall," she said stiffly. She still didn't like me despite all the hard work I put in alongside everyone else.

"Then I'll deliver it for you."

She set the tray on the table and turned her back to me. Kara's gaze darted between the two of us. I smiled at Kara before I picked up the tray and left.

Father wasn't at his paper stacked desk or anywhere else in the library. From the study, I heard his voice.

"We've stopped at one hundred and twenty-five," he said.

Silence greeted him.

I stepped into the room and caught Alec's hopeless gaze.

"None of that now. Have you already gone through the list?"

"Is there a need?" Alec asked, watching me set the tray on the small table. I took the plate from it and set it before him but stole one of his biscuits before I turned away. I doubted the cook would save me any dinner. Alec could share.

Father shook his head as I bit into the biscuit. I swallowed with a grin and sat to face Alec once more.

"Of course," I said, answering him. "You will need to converse with everyone who comes. Wouldn't you like to know their names and a little about them?"

"Very well. Mr. Hovtel, would you be kind and read the list for us?"

Father read the list and added a few comments about each guest. I kept my expression neutral when I heard Bryn and Edmund's names. Blye's name didn't bother me as much. I smiled when I heard Henick and his family would receive an invitation. I hoped they would attend. Alec's scowl only deepened.

"We had better add Rose's name," I said when Father reached the end.

They both looked at me, clearly surprised. I shrugged.

"She said she would be watching regardless. Consider the invitation your official acknowledgement of her observation, nothing more; and perhaps she will see the invitation as a gesture of goodwill."

I stood, knowing I needed to return to the ballroom.

"Where are you going?" Alec said.

The thread of concern in his words stopped me.

"For now, back to the ballroom. There is much to clean in a very short time." I hoped that inference would be enough to assure him that I meant to stay through the feast.

He nodded, and I left the pair.

Mrs. Palant, Egrit, and the girls were already hard at work scrubbing the floor. Seeing the room well occupied, I took the ladder outside and started to wash windows.

* * * *

The next morning, I woke with renewed ambition. At some point during the course of the night, I'd let go of my annoyance with Bryn long enough to realize Edmund might be the solution to Mrs. Wimbly's hectic schedule. Shortly after rising, I found myself walking toward Konrall to speak to him. This time, I brought Swiftly with.

"Benella, welcome," Edmund said when I walked into the bakery.

"Hello, Edmund. Allow me to introduce Swiftly. He is in Lord Ruhall's employ."

Above, the door to the second floor opened. I kept my smile on my face as Bryn descended. Her steps on the stairs slowed when she saw me, and her welcoming smile chilled. The arrival of another customer defused the tense moment.

"How can I help you?" Edmund said as Bryn moved to assist the other customer.

"Lord Ruhall is hosting a harvest feast. I would like to order two hundred pastries."

Edmund froze and Bryn stopped speaking to her customer to stare at me.

"I've had the sugar glazed kind from your bakery in the Water and enjoyed it immensely. However, I'm hoping you can work apples into a pastry for something out of the ordinary, something that would fit a harvest feast."

Edmund seemed to collect himself with a deep, slow breath, and Bryn went back to her customer.

"Apples...yes, I should be able to procure enough for two hundred pastries," Edmund said.

The customer left, and Bryn lingered by the counter.

"The estate has plenty, and I would be happy to send Swiftly back with the amount you need. They won't be ready for another two weeks," I said, knowing I'd just reduced the price he could charge. "Also, guests will be coming from the Water and a few even further afield. With so many guests sampling your sweet creations, you're sure to have new customers."

"This is for Lord Ruhall?" Bryn said, her voice heavy with disbelief. "Why would Lord Ruhall send you here to buy pastries?"

Since I'd already explained the reason behind the need for the pastries, I knew she was questioning why I was Lord Ruhall's emissary.

"Have you inquired after Father at all since you wed?" I asked. Her cheeks flushed, giving me her answer. "If you had, you would know he is no longer teaching but Lord Ruhall's man of estate. I'm assisting."

Bryn opened her mouth to say more, but a look from Edmund silenced her.

"Let's talk price in the back," he said, gesturing to the sitting room.

"No, thank you." I had no desire to visit that room again. "Perhaps the kitchen?"

Edmund nodded. When I moved around the counter, Swiftly followed; and I didn't mind his company. The kitchen had its own memories. Yet, when I stepped through the door, I couldn't recall them.

The back door stood open, letting in a breeze and light. No flour coated any surface. The old table was gone and a longer, thinner table had taken its place. There were also tall chairs near the high table. Edmund motioned to one and smiled at my questioning glance.

"It's easier on the back to switch from sitting to standing when working. The raised table helps, too."

"You look like you've quite settled in. Has business improved?"

"Not really. But perhaps this order will help."

"I think it will help both of us. I'll be honest, Edmund. After such a long enchantment, the estate struggles. It isn't what it once was, but Lord Ruhall is working hard to bring it back. Part of those efforts includes the harvest feast. It's not for the gentry, but for the merchants and common folk who depend on the estate."

"It feels as if you're trying to sell me something, Benella."

"In a way, I am. I'm trying to explain how you'll reach a larger market by baking for the harvest feast so when I tell you we can only pay a single gold for two hundred pastries, you won't kick me out."

Edmund sighed and his shoulders slumped, but he didn't kick me out. "That barely covers the cost of the flour, sugar, time to prepare—"

"I can also provide you with double the apples you'll need so you can produce the same pastries after the feast is over." He still looked troubled. "And promise a portion of next year's hazelnuts?"

His expression took on a speculative gleam. I sat quietly and waited for him to think over the offer. I was loath to part with a single gold piece but knew it only fair. If he didn't start receiving coin soon, there would be no baker in Konrall.

"You have a deal," Edmund said, offering his hand.

I shook it with a grin, feeling quite pleased with myself.

Swiftly and I left the bakery, together, after assuring Edmund I would keep him apprised of the progress of the apple harvest. I only hoped that promising him double the apples would leave enough for cider. If not, there was always spring water.

"He doesn't seem to like you any better," Swiftly said softly, interrupting my thoughts.

I followed his gaze and found Tennen watching us.

"His like or dislike is no bother to me," I said, looking away. "I've more important things to worry about."

"The feast will be a welcome respite because of your efforts," he said.

"I hope so."

We walked the rest of the way in silence. By the time we returned, we'd missed the midday meal. As I went to the kitchen for a quick bite, I heard a faint giggle. I walked slowly, listening. In the dim hall, just before I reached the laundry, I found a staircase leading up.

"I must be the least observant person here," I said under my breath.

At the top of the stairs, a hall led right above the kitchen and left above the laundry and formal dining room. Another faint peal of laughter came from the left.

A door opened to a large room. Inside, the children sat at small tables with the youngest in front and the oldest in back. A weathered man, dressed in a neat, yet worn, jacket decades out of fashion, wrote the letter D on the blackboard. He caught sight of me when he turned to his students.

"Welcome. Students, please welcome Miss Hovtel."

"Good afternoon, Miss Hovtel," they said in unison.

"What manners," I said with a smile.

"Manners, letters, and numbers, Miss Hovtel. I've found the letters and numbers do no good without manners."

I met the man's steady gaze, and he bowed slightly.

"Mr. Roost, at your service. I believe the last time I saw you, you were at the pond."

And, like that, I could see the resemblance in his features to those that had twice adorned the tree.

I smiled and gave a slight bow back.

"Do you have the supplies you need to teach this group?"

"Oh yes. The previous student did not use much of his supplies."

Alec had admitted to being a poor student.

"I'll leave you to your class then. Good afternoon children," I said, moving toward the door.

After leaving the schoolroom, I went to tell Father about my deal with Edmund.

Father sat at his desk, busily penning a letter. From the study, I heard a similar faint scratch of ink on parchment.

"Ah, Bini," Father said, looking up as he heard me enter. "How is the progress in the parlor today?"

"The second sitting room was almost finished yesterday. I hope we can start on the main ballroom yet today. How is everything here?"

"We've penned over half the invitations. By this evening, we should have two piles ready for the riders who will go out at dawn. I'll walk to the Water to hand deliver the ones in town."

"That is good news. I've made a deal with Edmund to make apple pastries for the feast. Twice as many apples as he'll need for two hundred pastries, for half the price he would normally charge. I'll need a gold to pay him when we deliver the apples."

Father nodded and made a note.

"Give my warm regards to Blye when you see her tomorrow," I said as I left.

Father nodded absently, already back to penning the next invitation.

Egrit, Mrs. Palant, and I used the rest of the afternoon to clean the parlor. Once we finished, Egrit went to press the curtains while Mrs. Palant and I set to work scrubbing the remaining windows. Once again, I skipped dinner and fell into bed exhausted.

When the bed dipped long after I'd fallen asleep, I barely roused. Gentle fingers began to untwist the braid from my hair. Sleep reclaimed me before he finished.

* * * *

When the sun hit my eyes, I groaned and rolled over. It took a moment to realize what the light meant. Sitting up, I looked at the windows. As I'd suspected, it was well past daybreak.

After a mad scramble of dressing and making my bed, I left my room and hurried to the ballroom. Both Mrs. Palant and Egrit were on ladders, using cloths tied to the end of long branches to dust the webs from the walls and ceiling.

"Why didn't you wake me?" I asked. Sun lit the room through the clean windows. The doors to the garden were wide open, and Tam whistled as he pulled up weeds from the immediate path.

"I tried. Lord Ruhall heard me and suggested I let you sleep."

Unsure how I felt about that, I changed the subject.

"I'm going to find myself something to eat in the kitchen and check on preparations while I'm there. I'll return to help."

The manor was quiet with everyone at their tasks. Father and the riders had left with first light, and Lord Ruhall was out hunting to replace the man who was helping Swiftly.

Mrs. Wimbly said little as I entered the kitchen and took a biscuit from a sack on the shelves. Mr. Crow nodded to me. He sat at the table, polishing silver and, it appeared, sorting through linens.

A swell of satisfaction carried me back to the ballroom and invigorated my cleaning efforts.

It was well past dark before I sought my bed. Just as sleep pulled me under, I reminded myself to search out Father to see how his visit with Blye had gone.

*   *   *   *

The bed dipped. His familiar fingers laced through my hair as they worked the braid free. I sighed, enjoying the feeling. When he finished, his arms wrapped around me and pulled me against his chest. His lips brushed the back of my neck. The sensation didn't disturb me. Instead, it comforted me; and I settled deeper into sleep.

Six

Egrit woke me with a chipper good morning and a tray.

"You didn't need to bring me a tray," I said, untangling myself from the blankets.

"Lord Ruhall has noted that you haven't been eating enough and thought to prepare you a tray. I met him in the hall, and I insisted it wouldn't be proper for him to bring it himself."

I glanced at her face and saw she was entirely serious.

"I walked these halls shrouded in nothing but mist," I said. "I hardly think bringing me breakfast improper at this point."

"Don't you? Perhaps Rose isn't just watching him. This is our chance to show her we won't let him become the man he once was."

She made a valid point. She set the tray on the small table and moved to help me remake the bed. If she saw the dent in the second pillow, she didn't comment.

Four days had passed since Rose's letter. Though I felt we'd made fair plans toward a passable feast, I still worried about the food we would provide.

"Has Tam checked the apple trees lately?" I asked.

"We walk out each morning at sunrise," she said with a blush, and I suspected frolicking as nymphs wasn't something they would forget soon.

"We tried one this morning. They're tart. Another week or two will be needed."

"We might need to start picking a few days early than that so Edmund has the time he needs to make the pastries," I said.

"Mrs. Palant and I were talking last night about the menu. We think smoked fish would be a nice addition," she said, touching on a subject I'd so far avoided.

"Smoked fish is a good idea. I think Mrs. Wimbly is salting or immediately preparing the fish being brought to her. I'll have Mr. Crow mention the idea to her. Any ideas for the main course?"

Egrit shook her head, looking worried.

"We have time. We'll come up with something."

She nodded and left the room. I lifted the cover from the tray and smiled at the egg tartlet. We needed to work on a new recipe. But, I doubted there was much else Lord Ruhall could make with the ingredients we had in the kitchen. That thought took me back to the source of my dilemma for the feast. Grudgingly, I acknowledged the impossibility of hosting the feast without using some more of the estate's gold.

With a sigh, I dressed then returned the empty tray to the kitchen.

Mrs. Wimbly's voice reached me before I entered.

"I told you, we're not a market. Lord Ruhall has no use for—"

"Henick," I said as soon as I saw the man in the door.

His frustrated expression melted when he saw me.

"It's all right, Mrs. Wimbly. I'll speak with Henick."

Mrs. Wimbly turned to scowl at me. The woman might know how to cook, but her personality remained unpleasant.

"He's trying to sell us potatoes," she said in a huff.

I smiled at Henick.

"Would you happen to have onions, too?"

Mrs. Wimbly threw her hands in the air and stomped from the kitchen. Kara kept her head down as she continued to prepare the midday meal.

"I do, but not with me. Father thought you might be interested in some produce since the manor probably has fallow fields," he said, waving to his wagon that waited just outside the door.

"Let's see what you have." I stepped out, moving toward the back of the wagon. My skirts tangled with my legs when I attempted to boost myself up, and I missed the days when I went about in trousers and had freedom of movement.

With Henick's help, I stepped up into the bed. Four large sacks rested near the front. They were tied with twine, so I easily opened the first one and pulled out a potato. Dirt sprinkled off as I turned it in my hand.

"How much for a sack?"

"I'll give you two sacks of potatoes and half a sack of onions for a gold and a promise to dance with me at the feast."

"You received your invitation, then?"

He nodded, his eyes twinkling.

"Yesterday. It was one of the reasons we knew you might be interested in potatoes."

"Well, you have a deal," I said, dropping the potato in the sack.

Henick reached up, and with a firm grip on my waist, helped me from the wagon. Inside the kitchen, something crashed. That woman...I sighed, pasted a pleasant smile on my face and motioned to the drive that wandered to the estate's gate.

"Shall we walk and discuss delivery?"

The corners of his eyes crinkled as he smiled knowingly.

"Yes."

We strolled side by side in silence until we passed the front of the house.

"Are you well?" he asked.

"Much the same. Memories plague me. I was thinking a fresh start in a new place might be the adventure I need to lighten my spirit."

"You want to leave, then?" Disappointment laced his statement.

"Not just yet. I'll be here to honor my promised dance."

"A dance I will look forward to."

We'd reached the gate and turned around. Walking from the manor to the gate took much less time without the tangle of living plants to impede a person.

"I can leave the sacks of potatoes and return with the onions in a few days."

"That will work perfectly. Thank you, Henick. I'm grateful that you and your father thought of us."

When we reached the wagon, he lifted the potatoes from the bed and set them by the door before climbing aboard. I waited beside the door and waved as he left.

"Benella." Alec's angry, clipped voice had me turning in surprise just as Henick rounded the front of the building. "What are you doing?"

Behind him, I caught Mrs. Wimbly glaring at me with an overly satisfied smirk.

"Purchasing potatoes and onions. Now we can serve individual meat pies."

Alec's gaze drifted to the direction in which Henick had disappeared.

I turned to Mrs. Wimbly.

"Please see the potatoes stored. Henick will return later with the onions."

She glanced at Alec expectantly as I moved to walk inside.

A moment after I cleared the door, Alec followed. He didn't speak as we left the kitchen; but in the hall, he caught me by the waist and pulled me into the laundry. His arm remained fixed over my stomach, anchoring my back to his chest. He leaned forward until his lips almost touched my ear. My pulse leapt.

"I said he was not to touch you." The low words spoken so close to my ear almost made me shiver.

"No," I said slowly. "You said he wasn't to kiss me anymore. And he didn't. Now, I need to let my father know of the deal Henick and I struck so Henick can be paid when he returns."

Instead of releasing me, Alec tangled his free hand in my hair.

"I don't want him touching you, either," he said. The menace in his tone had me submitting to the insistent, steady draw on my hair. His lips found the column of my neck. A tingle spread where his mouth touched. "From the first day you entered my lands, you were mine. No other will have you."

I shivered.

"Don't continue my torture, Benella. I miss you. I miss the way we spent our days together."

My heart skipped a beat. The memory of his mouth on my skin, of his hands gripping my thighs, dimmed the memory of the baker's touch. I missed the days we'd spent together too.

"Marry me," he said, surprising me.

"I cannot."

He dropped his hands and yelled his frustration. The sudden noise startled me. I spun to face him. His angry gaze pierced me.

"I asked you when I had nothing to offer but myself, and you refused me. I ask again, now offering you a title and modest wealth. But you refuse me still. What exactly am I missing?" He paced before me, his relentless scowl never turning away.

"My answer remains. I do not know you."

"How do you not know me? You know I can barely cook an edible meal, abhor arithmetic, and irritate easily. You know you need never fear me, that I would never harm you." He lifted his hand to stroke my cheek where he once had hurt me. "That I cannot sleep unless I am beside you. That you can calm me with a touch or a word. That I search you out just to hear you. You know there will never be another for me. That there is only you." He dropped his hand. "Yet, you say you cannot...I say you stubbornly *will* not. What is left to know?"

I stepped back from him and looked about the room.

"I gave up my freedom in exchange for my father's life, and the more I learned about you, the more I wanted to stay. I saw something in you worth helping, and my heart broke for you each time you tried to win back your freedom and failed.

"You say you need me. I've always known that. You asked what I still need to know..." I took a breath and pressed on. "When faced with the decision of saving the people here from re-enchantment or saving me, you choose your people. I understand your reasons. I'm not angry. Yet, I do not believe you can ever love me as much as I have loved you."

Alec turned scarlet, his gaze thunderous.

A cough echoed outside the laundry room, and Egrit stepped in.

"Lord Ruhall, Mr. Hovtel wants to speak with you."

Alec didn't glance at me as he stormed from the room. Egrit gave me a look I couldn't quite decipher then left.

I quickly made my way to the ballroom where I spent the rest of my day scrubbing the floor and avoiding Lord Ruhall. I would speak to Father about Henick tomorrow.

* * * *

A warm hand on my abdomen woke me. My stomach lurched sickeningly at the same time a tingle of awareness crept through me. I took a moment to remind myself it wasn't the baker touching me. He was gone.

Alec held me from behind with his arm draped over my waist. His hand didn't move but rested possessively on my bare skin just below my navel. He slept peacefully with me, just as he'd said.

Yet, knowing it was Alec didn't lift my unease at being touched by a furless hand. Breathing slowly through my nose, I tried to focus on a more pleasant memory than the baker. I remembered the beast kissing his way from my breast to my stomach and lower still. My breathing quickly grew shallow, and I warmed considerably. Perhaps that wasn't the best memory on which to dwell. I struggled to push away the recollection, but the feel of his tongue rasping between my legs lingered.

Dislodging Alec's hand, I rolled onto my stomach. Though I'd successfully banished my unease, it took a while for the new sensations to fade and for sleep to find me once more.

* * * *

The following morning, I woke before Egrit arrived. I quickly dressed and left the room. Wary of Lord Ruhall's mood, I chose to clean and forgo breakfast. The ballroom and connecting parlors were spotless, and Egrit and Mrs. Palant had agreed to start on the main sitting room at the front of the manor. However, the room remained empty and untouched.

Just as I was leaving, I collided with Swiftly.

"I'm sorry, Miss Hovtel," he said, quickly reaching out to steady me.

"No need for apology. I'm right and well." My heart still hammered from the unexpected impact, though. For half a moment, I'd thought him Alec.

"Meaning you can release her, Swiftly," Alec said from somewhere behind me.

Annoyance laced his words, and I recalled his reaction when Henick had walked with me. I inwardly cringed, and Swiftly immediately dropped his hand.

"Was there something you needed?"

Unsure to which of us he spoke, I remained facing Swiftly. Swiftly stepped away from me and looked at a point beyond me.

"I've run out of nails."

"There's a smith in the village, according to Miss Hovtel. Take this and get what you need."

A coin flipped through the air, and gold glinted in the early morning light. Swiftly caught the coin easily. He nodded and was about to turn away when I realized I'd be left alone with Alec.

"I should help," I said, moving to catch up to Swiftly. "I'm better at wheedling a fair price."

Alec remained quiet behind us.

It wasn't until we were halfway to Konrall that I realized what I'd done. I'd offered to face the people who'd been present at my near rape. My steps slowed noticeably.

"Miss Hovtel?"

My stomach clenched, and I struggled to breathe through it.

"Benella, you look pale. Are you feeling faint?"

Exhaling slowly, I shook my head.

"Not in the least. Just settling a moment in my mind."

"I can negotiate the price of nails," he said softly. "You need not accompany me."

"I swear I'm right and well. Besides, I must visit the candle maker. We'll need large, tall pillars for the feast. Bigger than anything we have."

"Then I'll take you there. You can inquire about candles while I speak with the smith. I'll return for you when my business is complete."

I nodded, glad I didn't have to return to the manor just yet and equally glad I could avoid the Coalre family.

The candle maker greeted me with a smile when he opened the door.

"Benella, welcome. Come in, come in." As soon as he stepped

aside, Swiftly turned away to go to the smithy.

"It's been too long, dear child. How are you?"

"Well, and you?"

He snorted.

"Well? I doubt well. I heard what happened." He patted my hand and led me to the chair near the fire. "Sit."

"You heard? From who?"

"Your sister. She needed candles. She's a mean one, that girl. Silly twit to try to put the blame on you. A harsh tongue for one carrying another man's babe."

My eyes rounded, and he laughed at me as he sat in his chair. "I'm old but my eyes and ears work well. There is plenty of yelling coming from the bakery of late. Edmund's a good man. Shame he didn't know about your sister before it was too late."

I had no idea what to say, so I remained quiet for a moment.

"Did you receive your invitation to the harvest feast?" I asked finally.

"I did. I hear we'll have some fancy apple pastries."

"And cider, meat pies, and smoked fish. The menu isn't set yet. Like everything at the estate, it needs work."

"So what can I do for you?"

"I need pillars to light the ballroom once the sun sets."

"Do you have stands?"

"How tall would they need to be?"

"About five feet to keep the flame away from the children. And wide to keep the flame from a lady's hair."

"We don't have them yet, but we will."

"I'm guessing you'll need a dozen big pillars. The fire will be lit, most likely."

"Yes."

He hummed to himself and looked at his shelves.

"I can do it, but it'll take all the wax I have. When the night's done, I'll collect the remaining wicks and wax. Since I'm taking more than half back, I'll halve the price. A blunt silver for each candle."

A little over a gold for a dozen pillars.

"The price is more than fair. Since you'll need to stay until the end, I'll have a room readied for—"

He laughed.

"There is no need for that. I'll walk home and sleep comfortably in my own bed."

"Then, I insist Swiftly bring you home. You'll have too much wax to carry safely in the dark."

"Very well."

Swiftly's knock ended my visit, and before I left, I promised to send payment the same day.

After we returned to the manor, I sent Swiftly back with the required coin while I helped clean the front sitting parlor. I was content to lend my assistance and avoid Alec. I'd upset him with my rejection and with my reason for doing so. No doubt he felt there was more to say on the topic. In my mind, there wasn't.

The next day, I successfully managed the same evasion. Though he did almost catch me alone in the laundry; however, his distinctive stride had given me enough warning to slip out the door. I'd waited around the corner with bated breath until he quit the room once more, cursing softly.

The nights proved more difficult as I continued to leave the door between our rooms unlocked. I'd debated locking them but thought it would only aggravate him further. Since he didn't accost me as I slept and only held me close, I continued to allow his nightly visits.

My feelings toward Alec were confusing. With a glance, he could change my pulse or just as likely annoy me. I found his dedication to returning the estate to its former glory admirable; but at the same time, I resented that he'd put it before me. I pitied him his continued scrutiny from Rose but wanted to shake him senseless for his close observance of me.

Rather than attempt to resolve how I felt, I chose not to think of it at all and drifted through my days, keeping busy with feast preparations.

Before twelve days had passed, much of the lower floor shined from our collective efforts.

* * * *

"Two weeks before the feast," Egrit said as she entered my room.

I groaned and burrowed under the covers.

"Come now. You have things to do today. Lord Ruhall needs you to go to the Water with Swiftly. The carriage is waiting for you out front."

I sat up in bed, pushing down the covers with the motion.

"Why am I going to the Water?"

"He didn't say." Egrit moved to my wardrobe and pulled out the dress she'd washed. She tossed it to me as I slid from bed. "But I'm sure it has to do with the feast. Swiftly probably knows more."

"Instead of the carriage, see if we can take the wagon," I said, unabashedly stripping from my shirt in my hurry to dress. "If we're going to the Water, we should take the spare milk we have."

"A sound plan."

"Have Swiftly meet me in the kitchen," I said as my head cleared the neckline of the dress. It took a moment for me to right myself and notice that Egrit was no longer there.

After quickly washing my face and teeth, I left my room. The rapid click of my boot heels echoed in the hall. It had been over a week since we'd last delivered milk. I wondered how much milk we had in storage and hoped it would be enough to give some to each home as we had before.

Swiftly waited in the kitchen and stood when I entered.

"Good morning," I said with a smile. "I apologize for the change in plans but thought we could take the milk as promised."

"I've plans for the milk, Miss," Mrs. Wimbly said from her place at the butcher's block. She was kneading dough and didn't look up as she spoke.

"Plans?"

"For soft cheese."

"How much cheese do you plan to make?"

"As much as the milk in storage will give me." A hard note had crept into her voice.

I studied her for a moment. She always seemed so busy with the food preparations she currently maintained. I wondered how she would find the time to make cheese, too.

"I see. How much milk is in storage?"

"Sixteen small barrels, Miss Hovtel," Kara said. Mrs. Wimbly's movements stumbled then resumed. Sixteen seemed a bit much for our small household.

"Thank you, Kara." I focused on Mrs. Wimbly. "How much soft cheese do you estimate a single barrel will provide?"

"Miss Hovtel, I have duties assigned to me by Lord Ruhall. I can't stand about chatting with you all day. If you'll excuse me..." She left the room in a huff, and I stared after her.

Despite Mr. Crow's admonition to treat me with respect, she seemed to be having a hard time of it. The why puzzled me as I'd been nothing but courteous to her.

"If you take all but three, there should be plenty," Kara said softly, watching the door.

"Thank you."

Once we had the wagon loaded—thankfully without Mrs. Wimbly returning—Swiftly helped me into my seat and clucked the horses to start our journey. While we navigated the drive, I kept a close watch on the barrels tied in the back to ensure they didn't jostle overly much. After we reached the main road, I turned toward Swiftly.

"What business would Lord Ruhall have at the Water?"

"We are buying a dress," he said with a slight smile.

"A dress? Why would Lord Ruhall need a dress?"

"He doesn't. You do."

"I have no coin. And if I did, I wouldn't use it for a dress. I have two, which is twice as many as I'd like."

Swiftly laughed.

"No need to worry about the coin," he said, reaching up and tapping his chest. Metal jingled.

"Whose coin?"

"Lord Ruhall. He asked that I remind you the purpose behind the feast is to help support the community by paying for local goods."

A concept I understood. However, supporting the community by impoverishing the estate would benefit no one. Rather than pointing that out, I decided to wait and see how much a new dress would cost. Since Blye had always made mine for me, I had no idea.

When we reached the trade street, the homes with children eagerly accepted the milk we offered. Barrels empty, we climbed aboard once more and rattled our way to the market district.

"Lord Ruhall thought you might want to try the seamstress at the end of the street," Swiftly said as we approached my sister's shop.

"No. I'd like to speak with Blye about the dress."

Swiftly made an odd face but slowed the wagon before her shop. He helped me down and followed me to the door.

"I'll wait here," he said, opening it for me.

I nodded and stepped in. Blye stood folding handkerchiefs on a small table. She looked up at the sound of the door, and the welcoming smile on her face faded when she saw me. She was probably hoping for a paying customer. Which I was. I smiled at her.

"Hello, Blye. I've come to see if you have time to sew a dress for me."

"Benella, I thought I said—" She glanced at the curtained door that no doubt led to the sewing room and started again. "No, I don't have time."

She'd been folding handkerchiefs. I doubted lack of time the reason. I studied her hard expression.

"Why?" I asked, unwilling to leave without hearing a reason for her attitude.

She released a slow breath with a shake of her head.

"Because I won't associate with loose women."

A small choking noise escaped me.

"And you consider me loose because a pig of a man almost raped me?"

"Benella, please. Just leave," she said with another nervous glance at the back room. She lowered her voice. "And it would be better if you never came back."

Her complete abandonment pierced me. I'd thought Bryn cruel; Blye was more so because she had no cause. Hers wasn't misguided self-recrimination but rather the shallow concern of what her peers might think of her.

Without another word, I turned and left.

Outside, Swiftly spoke to a beautiful woman with long blonde hair. His scarlet face and averted eyes distracted me from my anger.

"Swiftly?"

"Benella," the woman said with a small smile. Her voice sounded raspy and familiar. I studied her mouth and recognized Ila dressed in a simple, normal gown.

"I saw you and hoped we might talk."

"I'd rather not," I said with a glance at the Whispering Sisters' house. The place I had once thought filled with friends now seemed a house of lies. And it made me wonder why Ila sought me out.

"Not there," she said, following my gaze. "Just a walk if you think it suitable."

"I'm not concerned with suitability as much as I am preservation. Aryana has done enough—"

"I'm not here for her. I'm here for you."

Swiftly had watched our exchange; and when I looked at him in question, he shrugged.

"I will follow wherever you lead, Miss Hovtel."

"Well, then. Come, Ila. Let's walk."

Side by side, we slowly paced north along the street.

"Are you well?" she asked softly.

"Well enough, I suppose. How are you? I'm surprised to see you about at this time." It was nearing the hour when their clients would arrive.

"When news spread that Aryana was responsible for Lord Ruhall's curse, many of our customers did not return."

"I can hardly fault them."

"Nor do I. But now, many of us find ourselves idle. Without Aryana there to ensure our future, some have left for other occupations, thanks to their education. Two had offers of marriage."

"What do you mean? She's not there?"

"She gave us all a small fortune and disappeared not long after..." Conversation halted for several moments. "I heard some of what your sister said to you and am afraid you will find the same welcome at many of the seamstresses here."

"They condemn the wrong party," I said with a frustrated exhale.

"They do."

"It's just as well. I wasn't looking forward to another dress. I long for the days when I walked the woods in my sturdy shirt and trousers."

Ila chuckled.

"If you're willing, I would be glad to make your dress. We've grown adept at creating our own dresses because we've found the same welcome at most shops here."

I stopped walking and turned to Ila. The sincerity in her gaze and her words filled me with enough compassion that I answered more kindly than I would have previously.

"I would be honored and will wear it proudly."

She seemed relieved, and I wondered if boredom hadn't prompted the offer.

"What does the future hold for you, Ila?"

She shrugged and looked around. "I wouldn't mind finding a man willing to take me as I am."

"I wouldn't think that would be an issue. How old are you?"

She gave a small smile. "Almost twenty."

"Plenty of time to meet a decent man."

"Not here."

I looked around and caught the long glances aimed our way.

"No, not here," I said in agreement. "Come to Lord Ruhall's feast and be my special guest. There will be many faces there that I think you might not yet have seen."

Her smile widened. "I would be honored."

"Now, do you need my measurements?"

She laughed. "No need. I know them well."

"Payment?" I glanced at Swiftly.

He handed her the gold.

"I hope that's enough," I said with a question in my voice.

"It is. Your gown will be lovely."

With nothing more to say, I nodded farewell and followed Swiftly back to the wagon.

He and I rode back in silence. My thoughts were heavy and

unsuitable for company. My sisters shunned me; and though Ila sought me out, I wasn't ready to trust her or count her among my friends. I could count Egrit as a friend to an extent; however, she didn't treat me as a peer. Her affection for me ran closer to savior and part errant ward. I realized I was quite friendless. Now, more than ever, I wished I could leave the North.

Swiftly dropped me off at the front door and clucked the horse to bring the wagon to the barn. I let myself in and closed the door behind me. Though I wanted nothing more than to escape to my room, I turned toward the laundry to help press the table linens. Neither Egrit nor Mrs. Palant commented on my subdued responses to their active conversation.

Lord Ruhall had Father fetch me for a stilted dinner where Father glanced at me often, a knowing sadness in his gaze. I wondered what Blye might have said to him when he had gone to the Water. No doubt she'd accepted the invitation well enough, just not Father's presence. My heart was heavy for him as well.

Alec remained quiet throughout the meal, the set of his jaw becoming more tense with each moment until I finally excused myself.

With relief, I sought my bed.

* * * *

The sound of steps roused me. Someone moved about in my room. Before I could panic, Alec spoke softly.

"Why do you refuse to see I'm here?" Frustration laced his low words.

I knew he was speaking to himself. He didn't understand. I did see him. I knew he was there. And my longing for who he used to be was destroying me.

The pacing stopped and the bed dipped. He wrapped me in his arms, and I stayed awake long after his breathing lulled.

* * * *

I lay in bed after waking. My heavy heart wouldn't let me stand. I hated the need for the feast and my commitment to stay to see it through. I wanted to speak to my father and flee.

Pushing aside my despondency, I slid from bed. It was only when I stood and felt the air on my bare legs that I recalled I still slept in his shirt. Wrinkling my nose, I pulled it off over my head. It needed a washing. Though Egrit hadn't commented on it during the many times she'd come to wake me, I thought it better to return it to Alec's dirty laundry than to wash it myself.

After I washed and dressed, I strode across the room with the shirt.

Perhaps it was time to put aside my memories of the beast. His return was unlikely, and my continued hope for it, unfair. Twisting the handle, I pulled the door wide and froze.

Lord Ruhall reclined in a bathing tub on a rug at the foot of his bed. The wide expanse of his bare shoulders had me staring stupidly. I'd never before seen a man without his shirt. Not true. I'd seen all of Gen at the Whisperings Sisters. My stomach dipped and heat flooded my face as I recalled every detail of that particular lesson.

At the sound of the door, Alec turned his head and caught my gaze. The move brought more of his back out of the water. I swallowed and averted my gaze slightly to his shoulder and the tiny red marks there. Deeply puckered scars. As I stared, the small crescent shapes took on meaning, and my world pitched.

"Benella? Are you all right?" His words broke through my revelation, and I struggled to recall my purpose.

"Yes. Quite. I wanted to return your shirt. It needs a wash."

"Take a new one," he said, leaning back in the water once more.

The wardrobe stood just a few feet from the tub. My mind in a jumble, I absently dropped the old shirt to the floor and went to the wardrobe to select a clean one from the several waiting within. As I closed the doors, something tugged on my skirt. I turned. Alec had an arm extended from the tub and held the material in his hand. He looked up at me, his expression masked.

"Could you bring the soap for me?" He pointed to his dressing table near the wardrobe.

I absently nodded, and he let go of my skirt.

What did the scars mean? Could I have been wrong?

The well-used cake of soap was small and made me feel so guilty that I couldn't find a way around using estate gold for the feast. Soap in hand, I turned and brought it to Alec. The water did little to hide the strong length of his legs or the hard planes of his chest and stomach. He was so much bigger than Gen's lean frame. So much more interesting to study.

"The soap?" Humor laced his words.

I shook myself and handed over the soap before rushing from the room. In my own chamber, I went to the window and stared out.

The marks were unmistakably fingernails. Only one person had set her hand on Alec's shoulder. Rose. The morning the baker had almost raped me. Had Alec truly wanted to come to my aid? Though Rose posed no threat physically, her nails would have served as a reminder of what she could do with her magic. Why stop him, though?

The sun traveled the sky as I debated the possibilities. I needed to talk to someone. The only person left to me was Father. I knew he would listen, yet the reason behind the lackluster rescue of my near rape would be a potentially disquieting topic for him.

Sighing, I left my room and felt a small measure of guilt that I'd done nothing to help that day. Many of the rooms I passed had open doors and windows. Fresh air swept through the first and second floors.

I met Otta at the bottom of the steps.

"Otta, what are you doing out of the schoolroom?"

She looked nervous. I reached out, smoothed back the hair on her head, and gave her an encouraging smile.

"We stopped for the midday meal. Mrs. Wimbly had me deliver a tray to your father. I'm to return straight to Mr. Roost."

"I'll speak with Mr. Roost and Mrs. Wimbly. You should have no tasks during the day."

"Thank you, Miss Hovtel," she said before she scampered away.

As I continued toward the library, I heard what sounded like someone stomping on the floor. The sound came again. Not stomping. Something hitting the floor.

Lengthening my stride, I rounded the corner of the library door just in time to see a book sail from the study. It landed not far from the door with a loud bang. Cursing followed, punctuated by something hitting wood.

Father half-stood behind his desk, his shock clear. We looked at each other before I hurried to the study.

I ducked to dodge another book that Alec threw without seeing me. He was in a rage, his face red and his jaw clenched. He grabbed his chair and began to lift it high over his head.

"Alec," I said. Shock robbed my voice of volume, yet he heard.

He froze at the sound of his given name and turned his angry gaze on me. His chest heaved, and his eyes were dark. My pulse leapt at the sight. How many times had I faced him like this?

Cautiously, I walked into the room.

"Set it down," I said softly.

He yelled loudly and half-slammed the chair to the floor. I stepped further into the room and carefully approached him. I almost smiled. His mood reminded me so much of how he'd acted the time I'd locked myself in his room.

Once I reached him, I gently touched his face.

"What upsets you so?"

He closed his eyes, heaved a breath, and leaned his cheek into my hand. He stayed like that until some of the flush faded from his face. Pulling away from me, he reached for a crumpled piece of parchment and handed it to me.

Having a woman assist with your bath is not a wise decision. I am watching and will take from you all you hold dear if you continue with these transgressions. ~Rose

"I see," I said, though I didn't. How did fetching soap mean I had assisted with a bath? Aryana had assisted with my bath in a far more physical manner at the Whispering Sisters. Her assessment of the situation remained far from just. Then again, all her assessments seemed to run toward unjust. I thought of the marks on Alec's shoulder as I glanced up at him.

He looked ready to start throwing things again. He didn't seem cold at all, now, and I wondered if he ever had been. Could it be that he had only been trying to maintain control of himself? A control he still hadn't mastered by the looks of it.

Though I agreed he had a reason to be upset, his way of showing his disagreement needed to stop.

I glanced at the door and saw Mr. Crow and Father there.

"Mr. Crow, would you bring some spring water to the library?" He nodded and left. "Father, would it bother you if I read aloud while you worked?"

"No. Not at all," he said.

I turned back to Alec. "Would you care to listen to me read for a while?"

His gaze searched mine. So much anger and resentment churned there. Yet, I didn't think any of it was for me. Should it be, though? Perhaps I had misunderstood him. Or perhaps regaining my affection was another game. After all, if I'd misunderstood, why hadn't he come to see Father as Swiftly had said that day?

Instead of answering, Alec motioned for me to lead him out. I went to the couch before the fire and waited. He joined me with a book on farming. I smiled at the topic, recalling better times, and took the book from him. I reclined on the couch so my braid draped over the arm, and Alec sat on the floor. A moment later, I felt a tug on my braid, and I began.

Mr. Crow arrived with the pitcher and cups before I'd progressed more than a page. He quietly set everything on the table next to the tray already there, then withdrew as I continued reading about selective animal husbandry to create a stronger herd.

Alec's fingers combed through my hair as I read, and I hoped it soothed him as much as he soothed me.

Finishing the chapter, I closed the book with a snap then waited.

"Thank you," Alec said softly, removing his hands.

I sat up, moved over, and patted the spot beside me. He rose from the floor and took the seat.

"You have every right to be upset," I said, reaching to pour him a cup of water. "However, destroying your study resolves nothing." I handed him the cup and watched his expression.

His jaw clenched, but he nodded.

"She seems so fond of writing you notes. Write one back." I helped myself to a meat pie and waited for his reaction.

"And what would I say to defend myself? She is correct. I shouldn't have—" He looked down at his water.

"Alec," I reached out and took his hand in mine, "you're not the man you were. Don't let her keep punishing you for a past you've already paid for."

His hand tightened around mine a moment before he released me and walked back to his study, picking up the ejected book on his way.

I let out a long slow breath, then stood.

"I'll take this tray back to the kitchen. Do you need help with anything today?" I asked, looking at my father.

"No, Bini. We'll be fine here."

I left, carrying the tray to the kitchen, and once again not speaking to my father as I'd planned.

Seven

Mr. Crow stood at the open door, polishing the knocker.

"Would you like me to return the tray for you?" he asked, stepping forward.

"No need. I haven't eaten yet," I said.

He nodded and let me continue with the tray.

When I entered the kitchen, Kara kneaded bread at the block. Her nervous glance at me, then at the stairs to the cellar, only left me puzzled for a moment.

"Where is the milk?" Mrs. Wimbly shouted from the cellar.

"Sorry, Miss," Kara whispered as Mrs. Wimbly thundered up the steps.

I set the tray on the table and braced myself for a confrontation. However, when she saw me, she stopped in her tracks. Her face turned red, and the disapproving set of her mouth tightened. With a glare, she turned on her heel and left the kitchen.

"She'll go to Mr. Crow to complain," Kara said.

That Mrs. Wimbly went to Mr. Crow didn't bother me. She would likely find an unsympathetic ear there. However, it did concern me that she was spending time on worrying about milk.

"How are the preparations coming along?" I asked as I browsed the pots for any leftovers. I'd missed breakfast because of Alec in the bath and Rose's nail marks, and now I'd missed lunch because of his temper. I wasn't about to go hungry until dinner.

"By the fire, you'll still find some fish stew," Kara said quietly. "There are biscuits in the oven, too. We've stored a good portion of stag, boar, and fish for the winter. The menu for the feast still needs to be settled."

"Have we smoked any fish yet?" I skipped the stew, though it did look tasty, and helped myself to a biscuit.

"Not yet. Mrs. Wimbly plans to start that closer to the feast."

"Will that interfere with all the meat pies she needs to make?" I took a quick bite.

"I believe she hopes one of the girls from the schoolroom will help us in the days just before the feast."

"Perhaps in the evenings, but I'll stay true to my word. They will remain in the classroom during the day."

Kara nodded but I saw the doubt there. I needed to find Mrs. Wimbly and set her straight regarding the children and their roles. Still nibbling my biscuit, I left the kitchen.

Neither she nor Mr. Crow were by the closed front door. Wandering further, I heard faint voices from the library.

"...will not tolerate any more interference," I heard Mrs. Wimbly say from the study as I entered the library. "You hired me as the head cook, a position that requires me to complete preparation and planning each week."

I glanced at my father who sat at his desk. He met my gaze briefly then focused on his book once more, his expression set. Whatever the discussion in Lord Ruhall's study, Father did not approve.

Mrs. Wimbly continued in her agitated tone.

"My preparation and plans fall apart when others take it upon themselves to remove supplies without approval."

The woman had admitted to me that she threw much of the milk to waste. Why was she so upset? And why bring such a petty grievance before Alec? I continued toward the study and caught sight of Mr. Crow beside Alec.

"Mrs. Wimbly, who is taking it upon themselves to remove supplies and what supplies were removed?" Alec asked. Though his tone was calm, the tension from Rose's last letter remained in his hard expression.

I caught Mr. Crow's attention as I neared the study door, and his troubled gaze found mine. Nodding to Mr. Crow, I stepped into the study before Mrs. Wimbly could answer.

"I beg your pardon, but I believe I've upset Mrs. Wimbly by taking milk from the cold storage."

"You believe? Yes, you've upset me. You have no regard for—"

"Mrs. Wimbly," Alec said, "I would like a private word with Miss Hovtel. Thank you for bringing this to my attention."

"Very good," she said. She shot me a satisfied look and strode from the room. Mr. Crow moved to follow her.

"A moment, Phillip," Alec said.

Mr. Crow paused his departure and turned to look at Alec.

"Mrs. Wimbly is to leave my employ immediately. See her packed and delivered to wherever it is she came from."

"What? But why?" I asked as Mr. Crow moved to leave. "Wait, Mr. Crow." I held up a hand to forestall him and turned to Alec. "We need her. The feast is just weeks away. We can't possibly manage with just one cook."

Mr. Crow glanced at Alec who waved him from the room. An edge of panic grabbed me as I realized my plea had fallen on deaf ears.

"Alec, please be reasonable. She's done nothing to deserve dismissal."

He stood and moved around the desk. His carefully blank expression unnerved me.

"She has done nothing?" He stopped before me and lifted a hand to brush a strand of hair from my cheek. "Phillip said she's rude to you and refuses to treat you with the courtesy you deserve."

Very few had lately. The thought brought the hurt of my sisters' rejections dangerously close to the surface, and I quickly turned away.

Alec caught my arm and brought me back around.

"What's this, now?" he said, studying my face. A second later, he pulled me into a firm hug. "Surely, Mrs. Wimbly's dismissal isn't that upsetting. Even your father finds her disagreeable," he said against my hair.

Secure in his arms, the hurt from Blye's latest rejection eased. His hold felt so right. I leaned into the protection of his arms, allowing myself a moment of shelter from all life had been throwing at me lately. I wrapped my arms around his waist and breathed deeply of his familiar scent.

"You can speak to me, Benella," he said softly. "I'm here to listen. Always."

I sighed as I realized how much I needed just that.

"It's not your dismissal of Mrs. Wimbly. It's my life. I can't—"

His arms tightened around me so much that I looked up. His closed eyes, red face, and clenched jaw surprised me; and I knew I'd upset him. Removing my hold from his waist, I cupped his face.

"Alec, you're no longer listening."

He exhaled slowly, and his turbulent gaze found me.

"I am. You still want to leave. Don't." He closed his eyes once more and set his forehead to mine, a tormented man seeking sanctuary. What a poor pair we were, both seeking the same thing.

"I've made up my mind to stay and help with the feast. I won't abandon you."

"Say ever. Say, 'I won't abandon you ever, Alec.'"

I soothed my fingers over his jaw. His breath tickled my neck. When I said nothing, he opened his eyes. From the study, my father loudly cleared his throat, and I surmised we'd been quiet for too long.

"About Mrs. Wimbly?" I said, trying to step back. Alec's arms tightened, and for a moment, I thought he might not release me. Then, they fell to his sides. He studied me intensely, and I wondered what he searched so hard for in my expression.

Finally, he shook his head.

"Phillip will search for an immediate replacement. I would like you to help interview whomever he finds."

"Of course."

* * * *

That night, I didn't sleep until Alec came to my bed and wrapped his arms around me. I waited until his breathing deepened then turned in his arms. Lightly, I ran my fingers over the marks. The hard, puckered skin rose from the sculpted curve of his shoulder. Rose had marked him deeply.

As I lay there, I again struggled with how he'd stood there and calmly ordered the baker off of me. Were these marks enough to absolve him of his inaction? No. But they were enough for me to start questioning what happened after Tennen took me from the manor. Questions that I would never speak because I trusted no one to tell me the truth.

The most important in my mind was, why hadn't Alec come for me like Swiftly had said he would?

* * * *

In the morning, Egrit woke me with a letter and a coddled egg.

"A letter is never good news in this place," I said, sitting up.

Egrit grinned at me. "You're very perceptive." She left the room before I could say more. Sighing heavily, I unfolded the note.

> *Benella,*
> *Bryn and I have heard Lord Ruhall is in need of another cook. I know Bryn deserves less after her treatment of you, but would you perhaps mention her for consideration? Business remains slow enough that I manage the store and the stove well without assistance.*
> *Yours,*
> *Edmund*

Ungraciously, I did not want to endure my sister's presence on a daily basis. Yet, I knew her skill in the kitchen and knew we could do worse. However, it wasn't a decision I wanted to make without Father's input.

I dressed and carried my egg and the letter to the library.

"Good morning, Bini," Father said from his seat at his desk.

"Good morning, Father. I received a letter this morning."

"Letters bode ill here."

"My sentiments as well. I cannot ignore this one. Yet, I do not know how to respond."

I handed him the letter then sat on the chair near his desk. While he read, I ate the egg, enjoying the deliciously soft yolk.

"Hmm," Father said, sitting back. "What were your first thoughts after reading this?"

"That Edmund was correct. Bryn doesn't deserve my consideration. Then, I immediately felt guilty for having such uncharitable thoughts. Even if Bryn doesn't deserve the opportunity, Edmund does. For him to reach out...I think he truly needs help."

"So you'll speak to Lord Ruhall."

"Speak to me about what?" Alec asked, walking into the library. His gaze went to the empty eggshell and spoon that I held. "How was it?"

"Did you make the egg?"

"I thought with Mrs. Wimbly gone Kara might need some assistance in the kitchen."

A laugh escaped me. It couldn't be helped. The image of him wandering into the kitchen and offering aid...

"And her reaction?" I asked.

"As you might imagine. But after the initial shock, she gave me direction on how to soft boil the eggs for everyone's breakfast."

"Well done. You might not need to return to the kitchen tomorrow, though," I said, holding up the note.

He took it from me, scanned the contents, and frowned, studying first me then Father.

"You are both considering this, aren't you?"

I sighed and nodded. Alec looked at Father.

"With respect, your eldest daughter has shown her true nature again and again at the expense of both of you. For you, I will allow this, but if she causes trouble, she will leave as quickly as Mrs. Wimbly, family or not."

"I completely agree," Father said.

"Then, I should go speak with Edmund and Bryn," I said, standing.

"Take Swiftly with you," Alec said.

I agreed and left. Before seeking out Swiftly, I found Kara and Mr. Crow at the table in the kitchen. If they had been conversing, they stopped when I arrived.

"Good morning," I said. "Do you both have a moment?"

"Of course," Mr. Crow said.

I sat beside him.

"It seems word has spread of our need for a cook. I received a letter this morning with a possible replacement but wanted to speak with both of you first. Mrs. Wimbly wasn't agreeable, but she cooked well. I'd like to see an agreeable and competent person fill the position." The sister I knew now was not that person. I wondered at my reasoning, then, for considering her. Because we needed help. Any help. Yet, I would not subject Kara to another version of Mrs. Wimbly. If Bryn would only reserve her bad temperament for me alone, things would be fine in the kitchen.

"Miss Hovtel?" Mr. Crow said.

"My sister's husband has asked that we consider her for the position. However, I do not think she would be suited for head cook. I would prefer to see that position go to Kara."

"Me?" Kara said, her shock plain.

"Yes. You understand the workings of the kitchen and the staff. You work well with others. My sister has never had to direct anyone else." Not true. She had directed me plenty. But I wouldn't allow her to use Kara like that.

"My greatest concern as we approach the feast is keeping the expenses low. I propose that all kitchen purchases go through Mr. Crow, who can report weekly spending to Lord Ruhall." My bigger fear was that Bryn would find a way to filch coin from the estate, and I faulted that concern on my tarnished esteem of her character.

"Bryn does know how to cook and, with the knowledgeable direction you can provide, will be a fit addition."

"I look forward to meeting her," Kara said.

"As do I," Mr. Crow said, standing. "May I walk with you for a moment?" He offered me a hand up and indicated the outer kitchen door.

He didn't speak until we were on the path outside.

"Miss Hovtel, your presence here is an honor and a delight."

I smiled at his kind words, until I noted his very concerned expression.

"With respect, I watched your family for several days before you came to live here the first time, and I saw your hesitation just now as you spoke in the kitchen. Surely I am not alone in my concern regarding your sister's employ."

"Mr. Crow, you are far from alone. That is why I will not offer her the position of head cook and why I want purchasing to go through you. I trust her to cook, but little else. If you find her manner offensive or abrasive, Lord Ruhall and my father both insist she then be dismissed in the same fashion as Mrs. Wimbly."

He exhaled in relief.

"Very good."

"We need the help, Mr. Crow. If not, I would not choose her."

"I understand."

At the front of the house, I caught sight of Swiftly.

"If you will pardon me, I best catch Swiftly and visit my sister. The sooner she arrives, the sooner we will have the help we need."

After parting ways with Mr. Crow, I caught up with Swiftly and told him of my need to visit Konrall immediately. He turned and walked with me toward the gate.

"And what so urgently calls us to Konrall?" Swiftly asked.

"I need to speak with Edmund. He would have Bryn work in the kitchen with Kara."

"Do you think that wise? I mean no disrespect with the question..."

"It is only right that you question what concerns you. The enchantment taught you that, and I find no offense in it. It is wise to replace Mrs. Wimbly immediately. Time will tell if Bryn was the wisest choice."

He nodded, and we walked the rest of the distance in silence. Konrall seemed quieter than I remembered. Possibly because the schoolhouse remained closed. I needed to speak with Alec about that. The bakery doors stood open, but we found the front store empty when we stepped in, just another element to the uninhabited feel of Konrall.

I rang the bell at the counter and waited.

Edmund appeared from the kitchen after a moment, and he smiled widely when he saw me.

"Benella. Welcome. Did you receive my letter?" His hopeful expression firmed my decision.

"I did. It's the reason behind my visit. Lord Ruhall and Father were agreeable to hiring Bryn, not as head cook but as an assistant. Is she here?"

"Bryn," he called in answer. She came down the steps a moment later. When she saw me, her face closed of all expression.

"Yes?"

"Lord Ruhall will hire you as an assistant cook," he said. Where the news excited him, she revealed no emotion.

"When does he want me to start?" she said, looking at Edmund when she reached the bottom step. Her middle was just a bit thicker.

"Immediately if you can," I said.

"She can," Edmund said firmly.

Bryn turned away from him, still without even a glance at me and marched out the door. There, she stopped.

"Where's the wagon?"

Swiftly arched a brow at me. Edmund caught the look and flushed.

"Pardon us for a moment," he said before he strode out the door, grabbing Bryn's arm on the way. They moved off to the side to speak in hushed tones. Her shoulders stiffened to whatever he said, then she pulled her arm away and started down the road.

Edmund watched her for a moment before he came back in.

"Thank you for giving her a chance, Benella."

"I didn't do it for her," I said with a slight smile. "Enjoy your day, Edmund."

He smiled in return.

"I will."

Bryn had managed a healthy distance by the time Swiftly and I stepped out, and I was glad to let her keep it. We trailed her, and I witnessed her first glimpse of the estate. Her steps faltered for only a moment then doubled their pace toward the front door. Mr. Crow opened it before she reached it. When he closed it behind him and pointed to the left, I knew he would see her settled in the kitchen.

"Thank you for accompanying me, Swiftly."

"Whenever you have the need, Miss Hovtel," he said with a wink.

I grinned and moved to the front steps as Mr. Crow and Bryn disappeared around the side. For the rest of the morning, I helped clean wherever Egrit pointed.

Midday, I eagerly joined the others in the kitchen where a kettle of stew and a stack of bowls waited on the table. The children and Mr. Roost were already there. Mrs. Palant spoke softly to her son and daughter while Egrit sat by Tam. The mood of the room was relaxed and pleasant. Mr. Crow stood near the butcher block, watching Bryn as she ladled portions into three bowls and set a loaf of bread on a tray. As soon as she finished, Mr. Crow picked it up.

"I can take it," Bryn said quickly. Mr. Crow frowned at her, but she didn't seem to notice.

"There is a setting for you," he said, looking at me, "if you would care to join your father and Lord Ruhall."

I nodded and followed him from the kitchen.

"How did she do?" I asked.

"Fair. She questioned Kara about Lord Ruhall but asked nothing about you or your father."

I chuckled. Lord Ruhall was of interest in her eyes, and we were not.

"How did Kara deal with her inquisition?"

"Her standard answer was, 'Why should a cook know that?'"

"I like Kara."

"As do I," he said with the barest of smiles.

When we reached the library, Mr. Crow set the tray on the table and left.

Father, unaware of the world around him, continued to read. I doubted estate business kept him at his seat all day. The rows upon rows of books would tempt even the dullest scholar. Leaving him to his peace, I made my way to the study.

Alec likewise focused on a book and didn't immediately look up at my approach. With his brow furrowed in concentration, he absently rubbed his jaw. A healthy coating of stubble rasped his fingers. He'd removed his jacket and loosened his neckcloth. The sight of him thus made my middle warm, and I wondered again about the marks on his shoulder.

"Mr. Crow brought a tray," I said softly.

He looked up and warmth filled his gaze for a brief moment before it disappeared.

"Did you visit your sister?" he asked, standing.

"Yes. She helped prepare the midday meal under Kara and Mr. Crow's instruction. Instead of biscuits, we have bread."

He looked mildly interested.

"What were you reading?" I asked as he marked his page and stood.

"A book of basic arithmetic your father borrowed from Mr. Roost."

"Ah."

"Yes, ah. I have a man of estate who insists I must know the arithmetic to check my own records."

"I won't live forever," my father said from the other room. "And your next man might not be as honest."

"He hears everything," I said in a mock whisper. "Years of teaching."

Alec chuckled and walked around the desk toward me. When he reached me, he set a hand on my lower back and guided me to the library.

"I'm ready for a break. Let's eat."

* * * *

After a pleasantly drawn out meal with Father and Lord Ruhall, I carried the tray back to the kitchen.

Bryn was washing dishes, and Kara was absent. I brought the tray over to the sink and set it near the other dirty bowls.

"What is it you do here?" Bryn asked without looking up.

"I clean," I said, surprised she spoke to me.

"And eat meals with Lord Ruhall."

"With Father. Lord Ruhall chooses to join him."

She nodded slightly, straightened, and wiped her hands.

"Could you wash for a bit? I need to sit," she said.

"I'm afraid, Miss Hovtel is needed elsewhere," Mr. Crow said from his office, making me start.

Bryn gave an almost inaudible sigh and went back to washing. I turned to look at Mr. Crow, and with a conspiratorial wave, he shooed me from the kitchen.

* * * *

The next morning I woke with a stretch. Exhausted from a day of beating mattresses, I'd collapsed on the bed fully dressed. I had no recollection of Alec joining me; yet a blanket covered me, and my stockings were off.

I washed my face and went in search of food. In the kitchen, Kara and Bryn were already hard at work.

"Good morning, Miss Hovtel," Kara said when she spotted me.

Bryn looked up and frowned at me.

"Really, Benella. Your dress is wrinkled like you slept in it. You're in a Lord's house now. Go change so you at least *look* respectable."

I pressed my lips together. I was respectable, wrinkled dress or not.

"Bryn, go see if Tam has fresh milk for the children," Kara said.

Bryn dusted her hands on her apron and walked outside.

"Are you hungry?" Kara asked once we were alone.

"Very. Is there anything ready?"

"I can boil an egg for you. The biscuits will need another half an hour. There are also a few apples Tam picked yesterday. They should be ready for harvest tomorrow or the day after."

"I'll take an apple and come back later for a biscuit."

She grabbed the apple, and I held up my hand. With a grin, she tossed it to me.

"Thank you, Kara." Before Bryn could return, I hurried out of the kitchen and found Egrit in the laundry room.

"What will we work on today?" I crunched into my apple. The juice was only slightly tart and, in my opinion, perfect.

"Mrs. Palant is dusting the parlors in the ballroom so they remain clean. You can dust the front sitting room if you'd like. I am going to go through the second floor bedrooms that have been aired and cleaned." She had three of the large vats filled and lit a small fire under each.

"What is the water for?"

She straightened with a laugh.

"Benella, you are wearing yesterday's dust. It's for our baths tonight."

The idea of a bath in one of the large vats had me eagerly heading toward the sitting room. The sooner I finished the day's work, the sooner I could bathe. Once I eyed the room and recalled it had taken three of us more than a day to clean it, my enthusiasm faltered. With a sigh, I took my dust rag and set to work.

Several hours had passed when Mr. Crow found me.

"Miss Hovtel, your assistance is needed immediately."

I eagerly set down my rag and followed him from the room, hoping the assistance brought me to the kitchen. The apple had long since disappeared.

My anticipation of food dwindled as I neared the kitchen and heard a familiar voice. Blye stood in the center of the kitchen with her back to us when we entered. But she quickly turned at the sound of our steps.

"Why can't Bryn stop to talk to me?" she asked me. Annoyance painted her face.

I glanced at Mr. Crow who stood just slightly behind me and to my right. His focus remained on Blye. Why had he brought me here to deal with her? Facing Blye, I forced myself to relax and tried to forget our last, hurtful encounter.

"I'm not in charge of what Bryn chooses to do."

"He says if she stops working, she stops being paid. Why is it you can stop working?"

I laughed. At her. At the question. At the absurdity of the moment.

"Because I'm not paid."

She eyed me for a moment then seemed to decide I was telling the truth. With one last irritated glance at Mr. Crow, she began to explain her presence.

"I'm making Bryn's dress for the feast. I rented a carriage for two hours to bring it to her for a fitting because of the babe."

I sighed and glanced at Mr. Crow again. This time, we shared a calculating look. I didn't want to encourage either of my sisters to abuse Bryn's position. Yet, I couldn't ignore Blye's reasoning or her unspoken plea.

"A quarter of an hour should more than suffice," Mr. Crow said. "Miss Hovtel, I will leave you to show your sisters to an appropriate room."

Bryn and Blye shared an exuberant embrace that made me feel hollow. I turned away and listened to them follow me.

"If you're not paid, why are you here?" Blye asked as we passed the laundry.

"I'm here because Father is here, and I have no money to see me elsewhere. Would either of you care to visit Father?"

"I only have a quarter of an hour," Bryn said.

"And I must return to the shop as soon as I've finished," Blye said.

My face flushed with annoyance, but I said nothing as I led them to one of the smaller sitting rooms near the dining room. Egrit and Mrs. Palant had recently cleaned and aired it. I lit several candles and drew the curtains closed while Blye went to fetch the dress. Bryn closed the door and started undressing.

"What is he like?" she asked.

"Who?"

She rolled her eyes.

"Lord Ruhall." She stepped out of her dress and stood before me in her underthings.

"You've met him. Don't you recall what he's like?"

"That was when he was cursed. What is he like now? Is he handsome?"

The door opened and closed quickly as Blye stepped in with a sturdy, large bag.

"Who is handsome?" she asked as she set the bag on a lounge. She opened it and pulled out a pretty, lavender dress with a hint of lace trim.

"Lord Ruhall," Bryn said. Then she studied the dress Blye held out for her. "Isn't there more lace?"

"Not for the price you paid," Blye said. Bryn took the dress with a scowl and began to slip into it.

"Why would a married woman care about the handsomeness of a man?" I asked, watching the pair of them.

"Don't be dull, Benella," Bryn said. She laced up the front of her dress and adjusted the panel there. The clever design would allow the dress to grow with her.

"I wonder how many high ladies he's invited to the feast," Blye said. She tugged here and there and stood back to eye the dress critically.

"It's a feast for the local community. Why would he invite high ladies?"

"To start looking for a wife, of course. He's wasted enough of his life because of the enchantment and needs an heir for the estate," Blye said as someone knocked on the door.

I went to open it and found Otta in the hall.

"Mr. Crow sent me to tell you the quarter hour is up."

I smiled at the girl and gave her hair a gentle tug.

"And you should be in the schoolroom."

"Yes, Miss." She scampered off.

I closed the door and turned to face my sisters. Blye was already closing her bag, and Bryn was undressing. It didn't take her too long to change back into her normal dress.

"See if Benella can hang it for you until you leave tonight," Blye said as Bryn carefully laid her dress over the lounge.

"There is a spare room at the top of the stairs," I said to Bryn. "You can hang it in the wardrobe there."

"Good." She picked her dress back up and draped it over her arm. "I might need to leave it until just before the feast, so I can change at the last minute."

As I opened the door and stepped from the room, I heard a strange commotion, like the frantic rearrangement of furniture.

"Surely you're not working feast day," Blye said.

Bryn's reply escaped my attention as I hurried my steps to the end of the hall that opened to the front entry. The noise from the right almost covered Mr. Crow's arrival from my left. He glanced nervously toward the sounds then at me.

"Lord Ruhall, wait," Tam said distantly.

"Mr. Crow, see to my sisters," I said, just as something crashed. I lifted my skirts and dashed toward the sound.

I found Alec in the dining room. Several chairs lay in a broken heap already. Tam stood guard over the undamaged seats. But Alec wasn't eyeing those anymore. He was eyeing the stack of fine glazed plates at his side.

Mrs. Palant knelt near the fireplace, a forgotten bucket of dirty scrub water beside her as she stared at Lord Ruhall in shock.

I snatched up the bucket and hoisted the contents through the air in the general direction of Alec. The grey water doused him, just as he moved for the plates. The silence was immediate. Soot chunks stuck to his cheeks and forehead and littered his once white shirt.

His dark, angry eyes found me. His jaw remained locked, and his fists clenched as our gazes held.

"Mrs. Palant," I said calmly. "I apologize for the mess I've made on the floor. Would you fetch some rags so I can clean it?"

She said nothing, only rushed from the room. Under Tam's watchful and anxious presence, I approached Alec.

"This is unacceptable and beneath you," I said.

His eyes narrowed dangerously. I narrowed mine in return and leaned in so only he could hear me.

"I shall lock my door at night if you choose to lose control again." When I pulled back, his eyes were closed. He shook with his rage.

I looked at Tam.

"Lord Ruhall has sat behind his desk for too long. He needs fresh air and exercise, an abundance of it. And I have just the task. I need pillar stands for the feast. I thought tree trunks about this high would be just the thing," I said, leveling my hand to the height of my chest. "Make sure the limbs are thick and that Lord Ruhall does all the chopping."

When I finished speaking, Alec opened his eyes and left the room. Tam hurried after him.

Beside the door, I noticed a crumpled piece of paper on the floor. Another note from Rose based on Alec's reaction. I picked it up and straightened it as Bryn walked into the room.

"I just saw Lord Ruhall. It looked as if someone had dumped ash water on him."

Her words barely registered. They certainly weren't important. Nor was Mr. Crow's response.

"Mrs. Rouflyn, please return to your duties in the kitchen."

My heart continued to sink as I reread the brief message.

It is plain to see you cannot manage the estate alone. To continue as you are, a man, you must wed by winter solstice. Choose your bride with care. ~Rose

I crushed the note once more, truly feeling Alec's anger. She was punishing him because of my help? Help she'd instigated. The longer I stood there, the more I seethed. She'd played her game long enough.

"Mr. Crow, I have business in the Water and will return before dinner."

"Yes, Miss. Is everything in order?" he said, glancing at my hand.

"I'm not certain," I said, giving him the honesty he deserved. "If Lord Ruhall returns before I do and asks for me, say nothing of my leaving. We cannot give Rose more reason to doubt him."

Mr. Crow nodded.

Eight

Ila had said that Rose wasn't often at the Whispering Sisters. Yet, I had nowhere else to look for her. Well after the hour when the Sisters opened their doors to customers, I approached the back door. The guard who stood there let me through. Ila waited within. But she wasn't dressed in her veil, and smoke no longer clogged the air.

"Benella," she said warmly. When she stepped toward me to impart a hug, I eagerly accepted it.

"I'm not yet ready to show you your dress," she said, releasing me.

"I wish I were here for a fitting. I'm here for Rose. Aryana. Whatever we're to call her now."

"She's not here."

"Then, I'll wait and hope she returns."

Ila nodded and started to lead me down the familiar hallway.

"Where is everyone?" I asked.

She smiled at me over her shoulder.

"The men? Their numbers continued to dwindle until they stopped completely."

"How long will you stay?"

"At least until the feast. I want to see you wear your dress."

We went to the room where my father used to teach the women. A lounge and chairs now adorned the room. We'd only settled when the door flew open.

"Now, you want to talk to me?" Rose said, striding into the room. She wore a displeased expression, and she did not look old in either form or face. Seeing her so, angered me. It brought back the misery I'd suffered and continued to suffer.

"Silence didn't achieve the result I'd wanted," I said as Ila stood and left the room.

"And what result would that be?"

"For you to go away. You're punishing Lord Ruhall because of my help. That hardly seems just. If I leave, will you withdraw your demand?"

"Not at all. Your help proved that he cannot hope to manage his affairs on his own. Whether you remain or not, he needs a wife. Actually, if you leave, I shall be forced to move up the deadline to the feast. We wouldn't want him failing."

"Ha. I think you do want him to fail. You continue to punish him though he has paid for his past failings. Withdraw your edict."

"No. It remains. He has several months to woo his future bride. That is not a punishment; that is a kindness. Request that I change my mind again, and I will choose his bride for him and see them wed this night."

"Hateful woman," I said, standing. "I hope never to see you again."

The hurt that crossed her features was almost laughable. Did she think I would thank her for her cruel meddling?

When I reached the door, she spoke quietly.

"Thank you for talking to Ila. She was upset to think you might hold her to blame for anything that has transpired."

"Unlike you, I don't punish the innocent," I said without turning.

"When have I punished an innocent?"

With a scoff, I faced her.

"You've confessed that your manipulations brought me to the estate where I met with many manners of ill-use, disregard, and danger. The final event was your refusal to let the estate come to my aid, allowing the baker to nearly rape me. Was my time there not punishment? For surely I suffered more so than the enchanted beings of the estate who had the freedom to frolic and fuck without consequence or care during the duration of their stay."

Her eyes widened slightly, and her face flushed. "You would see no one punished. Instead, you label the guilty as innocent and let them carry on with their crimes."

I left, slamming the door behind me. My visit accomplished nothing but angering us both. I strode through the halls with clenched fists. Ila stood by the back door, waiting for me. Sympathy softened her features.

"Do you still wish me to attend the feast as your guest?"

I exhaled slowly and gave her a weak smile.

"I do. You are welcome to stay the night as well."

* * * *

A dozen candle stands were now scattered throughout the ballroom. Large, and thicker than my waist, they would work beautifully to hold the pillars the candle maker would bring. But it worried me that

Alec had felled them so quickly. I hadn't been gone long. Two hours, perhaps. The purpose of the task had been to allow him to vent his anger in a suitable manner. That he had completed the chore in such a small amount of time could mean that Tam had helped him. Or...Alec was still very angry.

Whisking out of the ballroom, I went in search of Alec. I found him in his study. He sat behind the desk and stared at his arithmetic book. He still wore his soot stained shirt, but his jacket and neckcloth were missing. Sweat dampened hair stuck to his forehead.

"The stands are very nice. Thank you," I said from the doorway.

He didn't look up, and the furrow in his brow did not ease in the slightest. I felt pity and sorrow for him. I wished Rose would leave him alone. He'd suffered through so much, already. And the injustice of her latest decision only added more.

"I saw the letter from Rose."

His jaw clenched and the grip on the book tightened.

"I'm sorry, Alec. I went to her to see if she would rescind her edict. She would not."

His gaze remained locked on the pages.

"There is time," I said, trying to console him.

He threw the book aside and rose from his chair to stalk toward me, his temper unsubdued by the recent hard labor. When he reached me, his expression shifted through emotions too quickly for me to attempt to understand his precise mood. He was angry, but more. Frustrated. Desperate. Weary. It all flashed in his gaze.

"Time for what? For you to change your mind?"

I swallowed hard and looked away. He still wanted me as his wife. Though I'd told him I didn't trust him to love me, which still held true, there was much more.

"Alec, the idea of marrying anyone upsets me. I cannot endure what the baker—"

He pulled me into his arms and hushed me. Cautious of his turbulent mood, I allowed it for a brief moment before I pulled away.

"You're spending too much time in here," I said. He was too active a man to remain sitting and studying for so long. He needed to moderate his pursuits to include activity each day. It might help with his temper.

"Would you consider helping with the harvest? According to what Egrit said, the apples should be ready any day."

"Will you be harvesting?"

"Of course."

A curious expression flitted over his features then disappeared.

"I will help. Will you read to me tonight? We can eat in the library."

I nodded. "I'll let Kara know we'll need a tray." I turned to go but looked back. "Don't give up hope."

I left him by his desk and went to the kitchen. When Kara saw me, she pointed to the table.

"Sit. You never came back for your biscuit and left before midday meal. I saved you some food."

Her concern had me smiling and dutifully following her order. While I sat, she went to the oven and pulled out a plate full of fish, carrots, and biscuits. My mouth watered as she set it before me.

"Thank you," I breathed just before taking a large bite of warm fish.

Bryn moved quietly about the kitchen, ignoring me. Her disregard allowed me to focus on my meal. It was only when I had a few crumbs left that I recalled why I'd come to the kitchen.

"Kara, Lord Ruhall has requested a tray for three for dinner."

Kara nodded and came for my plate. As I rose, I noticed Bryn's annoyed glance in my direction. I left without giving it thought.

* * * *

My belly was still satisfied when I joined Father in the library a while later. Alec read in the study.

"I heard there was a disturbance this afternoon," Father said discreetly.

I nodded and sat near his desk.

"Rose told him he needs to marry by winter solstice or suffer enchantment once more."

"We'd best start considering what preparations need to be made. Two feasts in a season will be a strain on the estate."

"The wedding feast must be simple, then. There were no requirements made by Rose. Only that he marry."

Father nodded and studied me for so long I looked away. Thankfully, Alec joined us and spared me from further scrutiny. As we ate, we discussed the estate coffers, which hadn't changed and shared reports on the feast's progress.

"I sent a note to the Head asking for suitable family entertainment," Father said. "He referred several local musicians who are happy to play for food, drink, and a bit of coin."

Relieved we'd managed yet another piece of the affair, I reported that the lower level was clean and ready for guests and the menu was tentatively planned.

"Tentatively?"

"Smoked fish, meat pies, apple pastries, and cider. I haven't thought of anything else we might offer without incurring an unreasonable expense."

"I think the menu will suffice," Alec said. "She seems to know exactly what we do. If it wasn't sufficient, we would have heard from her."

I knew he referred to Rose.

As soon as I finished, Alec stood.

"Would you read to me, Benella?"

He handed me a thin volume, and Father moved to go back to his desk.

"Of course," I said, accepting the book. I went to recline on the lounge, and Alec took his usual place on the floor. His hands tugged at my hair before I began.

He'd chosen poetry, sad pieces that brought melancholy more than cheer. I only read a few before closing the volume.

"Finished already?"

"Egrit has bath water heating. A warm bath would be more welcome than a cold one," I said, sitting up.

He accepted the volume from me.

"Will you read to me again tomorrow?"

I nodded and left, wondering what Father thought of how we behaved. It wasn't inappropriate, exactly. Yet, I still felt Alec's fingers in my hair.

* * * *

The bed dipped. Alec pulled me close. I sighed and sank deeper into sleep as his fingers trailed my arm.

* * * *

Tam had baskets waiting at the base of the trees when Alec, Swiftly, and I joined him. The other men were fishing, trying to catch as much as possible to smoke for the feast. With only four of us to harvest, the task before us was daunting.

Alec stripped off his coat and neckcloth and rolled up his sleeves as Tam started to explain how to use the poles. I found myself glancing at Alec too often and missing bits of the instruction. The marks on his shoulder and the reason behind them were never far from my mind.

Tam handed us our poles, and Alec followed me as I selected a tree on which to start.

Within minutes, it was obvious I would be of little help with the pole, so I set it aside and picked from the lower branches. Alec worked the top branches. He never moved far from my side, and our time together was reminiscent of our times before the enchantment broke.

It was well past midday before we had our first tree picked clean.

"We'll carry the baskets to the wagon," Alec said, looking at me. "Will you ask Kara to prepare us something to eat? We'll join you after we finish."

I willingly left them to carry the heavy baskets and walked the distance to the manor. Kara wasn't in the kitchen this time. Hiding my reluctance, I turned to Bryn.

"Could you please prepare four servings of something? We've finished with the first load of apples."

She glanced at me, marched to the stove, and pulled four biscuits from the oven. Setting them on a single plate, she handed them to me.

"Perhaps you should have eaten a few of the apples."

I will not break this plate over my sister's head, I thought to myself. I took a calming breath before I spoke aloud.

"I'm sure Lord Ruhall will be grateful for the lunch you've provided."

Her eyes narrowed slightly, and she snatched the plate back.

I watched as she grabbed three more plates and put a biscuit on each. Then, she sliced thick wedges of cheese and placed them along with pieces of smoked fish on the plates. By the time she finished, Swiftly had joined us.

"I'll bring them to the table, Miss," he said to me. "Go sit."

He joined me at the table and set a plate before me. Tam and Alec came in a moment later. Alec sat beside me. Bryn brought us water and fawned over Lord Ruhall, asking if he'd like more of anything. She had obviously forgotten his disdain of her when he'd been a beast and had us all hanging in vines.

As soon as we finished eating, Tam, Alec, and I returned to picking while Swiftly delivered the apples to Edmund. It didn't take Swiftly long to return with the empty baskets.

"He said that was more than twice what he needed and thanked us for it."

I eyed all the trees that still hung heavy with fruit. Letting the harvest fall to waste on the ground wasn't an option. What we couldn't use, we would sell.

Alec came to stand behind me as I stared up at the heavy branches.

"Are you tired?"

"A little," I admitted.

"We can continue without you."

"No, I prefer this over dusting," I said, reaching for my next apple. In truth, I didn't want the men having to work harder because of my absence.

When we returned to the manor several hours later, Alec went directly to the study, assured by Tam and Swiftly that they no longer needed his help. The two then brought the baskets of apples around to the kitchen, and I followed. Kara knew of our plans to press them for cider and directed the men to take them into the cellar. While Bryn prepared a tray for me to take to the study, Kara pulled me to the side.

"Your sister is very helpful. However, with all these apples, I'm not certain the two of us can prepare meals, smoke fish, press cider, and—"

"I will speak with Egrit and see if she and Mrs. Palant can help. The rooms on the first floor are clean, as are a few on the second floor. It should be enough to suit our needs."

With relief, Kara thanked me and went down to the cellar to check on Tam and Swiftly.

I turned to get the tray from Bryn. She stared at the door in shock. I followed her gaze and found Patrick and Sara there. Sara kept her attention on the ground.

"We're here to see Lord Ruhall," Mr. Coalre said. "My wife is seeking a position."

Anger heated my face. They'd stood idly by as the baker rutted over me and now wanted help? Hate had me clenching my fists at my side as I stood there stiffly.

Mr. Crow stepped from his office and eyed the pair.

"There are no positions currently open," he said.

Sara's face fell while the smith's grew red.

"I asked to speak with Lord Ruhall."

"Mr. Crow handles Lord Ruhall's staff," I said, drawing his attention. "There is nothing for Sara." Her face flushed. I noted the tears starting in her eyes, and I hated myself for the pity I felt. "However, there is work for you and your sons."

"And what would that be?"

"There are apples to harvest. We'll pay a copper for a filled basket."

"My time at the forge is worth more than that. As is Tennen's. I'll send Splane to help. Sara, too."

"It's the three of you or none. The forge lies cold most days, and Tennen has too much time on his hands."

The look Mr. Coalre gave made my knees weak with fear, but I didn't stop.

"Work for your bread or don't eat." I turned and left the kitchen before he could respond.

When I reached the laundry door, I stopped to lean against the wall and catch my breath. My hands shook.

"Miss Hovtel?" Mr. Crow approached me with concern, and I quickly straightened from the wall.

"Yes?"

"The smith and his sons will be here in the morning. Why did you offer them work?"

"Why did you and Father invite them to the feast?"

"Your father suggested them. I had the impression he was unaware of their involvement in what transpired and didn't speak out against it, fearing he'd want to know why." He glanced down. "I'd thought it the right thing to do. Was I wrong?"

I knew his doubt not only stemmed from his worry about me, but also from his past silence.

"I apologize if I sounded harsh. You were not wrong. I chose not to burden my father with all the details. I am glad you did not, as well." I sighed as I considered how to answer Mr. Crow's original question. "I offered them work because they should feel what it's like to labor for so little. The smith has not been a good husband and helpmate to his wife, and his sons are learning from his lazy and disrespectful ways. If they work hard, they could easily earn a blunt silver tomorrow. The choice is theirs.

"But warn Tam and Swiftly to keep close watch on them at all times and have Kara prepare a simple meal for Tam and Swiftly to take with them in the morning so they have no reason to leave the Coalre men unattended."

"You're concerned they will do something?"

"My past experiences have taught me to be cautious of them."

"Very well. I'll bring the tray to the library, Miss, if you'd like to wash first."

He left to fetch the tray; and after a hasty wash in the laundry, I joined Alec and Father in the library where the tray already waited.

"We've made such wonderful progress harvesting that Kara has asked for extra help in the kitchen tomorrow," I said, sitting. Father served me a plate, and we began eating. "And, interestingly, I also found help to harvest tomorrow. The smith and his sons." I held Alec's gaze as I said it and witnessed his grip tighten on his fork. "I agreed to pay them a copper per filled basket. After we press what we need for the feast, we can bring the rest of the apples to the Water to sell, making the expense of their labor profitable."

Alec studied me for a moment then nodded.

"A splendid idea, Benella," Father said. "I was thinking of having Kara press three times as much as we might need or as much as she can before she thinks they will go bad. I've come across a book on making wine and spirits, and it has detailed instructions on making hard cider. We could use the drink for future feasts or sell it to local taverns."

He was thinking of Lord Ruhall's commanded wedding. Such a celebration usually required wine, but a hard cider would do.

"You're right. We should use whatever we can. I plan to stay here to help Kara in the kitchen tomorrow."

"I'll do the same," Alec said. "With five men harvesting, it will likely take the three of us pressing the apples to keep up."

"Three?" Father said.

The genuine smile Alec gave my father warmed me.

"You have the knowledge, sir. We wouldn't know what to do without you. Kara and Bryn would be able to keep on their tasks with our help."

We ate the rest of the meal; and after reading to Alec, I excused myself and retired early. The day had exhausted me. I had barely lay in bed before sleep claimed me.

I only roused slightly when Alec joined me. And again later, when the languid caress of his fingers shifted from my arm to my exposed stomach. Too tired to speak, I simply rolled away from him, and his touch returned to my arm.

* * * *

Father, Alec, and I ate early in the study. We listened to Father explain the pressing process and then went to the small courtyard outside the laundry. While Alec brought up the baskets, Father and I worked the press. It was an interesting contraption with a large metal wheel and connecting crank. The apples went into the top holding chute; and as the wheel turned, the apples fell into the inner workings that crushed them. The juices and fine pulp slid down the exit chute and the peels and seeds fell into the waste bucket.

We all took turns working the wheel and feeding apples into the chute. When it was my turn at the wheel, my arms grew weary quickly, and I paused to watch the ease with which Alec lifted a full basket closer to the chute.

He caught me watching him and gave me a quick grin. Looking away, I tried to ignore the warmth that spread in my middle from his simple smile.

Tennen and Swiftly returned around midday with more apples, which they left outside the kitchen.

"How many baskets will we need to do?" I asked, feeling the burn in my arms.

"I've noted that we gain a bucket of cider for every three baskets. Estimating the servings for the evening, we need to press at least one hundred baskets. More would be better."

"How many trees were out there?" I asked Alec when he carried out some of the baskets the men had just delivered.

"Perhaps fifty in that field."

I stopped turning the handle.

"That field? There are more apple trees?"

"Tam mentioned there is another grove. A different apple. Green. Too tart for cider but he thinks they might store well over winter."

Even if we didn't need to turn the green apples, we still had the rest of the red to consider. I did the calculations in my head and decided I would end up pressing cider until my arms ceased to function.

"Interesting," Father said. "I'd like to try just a few baskets of green apples to see how they taste as a hard cider."

Something must have shown on my face because Alec stopped loading apples and walked toward me.

"Let me turn the wheel for a while," he said. "See if Kara knows where the old barrels are to store the cider."

* * * *

By nightfall, we had several barrels of cider stored in the cellar and many baskets waiting for the press the next day. Mr. Crow had paid the Coalre family and reported that the men would return the following day.

I went to bed weary. My arms didn't want to cooperate enough to undress, so it took much longer than usual, and I was still awake when Alec quietly entered my room. I pretended to sleep as he pulled me against his chest.

His fingers trailed along my arm. I sighed sleepily, soothed by the motion...until I felt my shirt lift. A moment later, his fingers trailed lazily along my stomach. They moved from bellybutton to ribs, blazing a little further south and north with each pass.

My thoughts scattered, and my pulse quickened as I recalled the last time he'd touched me like this. Remembered sensations swamped me anew, and my breathing grew shallow as my body heated.

His fingertips skimmed the underside of my breast. The raw need that ignited startled me enough that I sat up in bed and twisted to stare down at him.

The moonlight glinted in his eyes as we watched one another.

"What are you doing, Alec?"

Slowly, he lifted a hand and lightly brushed a knuckle over my nipple. My chest tightened with longing.

"Do you fear me?"

"No," I answered, honestly, wondering why he would think that.

He lifted his hand and drew his palm under my shirt and up along my side. My breath caught at the need I felt. He tried to pull me toward him, but I resisted. I had to because I wasn't thinking straight.

"Leave, Alec. Leave now, and I won't bar my doors. Persist, and I'll call for help and bolt the doors every night until the day I leave."

Because I would need to leave, I reminded myself.

I saw his temper flare, but his only reaction was to withdraw his hand and leave my bed. He stalked across the carpets and quietly closed himself into his own room.

It was a long while before I fell asleep.

* * * *

As soon as I opened my eyes, I hurried from bed and dressed. With the feast so close, we couldn't afford to have Alec losing his temper after my rejection the night before.

Instead of finding him upset, I found him reading in his study. When I hesitated in the doorway, he glanced up at me.

"Are we to press cider so early?" he asked as he set the book aside and stood. He looked completely relaxed and not a bit upset with me.

"Uh...yes. Have you eaten?"

"Not yet. And you?"

"No."

"Then we'll see what your sister can offer us before we begin today's work."

He held out his arm, and I hesitated. Once before, I'd mistaken his courtesy and patience for coldness. Yet, according to him, it had been a mask to hide what he really felt. What was he hiding now?

"Perhaps I shouldn't," I said, considering the courtesy he offered.

"Perhaps you're right."

His accepting, genial mood worried me.

He motioned for me to lead the way, and I did.

In the kitchen, the table was set with bowls, and a kettle of oats waited with a pitcher of fresh cream. Kara and Bryn were absent. I spooned us both a portion and saw they'd added apples to the oats. Topping the bowls with cream, I sat across from Alec.

"You seem in a good mood today," I said carefully, watching him eat with enthusiasm.

"I am."

"Does that mean you've accepted that you need to wed soon?"

He paused eating to look at me. A serious light crept into his gaze.

"I have."

My stomach gave a nauseating turn.

"Very good," I said softly as I lifted the spoon to my mouth.

Bryn walked out of the dry pantry just then. Though she didn't acknowledge us, I knew she'd heard he needed to wed. Tonight, everyone in the village would know. Within a day or two, many in the Water would know as well. My face flushed at the thought, and my stomach continued its sickening churning. I struggled to remind myself that Alec wasn't the beast I'd once loved. It was kinder to let him go and start anew. Kinder for us both. And, having those around us know about his need to wed might not be a bad thing. If Alec had settled his mind on wedding someone, he needed to start meeting his options. And once the female population heard he meant to wed, his options would come to him. I struggled to continue eating.

He finished his food first and stood.

"I will see you outside," he said.

Bryn stopped adding things to her kettle and stared after him, no doubt waiting for him to leave so she could question me. However, Kara came up from the cellar, carrying a half basket of apples. Alec passed her with a polite nod.

"I hope it's all right to take some," she said, looking at me after he left.

"Certainly. We'll have more than I'll care to press. Plenty to make cider for the feast and any future entertaining the estate may need to do."

I forced myself to finish breakfast quickly and fled the kitchen.

Alec was already outside pressing the baskets of apples we'd stored in the laundry. Father joined us not long after, and we spent a companionable morning and afternoon together making more cider.

Bryn finally caught me alone as I washed in the laundry before dinner.

"Is he truly seeking a wife?" she asked in a hushed tone. She didn't wait for an answer. "Did you tell Blye?"

"Tell Blye? Why? Both you and Blye were quite clear in your refusal to speak with me ever again."

"We didn't understand you were in Lord Ruhall's confidence."

I stopped drying my hands and turned to stare at her.

"Your selfish ways continue to astound me," I said.

"Me, selfish? Hardly. You should have told Blye when she was here.

She could have introduced herself as a prospect. In fact, you should invite her for tea and introduce her yourself. If they married, we'd be related to the Lord. Edmund and I wouldn't need to work like this, then."

I threw my hands in the air.

"Do you have any idea how futile that would be? Do you honestly think he doesn't remember you or Blye? He knows your characters and wants nothing to do with either of you. He tolerates you here because Father and I asked him to. Stop thinking of yourselves. Start thinking of your babe and your husband. He likes and respects his occupation, and you did too once. Change your ways, Bryn, before you find yourself alone and unloved. Never forget you have another man's babe in your belly and that Edmund could choose to annul your marriage."

She paled and trembled, but her fear didn't stop her anger.

"I hope Lord Ruhall weds soon. You preside over the staff and sleep in the Lady's room as if the role was yours. But you're too stupid to take it."

She turned and left. I didn't move.

She was right. If Alec did meet someone, what would she think of me occupying the Lady's room? Many of the bedrooms on the second floor had been cleaned now. There was no reason to remain where I was.

Instead of joining Alec and Father in the library for dinner, I went to my room and gathered my things. I looked around the room with sad eyes. It had been my home for so long.

Father found me as I left the room with my arms full.

"Will you dine with us?"

"Yes, let me just set these things in my room."

He made no comment when I picked the room next to his and placed my few possessions there. The spare dress, my shirt and pants, which I hadn't worn in ages, and my hairbrush and hair oil.

After straightening the Lady's room, I closed the door behind me for good and joined them for dinner.

* * * *

A crash woke me. Lying still, I listened with a hammering heart. Another crash followed.

"Damn her!"

Alec's roar echoed in the hallway. Cowering under the covers crossed my mind. Instead, I rose and tiptoed to the door. Something crashed again, and I jumped. He would wake the house if he hadn't already. Nibbling my lip, I opened my door.

"Bini?" Father said quietly. His door stood open, and he held a lit candle.

"Yes," I said, just as softly.

Suddenly, all sound stopped. I turned to look down the hall and saw Alec standing just outside his door. As soon as our gazes met, he started toward me.

"Perhaps you should fetch your wrap," my father said. "It appears he would like to speak to you."

Then he withdrew from the hall, closing his door. I blinked at his abandonment.

"Benella," Alec said, startling me. I spun and found him just inches from me. "Why are you not in your room?"

I swallowed and stood straight.

"I am in my room. If you recall, I only took the Lady's room because no other had been cleaned. Most are now clean, so I could choose."

He opened his mouth, ready to argue, and without thinking, I stepped closer and pressed my hand over it.

"Listen. Many people will be here in just a few days. Some might ask to spend the night. How would it look if I slept in that chamber? Especially, when most who attend know what the baker tried to do."

He growled and grabbed my wrist. Then, he surprised me by licking my palm before pulling my hand from his mouth. The tingle almost distracted me from what he said next.

"Marry me, and you need not worry what they think."

I curled my hand into a fist. I stared at him for a moment, confused. He had told me just that morning he'd resolved himself to marriage. Had he meant to me?

"I cannot," I said. But I struggled to remember why. His abandonment of me after the baker attacked. Yes. I questioned if he truly cared for me.

Even in the dimly lit hall, I caught the scarlet hue of his face.

"Then I damn what they think and damn the feast. If I cannot have you, I will have no one." He turned and strode back to his room, slamming his door.

Surely, he did not mean that.

* * * *

Alec said nothing when he joined us outside at the press. Though he was late, I was glad to see him. Many baskets lined the laundry. So many that Tam, Swiftly, and the Coalres ran out. On their last delivery, they had created a small mountain outside. Father and I fed the apples in as Alec turned the wheel with aggressive force.

His gaze tracked my movements, yet he made no comment. It

wasn't until near lunch, when Father walked inside for a drink, that Alec moved away from the press. I stood quickly, dropping the apples I'd been about to place in the bucket.

"Return to your room tonight."

"That is not my room."

He snarled and ran his hand through his hair. I backed away a step and tripped over the bucket. Before I could fall, he wrapped his arm around me and pulled me tight to his chest.

A shiver stole through me at the contact. His frown faded as he studied me. He brought his other arm around me and slowly smoothed his hand up my back. When he reached my neck, his fingers speared into my hair. My breathing became irregular as I realized he intended to kiss me.

I lifted my hands and gripped his coat.

"No," I whispered.

"Yes." He started to close the distance.

"Ah-erm."

The noise gave me the motivation I needed to pull myself from his embrace.

Father stood by the door, looking decidedly embarrassed. He held two cups.

"I thought you might both be thirsty."

"I am. Thank you. If you'll excuse me, I need a private moment."

I took the cup from him and left, heading toward my room for some quiet and perhaps a nap. However, it wasn't meant to be.

The door opened to a disaster. The mattress lay shredded on the bed frame, and for a stunned moment, I just stood there. Then I realized what had happened and stomped my foot. Alec's late arrival wasn't due to sleep but manipulative destruction. He thought to drive me back into the Lady's room. I wouldn't go back, and the estate couldn't afford for me to choose another room. I would need to sleep on a ruined mattress.

Breathing through my anger, I left my room just as I'd found it. When I rejoined them for lunch, Alec watched me closely. I gave nothing away then or through our dinner.

"Will you read to me, Benella?" he asked softly just before we finished.

Father excused himself to look at books on one of the far shelves.

"I've slept poorly these last few nights and pressing cider is tiresome work. I would prefer to retire early."

He bowed his head as if in acceptance. I knew better. He hid his smile.

* * * *

Sleeping on a torn, lumpy mattress made my slumber restless and light. The slightest noise roused me as did the slamming of Alec's door at some point during the night. I lay awake a long while after, straining to hear the slightest noise, but all was silent. The quiet was worse than the previous night's rage. What was he planning?

The next day, he glared at me over breakfast and maintained his surly mood throughout the morning. When he excused himself from our midday meal, I wondered what he would do next.

Later that evening, when I stepped into my room, I discovered a large space where my bed and torn mattress had once existed. I hoped he hadn't destroyed the bed further when removing it. Backtracking, I went to the laundry and took what blankets and bedding I could to make myself a nest on the floor.

Exhaustion did not aid me to sleep. My mind refused to calm. I considered Alec's anger over my change in rooms. He had agreed he needed to marry. Surely his comment about only marrying me was false. He would do what was needed in order to maintain his freedom. Wouldn't he?

Nine

My back objected when I rose the next morning, and my arms begged to be left alone as I dressed. Had I an actual bed, I would have remained in my room several more hours and ignored my protesting stomach.

I opened my door and squeaked at the sight of Alec. He hadn't made a sound in the hall to warn me that he stood just outside the door. His eyes were bloodshot, and he wore the same clothes as the prior day.

He scowled at me.

"I vow, tonight you will sleep where you belong."

He turned and walked to his room. I stared after him and hoped he would stay in his room to rest nearly as much as I hoped he would continue to help us press the apples. After his door slapped shut, I quietly left my sanctuary.

When I entered the kitchen, I found Bryn and Kara hard at work. Bryn rolled out thin sheets of dough while Kara sliced apples, equally thin.

"Good morning, Miss Hovtel," Kara said with a smile. "Would you care to sample one of the apple tartlets we're making?"

"Please. I'm starving and will sample anything you set before me."

She smiled as she went to the warming oven where she withdrew a full plate.

"I'd hoped you would be hungry," she said as she brought the food to me.

On the plate, she had several types of tartlets, bits of apple that looked brown, and a serving of thick oats mixed with more brown bits of apple.

"May I sit with you?" she asked.

"Of course."

She studied me closely as I sampled everything, and I knew she was waiting for my opinion.

"The tartlets are delicious."

"Good. With Lord Ruhall's intent to marry, Bryn and I thought we might need some form of refreshment in supply for any callers."

Bryn was a gossip. I'd known that. Yet, it still irked me that she'd told Kara.

"A sound plan. This bit here," I said, pointing to the brown apple pieces. "It was surprisingly sweet. I'd thought it burnt at first glance." I popped the last morsel into my mouth and chewed.

"We set some of the slices in the warming oven last night to dry them. Often, stored apples rot too fast. Dried apples last much longer. I used the dried pieces to sweeten the oats to show you how they could be consumed."

"It was very tasty," I said.

She smiled broadly.

"I'd hope you would say that and allow me to dry some more."

"Take as many apples as you want. The fewer to press, the happier I will be."

She thanked me and took away my empty plate. Sated, I walked out the laundry's door and found Alec already at the press.

He cranked the handle ruthlessly. Knowing him to be in a mood, I carefully did not turn my back to him as I filled a bucket with apples. He watched me approach and narrowed his eyes as I dumped the fruit into the chute. The way he acted reminded me of our earlier attempts to pent up his energies in the moments just before he would run and find the wood nymph.

However, Egrit was no longer his target. I wasn't sure what to do about him.

Father joined us before I'd added the fourth bucket, and I almost sighed with relief. He moved to help me fill buckets, and Alec continued with his wheel.

We worked a long while that way before Father offered to take a turn at the wheel. Alec quickly agreed. Neither Father nor I could compete with Alec's endurance, but we tried to help.

As I bent to pick up more apples, something brushed against my backside. A hand gripped my hip. I straightened with a blush and glanced at my father who busily turned the wheel. Glaring at Alec, I pushed him back a step.

"Stop this," I whispered.

"No," he said, not bothering to lower his voice.

"Beast," I hissed.

He grinned at me.

"I need to rest," Father said suddenly. "This work is taxing me."

And faster than I could blink, he left me alone with Alec in the courtyard.

As Father's steps faded, Alec's grin widened. He'd rolled up his sleeves at some point during his labor, and his shirt was damp with sweat. My heart skipped a beat. He took a step toward me, and I retreated in time as if we danced. His eyes narrowed, and he reached out to grab me. I ducked under his arm and sprinted for the door. Behind me, I heard apples tumble and his curse. A glance showed him on the ground due to a tipped basket. I didn't hesitate but fled to the kitchen.

Kara looked up in surprise as I burst into the room.

"Kara, do you have a pitcher of cold water?"

"Yes, right th—"

I rushed to where she pointed and snatched up the pitcher just as Alec stomped into the room. His gaze immediately landed on me. We stared at each other, both of us breathing heavily but for different reasons. Anger and lust fueled him. Fear had me tossing the contents of the pitcher in his face.

For a moment, stunned silence claimed the kitchen.

"Benella!"

I ignored Bryn's censure and stared at Alec, awaiting his reaction. Mr. Crow stepped from his office.

"Is there a problem, Lord Ruhall?" he asked.

Alec's eyes narrowed on me briefly.

"No problem. I think I'll go change." He turned away and said over his shoulder, "Have Miss Hovtel take a tray to the library."

I swallowed hard, glanced at Mr. Crow, and shook my head slightly. Alec wasn't done with me; but, I wasn't foolish enough to enter into whatever game he saw us playing.

Mr. Crow turned to Bryn who stared at me with her mouth open.

"Mrs. Rouflyn, please take a tray to Lord Ruhall."

She nodded and started preparing a tray. I watched her for a moment, knowing Alec would only become more impossible when he saw Bryn.

"Mr. Crow," I said, "how many pitchers do we have?"

"Several, Miss Hotvel."

"Good. Each room needs a full pitcher of water. When we run out of pitchers, use buckets just inside the doors."

"I will see to it myself," he said with a bow before he left the room.

I left the kitchen and tried to decide where Father might be. Most likely the library, the very place I did not want to go. Hoping Alec still changed, I cautiously hurried through the halls and paused outside the library door. When I peeked inside, I found Father reclined on the lounge, comfortably reading a book.

"With respect, you're not so old as to be taxed enough to warrant an afternoon nap," I said, entering the room. "Why did you abandon me? Twice now."

"Abandon? Never. I trust Alec to keep within the boundaries you've established with him."

I snorted. I didn't even trust Alec to keep within the boundaries.

"Bini, you've upset him."

"He has upset me." I crossed my arms.

"He told me you've rejected his proposal more times than he has toes. His words."

My arms fell to my sides. Counting the times he'd asked me as the beast, I had rejected him that many times. Father sat up and patted the lounge next to him.

"Why, Bini?"

I sighed and sat beside him.

"Because of so many reasons. What happened with the baker makes marriage a less than appealing state, and it broke my trust in Lord Ruhall. I also thought I didn't know him; but lately, I'm wondering if I say no because I don't know myself."

He wrapped an arm around my shoulders and hugged me to his side to kiss my temple.

"Of all of us, you know yourself best. Trust your heart and your head to lead you to the right choice."

Mr. Crow entered the room and discreetly set a bucket of water just within the door.

"Thank you, Mr. Crow," I said to him.

He gave a single nod and left.

"Should I ask?" Father said.

"Probably not."

A few moments later, Mr. Crow returned.

"There is a caller for Lord Ruhall. I've put her in the front sitting room."

A caller? So soon?

"Please have Bryn provide refreshment and let Lord Ruhall know. I believe he's in his room, changing."

Mr. Crow didn't move. I watched him glance at Father before focusing on me once more.

"It's your sister, Blye."

"Don't bother with the refreshment."

"Benella," Father said chidingly.

"I understand you must love your children, but I will not encourage what she intends with pampered attention and sweet treats."

Mr. Crow nodded and left the library. I stood, too.

"I should try to dissuade her. In Alec's current mood, I don't believe he will tolerate her attempted manipulations well."

"I quite agree," Father said after a weary sigh.

I left him on the lounge with his book and sought out my sister. I found her sitting serenely in a new dress, drowning in yards of pink lace.

"Hello, Blye."

"Benella," she said indifferently. "Is Lord Ruhall on his way?"

"I haven't the slightest idea. Why are you here?"

"As if you don't know. You've always been close mouthed, but how could you keep such news as Lord Ruhall's need to wed to yourself? You weren't hoping he'd marry you, were you?"

The heat of anger colored my cheeks as she continued in a patronizing tone.

"You're not precisely the model of a lady. Pants, fishing, hunting, foraging..." She shook her head.

"You didn't so disregard those skills when they kept you from starving. And what skills do you possess that you think might tempt him to forget your groveling pleas for mercy when he asked you to stay with him in exchange for Father's life?"

She didn't look the slightest bit put off by the reminder. Instead, she fluffed her skirt and smiled serenely.

"He's no longer the beast."

"He is the same, only changed in form. He's forgotten nothing. Spare yourself humiliation or worse. Leave."

A throat cleared behind me. I turned and saw Mr. Crow.

"Miss Hovtel," he said, looking at Blye. "Lord Ruhall is unable to take callers today."

"Will he be available tomorrow?" she asked, crossing the room to stand before Mr. Crow.

"He will be unavailable to all callers until after the feast. He begs you understand the time and attention it takes to coordinate such an affair."

"Of course," she said serenely.

"Might you want to see your father?" he asked.

She waved a hand negligibly.

"I haven't the time. I must return to the shop."

"I will see you out," he said with a bow. Since he left her no choice, she followed him from the room.

With effort, I pushed my sister's visit from my mind and focused on the problem at hand. Alec was angry with me; and if he hadn't already realized I wasn't in the library waiting for him, he would soon. Thinking quickly, I went in search of Egrit.

I survived the rest of the day by sending Mrs. Palant to help with the press while I helped Egrit dust. Egrit didn't comment on the change. However, she did ask if I was well several times throughout the afternoon because I jumped at the slightest sounds.

By evening, I'd exhausted myself with worry over what trouble he might cause next.

When I went to my room, the nest of blankets remained as I'd left them. I carefully locked the door and undressed for bed. It didn't take me long to fall asleep.

* * * *

Fingers trailed over my skin, tracing a burning path from navel to knee. I woke with an aching need that smothered any sense of worry. Turning my head, I found Alec beside me. I blinked at him, trying to focus. How had he gotten in?

His dark gaze held mine as his fingers barely missed the v of my legs. My breath hitched, and I almost forgot my question.

I closed my eyes and turned my head away to escape his focus. The pillow shifted under me, and I became aware that I lay on a bed, not the floor. I opened my eyes once more and saw his wardrobe. He'd moved me.

His lips suddenly skimmed along my neck. I sighed, and my eyes drifted closed. His fingers continued their languid strokes, tempting me, begging me to part my knees and give them access. I wanted nothing more than to give in to his seduction. My need almost robbed me of thought and will, as did his fingers and mouth.

I needed to deny him. Why? I couldn't remember...

He nibbled his way from my neck to my shoulder. My skin tingled with fire and life. Then he licked my collarbone. He lifted his head and moved so his mouth hovered over my left breast. He exhaled, the hot air creating an ache. I knew what he intended, and I wanted it more than I wanted my next breath.

"You are mine," he breathed against my skin. His fingers continued to dance along the v of my legs. His tongue brushed against my nipple then disappeared, leaving me unsatisfied. I whimpered and arched.

"Agree to marry me, and I will give you what you desire."

The words chilled me as if a pitcher had doused me. Marriage. He needed to marry or be re-enchanted. I balled up my fist and swung at him.

"Manipulator. Beast," I cried as my fist connected with his cheek. He grunted and grabbed both my hands. I pulled back hard and tumbled from the bed.

Tired and frustrated, I couldn't prevent the tears that welled in my eyes.

"Why? Haven't I been punished enough?"

"Punished?" He sat up and looked down at me. "Do you really see my touch as punishment?"

"Do not twist my meaning. It's not your touch but your cruel manipulations to gain your own ends. Stop this, Alec. I want sleep."

"As do I," he shouted at me.

"Then why are you awake touching me?"

"How else am I to get you to stay?"

The tears spilled over.

"That is the problem, Alec. You cannot force me to stay. You can only ask and leave the choice to me."

His shoulders slumped, and his hopeless expression tugged at my heart.

"Please stay the night with me, Benella. I cannot sleep without you by my side."

I considered him a long while. Saying yes would ease whatever madness gripped him now, but it would not ease my conscience. He would marry soon. Sleeping with me like this was wrong. Yet, his desperate expression and bloodshot eyes moved me to compassion.

"I want my nightshirt back. And my underclothes."

"Yes," he said quickly. He rose and retrieved them from the bottom of his wardrobe.

Once I had the shirt about me, I sat on the edge of the bed.

"Lie down," I said.

He immediately obeyed but then pulled me down with him. He tucked me close to his chest and rested his chin on the top of my head.

I held still and waited for his breathing to slow. Once each exhale came in an even rhythm, I eased from his arms. He didn't stir. I covered him with a spare blanket and quietly left his room.

* * * *

The next day looked as if it would play out no better than the prior day when I heard Alec pacing in the hall. He whirled at the sound of my door opening. I hesitated near the threshold, close to the pitcher of water Mr. Crow had considerately placed within.

"You left me," he said with an angry scowl.

"It wasn't my place to stay. I should not have been there to begin with."

He opened his mouth to argue, and I stepped close to take his hands in mine. The action stopped the forthcoming rant. He gripped my hands firmly and watched me with mixed emotions.

"Alec, have patience. The feast is a mere five days from today. You might meet someone then." He made a sound of disagreement. "Or perhaps officially announce your intent to wed. If you can just hold yourself for a few more days, your life might unexpectedly change for the better."

"I don't want my life to change unexpectedly. I want you."

He pulled his hands from mine and left me in the hallway.

For a brief moment, I considered finding Egrit to see if she would consider helping with the press. Then, I slowly followed in Alec's wake. Hiding from him did no good. Avoiding him made things worse. Perhaps if I did the opposite, things would then improve.

We worked together throughout the morning. He watched me continually and used any opportunity to touch me. When he invited me to join him in the library for the midday meal, I accepted after he also invited Father.

The meal didn't last long. As soon as Alec finished his portion, he stood and began pacing just behind my chair. I felt as if the beast was back, waiting to pounce. I took my last bite and set my plate back upon the tray. Before I could swallow, Father quickly excused himself to return the tray to the kitchen.

The sound of Alec's pacing stopped. I stood and turned. With a determined glint in his eyes, he waited, poised just behind my chair. Instead of finding an excuse to leave, I stayed where I was. He seemed to calm when he saw I wasn't about to bolt.

"Thank you for a lovely meal," I said softly.

He exhaled slowly. If he still had fur, I had no doubt I would have witnessed his hackles lowering.

"Will you read to me after dinner?" he asked.

"Yes, if you will tell me how you entered my room last night."

"So you can bar me from entering?" he asked with a scowl.

"I won't need to bar you if I have your word that I will remain in my room all night tonight and have no cause to lock my door."

He considered me for a moment then reached into his pocket. He withdrew a key and handed it to me.

"I asked Phillip for the master key. I had to wait half the night for him to leave his post outside your door." The petulant way he said it almost made me smile.

"Mr. Crow is a good man. I'll return it and let him know he need not worry tonight?" I ended it as a question because I wanted Alec's agreement. When he nodded, I smiled. "Then, I will read to you for as long as you like."

*   *   *   *

After dinner, Alec brought me a tome of enormous proportions, and I read until my voice objected. The whole while, he sat on the floor and ran his fingers through my hair. When I closed the book, he stood and offered me his arm.

We walked together to our rooms, and he bade me goodnight at my door. His civility eased my mind enough that I kept my promise and did not turn the lock.

In the morning, the warm place in the blankets beside me told a truth. He'd come to me, and slept beside me, but had left me unmolested.

The next three days followed a similar pattern. If I behaved in an accommodating manner, he adhered to the boundaries I'd set, with the exception of sleeping in my room. He continued to let himself in, though I had asked him to cease.

In those three days, the stacked barrels of fresh cider lined one full wall of the cellar, and the men completed the harvest of the red apples. Mr. Crow paid the smiths their due and let them know there was no further work for them. If they were smart, they would hold tight to their coin.

Bryn and Kara continued to cook and prepare everything brought to them. Cloth-covered, wooden platters of smoked fish crowded the cellar on every spare surface. Kara even managed to turn a large amount of herbed soft cheese from the goat milk that I'd neglected to take to the Water the week prior.

The day before the feast, we finished pressing the remaining apples early in the morning while Bryn and Kara started the meat pies.

Everything was progressing nicely, and I felt a sense of calm until midday.

Alec, Father, and I were in the library, eating and discussing last minute details when Mr. Crow interrupted us.

"Lord Ruhall, a guest for the feast has arrived early. Egrit is showing her to a guest room...near her father's."

Blye. Mr. Crow and I shared a look before I glanced at Alec.

"Perhaps you should lock *your* door tonight," I said.

Alec ignored me and turned to Phillip.

"Let Kara know we'll eat in the dining room tonight with our guest. Nothing formal, just a change in scene."

Mr. Crow nodded and left.

"I'll take the tray to the kitchen," I said, standing. "Alec, will you help me in the ballroom? We should start moving the tables and chairs in."

He seemed pleased that I'd asked him and nodded.

We met a few minutes later in the ballroom. Alec had brought Swiftly with him to help. I directed them where to place the food and drink tables, then helped bring in some of the lighter chairs for the older guests like the candle maker.

Less than an hour had passed when Mr. Crow found us again.

"Miss Hovtel, there is someone here to see you. She gave the name Ila."

I was elated she'd decided to come early.

"Thank you, Mr. Crow." I turned to glance at the tables. "Can you bring Kara in here to see if this will be enough room for the food? I'd like to set it all out right away tomorrow so everyone can join in the feast."

He nodded, and I left him in the ballroom so quickly that he had to call after me.

"She is in the sitting room, Miss."

I waved to show I'd heard and kept going. I desperately needed a friendly face and an escape from my troubled thoughts. I hoped Ila would provide both.

Ila didn't sit on a chair as Blye had but wandered around the room to study interesting objects here and there. When she heard me enter, she turned with a hesitant smile.

"Ila, I'm so happy you're here. Will you be staying the night?"

I hugged her warmly when I reached her, and after a slight hesitation, she hugged me in return.

"I'm glad you're happy to see me," she said. "I wasn't certain."

"Nonsense. I'm delighted. And I would like you to stay. Blye is here early as well, and I would enjoy a companion who doesn't ignore me."

Ila laughed, a husky sound and a bittersweet reminder of our shared past, as she pulled back from our embrace.

"I will stay, then, and protect you as I am able." She turned and gestured to a small trunk just inside the door. "I brought your dress."

It was hard to keep the joy on my face. The extravagance of having a formal dress still annoyed me. Even my serviceable dresses annoyed me at times. What would I do with a lace-ridden dress? Owning something that could only be worn once, maybe twice, made little sense.

"Don't look so cornered," Ila said. "Through your visits, I've grown to know you. I think you'll be happy with what I've brought. Would you like to see it?"

"I apologize if I looked unappreciative, I'm nothing but grateful. Yes, please do show me."

Ila moved to the trunk and opened it. With her back to me, she lifted something from within, shook it out, then turned. The cream dress adorned with golden and burgundy threads stunned me. No lace trimmed the square neckline; the parallel patterns of the threads were enough of an adornment. The pattern continued down the length of the skirt as well. From a distance, it would appear a solid cream color. Only on closer inspection would someone realize the beauty of the material. The only lace on the creation hung from the sleeves that stopped at the elbow.

"It's beautiful," I said, reaching out to touch it. The fine, thin material reminded me of the dress I'd worn to my sister's wedding.

"There is an underskirt if you want more volume, or you can wear it without."

"I cannot wait to try it on," I said with honesty.

"Not until tomorrow." She smiled at me, then turned to tuck it into the trunk once more.

"You're sure it will fit?"

"Yes. I have no doubt."

After asking Mr. Crow for a tray, Ila and I enjoyed a quiet afternoon talking. Before dinner, I showed her to her room then walked with her to the dining room where we found Alec, Father, and Blye already seated.

"I apologize," I said. "I didn't think us late."

Alec stood as we approached the table and pulled out the chair to his right.

"You're not. We were early, Miss Hovtel."

Blye, who sat beside Father, narrowed her eyes at my placement next to Lord Ruhall. I sat and let him push me in. He gave the same courtesy to Ila, who sat beside me and across from Blye.

"Hello, Mr. Hovtel," Ila said softly.

Father smiled at her.

"It is good to see you again, Ila. How are your sisters?"

"Well, thank you. A few have found husbands since we last saw you."

Blye's gaze bounced between the pair before understanding dawned. Her lips thinned in disapproval. I ignored her.

"You should see the dress Ila made me, Father. It is truly stunning."

"I look forward to seeing it tomorrow," Alec said, his eyes on me.

Mr. Crow's arrival saved me from needing to respond. He entered the room slowly, carrying a heavily laden tray. I stood quickly and went to help him.

"Thank you, Miss," he said. "It wasn't heavy when I left the kitchen."

"I had the same problem with the press. The handle turned with ease the first few times."

I set it on the table and moved aside so Mr. Crow could serve us.

Alec again helped me sit. This time his arm brushed against mine. No one seemed to notice as Mr. Crow began to set our soup bowls before us.

"This looks delicious. Thank you," I said when my bowl waited before me. Orange and thick, the aroma hinted at squash and onion.

The table grew quiet as we ate. I was surprised when Mr. Crow returned a short while later and held the door open for Kara. She carried in a large platter with a roast surrounded by peeled potatoes.

She set the dish on the table as Mr. Crow took our bowls and replaced them with plates. The first slice of roast she set to the side. The second slice she set on Alec's plate. The smell made my mouth water.

"Thank you, Kara," Alec said after she added potatoes. He waited until we each had our portions before picking up his fork. I beat him to the first bite. The last time I'd eaten roast escaped me. While enchanted, the estate or the beast usually fed me finger food.

I chewed slowly, savoring the flavor and remembered. It had been at the Kinlyn's. Mrs. Kinlyn had served us roast, and I'd met Henick for the first time. I smiled and took another bite.

"The roast pleases you," Alec said. I noticed he no longer ate but only studied me.

"Very much. It's been a long while since I last tasted roast." I took another bite.

"Roast isn't typically served here?" Blye asked.

With my mouth full, Alec answered her.

"A stew is much easier for the kitchen to prepare while they try to shore the winter stores."

"I'm honored you had a special meal prepared for us, Lord Ruhall," Ila said.

Blye's lips thinned again. Her distaste for Ila was obvious, and I wanted to kick my sister under the table.

"I'm honored you could join us, Ila," Alec said. "Tell me what news you have from the Water."

And with that, he let Ila lead the conversation and Blye sulk quietly in her chair.

* * * *

Egrit woke me with a knock on my door. The place beside me still held Alec's heat. He always managed to come and go without being caught. Too many years prowling as a beast had honed his nocturnal skills.

"Good morning," she said softly when I opened the door. "I started water heating in the laundry so the children can wash before the feast. Tam is bringing bath water to Lord Ruhall's room. Would you like him to bring some to your old room, too?"

"Would he mind?"

"Not at all. Mr. Crow said that we have no duties today other than setting up for the feast. Tam and I still milked the goats and collected eggs, though."

"Tell Tam thank you for his hard work. You too," I said, reaching out to touch her arm.

"You're welcome, Benella. The water should be in your room in an hour."

I nodded, and she walked away. Down the hall, another door opened and Ila stepped out to wave to me. I joined her and saw my dress laid out on her bed.

"Should we take it to your room?"

"I'm going to use the Lady's room to bathe. Let's take it there." Better she thought me overreaching than for her to see I had no bed in my room. She picked up the dress, and I carried the underskirt and matching slippers.

"This is truly amazing." I spoke softly in the hallway, not wanting to wake Blye or Father.

"I cannot wait to see you in it. Let me know as soon as you have it on."

I opened the door to the large room. It was just as I'd left it. We set everything out on the bed, and I pulled the tub out from under its table.

"Let's see if there's anything to eat in the kitchen," I said, ready to leave the room before Alec heard something.

Ila agreed, and we left the room to search out food. Giggles echoed in the laundry as we passed the room. I caught sight of Otta in the doorway and waved.

Kara was alone in the kitchen, frantically moving about.

"Where's Bryn?"

"She hasn't arrived yet."

I hoped everything was all right.

"Can I help?" I said, moving to stir whatever bubbled over the fire.

"Please. I have biscuits in the oven, eggs boiling over here, stew boiling over there for the remaining meat pies, I need to roll out the dough..."

She looked ready to cry. Ila stepped forward.

"I'll watch the biscuits and eggs and set the table for the children. You roll out your dough."

Between the three of us, we settled the kitchen to its typical morning rhythm. In no time, we had the table set, the eggs in a bowl, a pitcher of fresh milk ready, and the biscuits from the oven. The children started to trail in; and when Egrit saw us, she shooed us to the table.

"Eat," she said. "I wonder where Bryn is. I saw her walking down the lane earlier."

I frowned, wondering what might have happened to her, and sat at the table. The children were excited for the feast. Otta and Retta spoke in quiet tones about the possibility of dancing with boys their ages.

"I promise there will be a few in attendance," I said, thinking of the Kinlyn boys.

As soon as Ila and I finished, we started the trek back to our rooms. When we passed the dining room, I stopped short at the sound of both Bryn and Blye's voices. I waved Ila to go without me and waited until she was out of hearing before I stepped into the room.

They both sat at the table, one on each side of where Alec usually sat.

"Is breakfast almost ready?" Blye asked.

They were waiting to be served breakfast. I closed my eyes and took a calming breath.

"Benella? Are you well enough to fetch Blye and me a tray?"

I opened my eyes, looked at them once more, then turned to leave, swallowing what I would have liked to say to Bryn.

When I spotted Mr. Crow in the entry, I hurried to his side.

"Bryn is sitting in the dining room while Kara is struggling to prepare the feast."

"I will address the issue immediately, Miss Hovtel."

"Thank you, Mr. Crow. If more help is needed in the kitchen, please let me know. Kara looked near tears this morning."

I stalked to the ballroom, seething because my sisters were so arrogant and selfish. After closing my eyes and counting backward for several moments, I calmed enough to view the progress within the room. Tables lined the wall near the north parlor. Linens already covered the tables. A mountain of napkins and small plates waited at one end.

Chairs lined the wall near the fireplace and several more near the garden doors for the musicians. Someone had thoughtfully gathered fall's last wildflower blooms and placed them in vases on the tables and around the base of each wooden candle stand. The simple decorations were beautiful.

Satisfied everything was ready, I went to my room to grab my brush and hair oil. With the items in hand, I returned to my old room. The tub waited, full of steaming water. Setting everything within reach, I stripped my clothes and slid into the water with a sigh. Less than a minute later, a door opened.

I turned my head and met Alec's gaze. While he crossed the room, I cursed myself for not thinking to lock the door. Ila's company had too successfully distracted me from my troubles with Alec.

"Stop there," I said quietly.

"It has been more than two months since I watched you in the bath." He stepped close and circled the tub.

I crossed my arms to shield what held his attention. It only encouraged him to squat beside the tub.

Keeping my gaze, he leaned close.

"You are most precious to behold as you are, without clothes and pink from the water." Closer still he came, his intent clear when his gaze dipped to my mouth.

I lifted one hand and flicked water in his face.

Angrily, he leaned in, held the back of my neck, and pressed his lips to mine. I turned my head, unwilling to part with a single bit of affection for the impertinent man, and splashed him again. He quickly stood and stepped out of danger.

"Behave yourself tonight," I said in a harsh whisper. "There will be plenty of cider for me to douse you."

"Me?" He plucked at his wet shirt. "I will behave if you behave," he said.

"What do you mean?"

"If you cause issues, such as throwing anything at me, or disagreeing with me in front of the assembled, I will ruin the feast."

With that, he left me. I frowned after him, trying to understand his threat. What did my behavior have to do with the feast? His was under scrutiny, not mine. And why threaten with the ruination of the feast when that would result in the return of the enchantment?

Still puzzling over it, I continued my bath.

* * * *

I didn't attempt to put on the dress until I'd combed my hair dry, which seemed to take ages. The soft material danced upon my skin as I let it fall down my raised arms and over my head. The bodice had a double panel, so I went without my bindings. The lacings, once tightened, pushed my breasts up so they mounded ever so slightly over the top. Even through the stretched material, I could see the shape of each breast. The full underskirt provided a bit more modesty.

After stepping into my slippers, I left the room to show Ila. She opened the door after my first knock. Her dress was equally beautiful. Dyed a deep red-brown, the fine material was edged with cream lace at her sleeves. White threads created a swirling pattern along her hem.

"It's beautiful," I said. "Perfect for fall or winter."

She smiled, stepped aside, and waved me in. "Your dress fits nicely. Come in. Let me braid your hair."

I sat on a low stool while she stood behind me and patiently created braid after braid within my loose hair. Then she swept the mass up and started pulling out the braided sections to weave them into unbraided sections. When she finished, she handed me a mirror.

"Ila, you are very talented. I would offer to help braid your hair, but it would look nothing like this."

"Don't worry. I plan to wear mine in a simple braid. You should go now and check that everything is ready."

Ten

Mr. Crow stood ready at the door but waved me over when he saw me.

"You are most lovely, Miss Hovtel."

I smiled at his sincerity.

"Thank you, Mr. Crow. You look very fine yourself." He wore his usual dark jacket and pants but had taken care to polish his shoes until they reflected even the tiniest bit of light.

"I want to keep you apprised of your sister's behavior. She has been warned. If she ignores her duties again, she will be dismissed. She also lost half a day's wages."

"A fair consequence for her actions," I said. "I'm going to check on the kitchen and see when Kara thinks we should start bringing out the food. How much longer until you expect guests to arrive?"

"Within minutes, Miss. There are always those who want to be early."

I hoped the candle maker was among them. While heading toward the kitchen, I checked the rooms I passed and found everything in order. After weeks of preparation, it seemed the estate was ready to hold its first feast in fifty years. I hurried my steps.

Kara stood alone in the kitchen. Trays of carefully stacked meat pies crowded the table.

"I sent Bryn to get ready with your other sister," she said as soon as she saw me. "I'm just waiting for this last batch of pies to come from the oven."

"It smells like heaven in here," I said, leaning over the pies. Heat radiated from them. "How did you get so many done so quickly?"

"I under baked several batches yesterday, so I would only need to brown them today. I had crust ready in the cellar, too, for rolling this morning."

Flour dusted her apron and face.

"I will watch the oven. Go ready yourself. Mr. Crow says he expects guests soon."

"I have everything right in here," she said, pointing at the servant's room. "Call out if you need anything."

After Kara ducked into the room, Ila entered with her hair plainly braided. I was glad for her company. Worry over Alec's threat kept churning through my head, and I needed a distraction.

"I thought you might be here," she said, studying the meat pies as I had.

"Though I have no love of cooking, I do so enjoy eating," I said with a grin. "Kara is dressing while I watch the oven for her."

Ila kept me company until Kara reappeared. She wore a plain, light grey dress very similar to the one she'd worn before. Her hair remained in its typical bun.

"Do you have any hair ribbons?" Ila asked.

"Yes. A black one and a grey one. Do you think I should use one of them?" She reached up to touch her hair.

"Yes, but not in your hair. Let me show you." Ila stepped into the room with Kara and a moment later Kara reappeared with a black ribbon tied around her neck with the bow in the back.

"Lovely," I said. "That such a simple thing can so enhance one's appearance amazes me."

"I agree," said Kara. "Where did you learn this?"

Ila gave a small smile.

"I have many sisters who are well traveled."

"You are lucky, then, to have them."

"I agree," Ila said.

"Are we ready to start carrying the food to the ballroom?" I asked.

"Yes," Kara said. "The cider should probably go first. I imagine the guests who choose to walk will be thirsty."

Ila stayed in the kitchen while I went off to find help. Tam and the other men returned with me and carried up more than a dozen small barrels before starting on the trays.

Outside the kitchen door, I heard the rumble of a wagon and went to see who had arrived. Edmund waved at me then set the brake and jumped down from his seat. Beside him, the candle maker held several thick pillars in his arms.

The men, having just returned from the ballroom, helped Edmund unload his pastries and took the pillars from the candle maker. Satisfaction coursed through me at seeing everything coming together so nicely.

"Where's Bryn?" Edmund asked after the last of his trays disappeared. Kara and Ila were carefully arranging the last meat pies on a tray.

"Dressing with Blye."

"Shouldn't she be helping?"

"Kara said she could dress."

"You're dressed and helping."

"I am." I patted his arm. "How have things been going without the extra help in the bakery?"

"Fine. It's quiet, though." His expression said he missed her.

"If you'd like, perhaps your wife should stay home with you for the next few days. I expect it will be quiet enough here."

"I would like that. I think she would, too."

"Go find her and tell her. And enjoy yourself tonight, Edmund."

He walked out, leaving Kara, Ila, and me in the kitchen.

"Are we ready?" I asked them.

"We are," Ila said, coming to hook her arm through mine.

"Thank you for your help. I truly appreciate it."

"It's what a friend would do."

We walked out of the kitchen and soon heard the buzz of voices from those guests who had already arrived. In the main entry, I gave a warm greeting to the butcher and introduced both Ila and Kara. His daughter found Retta, and the pair went off to the ballroom.

The general gaiety of the crowd had me smiling at everyone who stopped to say hello. I spotted Sara and her family in the crowd and followed Tennen's narrowed gaze to Bryn, who stood beside Edmund. Edmund had his arm around Bryn's waist, and she was looking up at him with complete focus.

"Miss Hovtel," Alec said from behind me, "you look lovely."

I turned to look over my shoulder and found him just inches from me. He wore a dark jacket and matching pants. Like Mr. Crow, his shoes were highly polished. His neckcloth was precisely tied and set against his neck. He was devastatingly handsome and looked every inch a lord. However, the heated gaze he raked over me stole the respectability given by his clothes. And it made my pulse flutter.

Tonight he must announce his intent to wed, I reminded myself. The sting of that realization helped ground me in the reality of our relationship. I would leave, and he would wed. Hopefully, in that order.

"Might I return the compliment, Lord Ruhall," I said politely.

"Lord Ruhall," a man I'd never met before said, claiming Alec's attention.

I quickly moved away and spoke with several of the students my father used to teach.

Before long, the sounds of music drifted from the ballroom, and the crowd slowly migrated that way. As we moved, I caught sight of a woman in a pale pink dress tiered with ruffles. The volume of the skirt was so much that no one could walk too close to her. Though the dress was pretty—if one had an affection for ruffles—it was far too overstated for such a simple gathering.

The wide neckline set the sleeves from the woman's shoulders, and her side swept hair bared her neck, which she held regally erect. She turned her head, and I caught sight of her profile. Blye.

Her sewing must be lucrative, indeed, to afford such a dress. When would she ever wear it again, though? I watched her glide into the ballroom and look around. Her gaze slid right over me and settled on someone not yet in the ballroom. I turned to look back in the hall and found Lord Ruhall walking slowly as he listened to what the man beside him said. I wanted to shake my head at my sister for her wasted efforts.

"Would you care to dance?" someone said as he gently tapped my shoulder. I turned to find Bolen, one of the Kinlyn boys, bowing to me.

"I would be delighted, sir," I said, returning his humor and pushing Blye from my mind.

Bolen led me to the floor, and we joined the others already there in a simple dance. He kept his hand politely at my waist while he held my other hand.

"How have you been?" I asked. "I heard you were able to fish."

"I am well, thank you. We've been fishing more now that the crops are in. Parlen finally got his wild pig with Da's help." He regaled me with their story and had me laughing. "He wanted to dance with you so he could tell you himself, but Ma said..." A blush painted his cheeks.

His mother hadn't wanted Parlen to dance with me. But why? I could think of only one reason. The baker. Yet why then let another son dance with me?

"Did your mother think me unsuitable to dance with?"

"Not at all," he rushed to assure me. "She said it would be improper to dance with a woman so much taller than him."

I puzzled for a moment then laughed aloud as I realized young Parlen would have been level with my breasts.

"Well, there are many girls here who are very close to his height. I hope he asks some of them."

The dance ended, and before I could leave the floor, I had another offer to dance. I vaguely recalled seeing the boy while I'd attended school but could not recall his first name. His family lived on a patch of land to the south, like the Kinlyns.

Another song saw a new partner waiting for me; and as I danced, Blye's words about how unsuitable I would be rang in my ears. How could I be so unsuitable and dance with so many while my perfectly suitable sister stood on the side without a single offer to dance? Blye circled the ballroom, chatting to those she knew and casting long looks at Lord Ruhall.

When the song ended, I found myself facing Henick. He took up my hand and gently held my waist as I rested my palm on his shoulder. A new song began, and he led our moves.

"Did you know there is a line to dance with you?"

"Surely not," I said, looking around. I caught Alec's thunderous frown before Henick's laugh returned my attention.

"It's true. Not an obvious line, but it's there all the same. Bolen was smart to grab you first."

"Your brother was a fine dancer. As are you. I hope the other women here find the same attention as I've received."

He smiled.

"A few might. But none are as pretty."

I blushed and glanced away. My gaze collided with Alec's again. He tracked my dance with Henick, clearly unhappy. When he saw me looking at him, he jerked his head to the side, a motion to show me he wanted me to leave the floor. I returned my gaze to Henick, determined to ignore Alec and his threats.

"Perhaps you'll allow me to introduce you to a friend who might be one of those few?" I asked.

"I would be honored."

On the next turn of the room, Alec wasn't where he had been. Before I could worry, the dance ended; and I asked Henick to walk me to the drink table rather than let another partner sweep me into the next set.

Drink in hand, I turned back to observe the room and caught sight of Alec weaving his way through waiting dancers. Unbeknownst to him, Blye moved toward him from his right, their paths set to intersect. She stepped in front of him just as the music started. He frowned at her then, glancing about, held out a hand.

Ila approached Henick and me and noted the direction of my gaze.

"Your sister is bold," she said.

I nodded slightly then focused on my friends.

"Henick, this is my friend, Ila."

Henick smiled and bowed over her hand. Within moments, they were fully engaged in conversation. It gave me time to observe Lord Ruhall and Blye.

He swirled her around the room at an aggressive pace. His gaze wasn't on her but was searching the dancers around them. She didn't seem to notice his distraction for she tilted her head back, laughed, and moved closer to him. Everyone turned to watch them. Her skirts flared out prettily, and I had never disliked my sister so much as in that moment. She only wanted him for his wealth and would ruin all the hard work Alec, Father, and I, along with the rest of the old staff, had put into this affair and the estate.

I wished he would announce his intent to wed. Blye certainly wasn't an option for him.

As soon as the song ended, I excused myself and approached the pair, planning to pull Blye aside to speak to her.

"Lord Ruhall, might I have a moment with—"

"Of course. We can speak as we dance," he said, releasing Blye abruptly and pulling me into his arms. He twirled me onto the floor before I could protest. We moved together as we had to the sweet bird song that day long ago. I couldn't deny I felt a thrill being in his arms. I tilted my head back to study him. His deep blue gaze remained locked on me, and I struggled to keep my wits about me.

"I meant to speak with my sister."

"Whatever for," he said, pulling me closer.

His body brushed against mine as we moved. I tried to gain distance but his hard hold wouldn't yield. So, I gripped his shoulder, fighting to remain upright during the dizzying pace he set.

He leaned in and breathed in near my neck, sending a shiver racing through me.

"That scent..."

"My hair," I said. I hadn't oiled my hair since the enchantment had broken.

Knowing it was dangerous, I allowed myself to relax. Just for a few moments, I wanted to pretend he truly loved and cherished me above all else. That he and I were together and happy like we'd been before the baker.

"I need you," he whispered. "More than the air I breathe. More than my freedom."

My heart thumped painfully at his words, which were so close to what I'd just been thinking. I pulled back again, searching his gaze for answers I so desperately needed.

"Don't forget that in the next few moments," he said with a wild look.

We stopped twirling and before my world righted itself, I was alone in the center of the room.

"Your attention, please," Alec called from near the drink table. "Everyone take up your drink for I would like to toast this feast."

While I wondered how he'd crossed the room so quickly, those on the floor left to obtain drinks; and those crowding the edges of the room, moved closer, filling in the empty dance floor around me.

"Raise your cups," Alec said, raising his own.

My pulse leapt. Would he announce his intention to wed now? My stomach gave a sickening twist.

Alec's gaze met mine, and my heart shattered all over again.

"To a merry harvest feast," he said loudly and clearly. "The first the North has seen in too many years. And I owe the success to Miss Hovtel, the beautiful, kind, and intelligent woman who has just consented to marry me."

My mouth dropped open as cheers erupted throughout the room. Alec's serious and slightly angry gaze held mine as he drank deeply. It was almost as if he were daring me to refute his claim. Suddenly, his words made his plan clear. He had just said that he needed me more than his freedom. He had warned me he would ruin the feast if I acted out against him in any way. If I rejected him here, now, he would do as he'd promised. He would ruin the feast and force Rose's hand.

My first reaction was anger. He'd planned to snare me all along. Then, I began to wonder what he had to gain by doing that. Me. Just me. Could he truly care for me so much? Hope spread like wildfire, worrying me. I needed a moment to think.

Well-wishers pressed close, blocking Alec from my sight. I nodded, smiled, and thanked those who congratulated me. The music struck up once more, and most of those around me moved away to clear the floor.

Purposefully, I made my way to the open garden doors. The sun had begun its descent, casting long shadows in the garden. Overgrown as it had been, there wasn't much to see as my gaze swept the area. A movement to my right caught my eye but before I could focus, someone stepped out of the ballroom behind me.

I turned and saw Alec by the door. Behind him, dancers moved in time with the music, a bustle of motion compared to his still watchfulness. We eyed each other for several long moments.

"Why?" I said. "You lied to everyone and, through your threats, forced my silence. What kind of Lord does that make you?"

"A desperate one, I should think."

"Desperate?"

He let out a frustrated sigh.

"I've asked you to be my wife countless times to which you always answer no."

"With reason," I said in exasperation.

"Reasons that can be overcome. You care for me. You admitted it. Yet, you stubbornly refuse to believe I care for you. You have fears about being a wife but won't trust that I can be patient, though I've spent the last fifty years practicing patience."

"I would hardly call that patience."

He ran his hand through his hair. I watched him struggle to control his temper.

"Your unwillingness to see reason forced this lie. Have no doubt I will carry through with my threat. Whether as the man you loathe or the beast you once loved, I will have you."

Again, pretty words. Could I trust them?

He turned and strode once more into the ballroom, and suddenly, Aryana's words rang in my mind. "Lies are necessary when truth fails." What truth had failed? My heart wanted to swell at the answer I found there. His love for me, because of my shattered trust in him and in men.

I turned away from the door and watched the sky change from blue to azure. High above, the first star sparkled in the darkening sky.

"Do you think this will change anything?"

I whirled at the sound of Tennen's voice. He stood just outside the door, partially hidden by the growing shadows. Surely, he wouldn't be so foolish as to try something with so many nearby to come to my aid.

"Yes, I do," I said, answering his question. "It will make you hate me more. A hate I do not deserve."

He snorted in disbelief and walked back into the ballroom.

Inside, the lit pillars and fire gave the large room a soft light. Near the food tables opposite the door, Alec watched me. His gaze followed Tennen briefly before returning to me. His observation made me feel safe, and I considered our engagement once more. If I were honest, it relieved me that he'd taken the decision from me. My heart hadn't forgotten his affection, though I'd desperately wanted it to. Could I dare allow myself to love him once more?

"You will make a fine Lady," Otta said softly, "if you can stop seeing innocence in everyone." The unexpected sound from behind startled me, as did the familiar words. I spun to face her.

Her small face began to transform, and I gasped as I recognized Aryana. I grabbed her wrist and quickly pulled her into the shadows.

"Speak your mind then leave," I said once I knew we were out of Alec's sight.

"You invited me."

"As yourself. I tire of your games. When will you leave the north and Lord Ruhall in peace?"

"When he is wed and settled. I'm not so certain you will be his wife, as he so clearly desires."

"And I'm not so certain you will leave us in peace when we are finally wed."

"Despite the trap he's laid for you, I could help you leave if that is what you wish."

I stared at her for a moment.

"I think that is what you wish. As Otta, you have watched for any excuse to return the curse. Speak true now. Why do you hate him so?" Then a thought occurred to me. "Did he hurt you like he did Egrit?" Compassion warred with distaste. "If he did, I must remind you that you allowed, no, encouraged his abuse of you. You forced it by purposely setting his freedom on a task he would misinterpret. Yet, I would understand if you did harbor hatred."

"No, he never hurt me. Egrit needed to learn a lesson as much as he did," she said with a sigh and a shake of her head. "Such a high price to pay."

"Was that why you allowed Tennen to take me? Was I to learn a lesson? If so, I believe I failed."

Her expression softened.

"Rape is never a tool to teach."

"But Egrit..."

"She was willing through it all, Benella. I thought she told you as much. She could have solidified at any time. She wanted him to use her, to find favor in her. She wanted to please him over her own self-preservation. That was the lesson she needed to learn. To put herself, her safety, before his desires. To value herself, she needed to learn to say no."

Aryana glanced over my shoulder, and her form began to recede into Otta once more.

"I will be watching," she said before ducking into the bushes.

"Miss Hovtel, Lord Ruhall requests that you come back into the light. He is concerned," Tam said from the doorway.

"I'll come inside," I said, moving toward him. "Will you dance with me?"

"Me?" He looked surprised. "I shouldn't think it suitable."

"I'm still the same. And, this is the harvest feast. If you dance with me, it will let the others know it's all right to do so as well."

"I would be honored," he said with a bow.

For the next hour, I twirled about the dance floor with various partners, carefully avoiding Bryn and Blye, who both seemed intent on speaking to me. When my feet grew tired, I begged my partner for a small break. Ila found me on the side of the room and offered me a glass of cider.

"I saw you dancing with Henick," I said. The Kinlyn boys were availing themselves to any willing partner and were truly making the feast a merry event.

"He's kind."

"And handsome, too," I said with a small, knowing smile. "I believe he and his brother are looking for wives."

She looked off in his direction.

"Do you think he will care?"

I knew she meant about her past.

"As you said, he is kind. I don't think he will mind at all."

She turned to study me then changed the subject.

"Lady Ruhall," she said. "That will be a change."

"Yes. Quite a change."

"You don't sound certain."

"I'm certain there will be a change. I'm not certain if it will be a positive one."

She leaned closer with a concerned frown.

"You've no wish to marry him?" she asked in a hushed tone.

I chose my words with care.

"The suddenness of the announcement and the reactions of a few have me doubting my wishes."

She straightened with a sigh and patted my arm.

"Follow your heart. It will lead you true."

I thought of Bryn and her infatuation with Tennen.

"Sometimes, I think the heart isn't a good leader," I said softly.

Before my cider had time to warm, Alec found me from across the room. His serious gaze held mine as he wove through people to reach my side. My heart gave an erratic beat.

"Will you dance with me?" he asked.

The reality of the announcement gripped me. He was mine. Should he be? Was this what I wanted? I thought so because the idea of him marrying someone else truly upset me. Yet, I still doubted his affection for me. I believed he cared for me, but did he care for me more than he did the estate?

He held out his hand, waiting for my answer.

"Yes. I'll dance with you."

He took the cup from my hand and set it on the table. My pulse leapt as he captured my fingers and led me to the floor.

He placed a sure hand at my waist, and we joined with the swirling dancers. He held me close, and I struggled to remain indifferent to his touch, my heart and my mind conflicted. What would a life with Alec, Lord Ruhall, mean for me? Bryn and Blye thought it meant luxury, but I knew better. There was little money; but even if it was plentiful, I wouldn't be interested in it. I wanted a marriage of love and consideration. Would I find that?

His gaze never left me, and the longer we danced, the more he frowned.

"What are you looking for when you study me so intently?" I said to distract myself.

"A hint, a sign of what you're thinking, what you're feeling. Before, I could read you so well. Not now."

"Before I knew what I thought and felt. Now, I don't," I said honestly.

He looked away for a long moment, and his hand on my waist gripped me tighter. When he viewed me once more, he seemed tormented.

"Do you still intend to leave, then?"

"No, Alec," I said softly. "I plan to stay and marry you."

"Why?"

"Because you said I would."

My words hurt him. I saw it in his expression and felt it in his arms but didn't understand why. Worried what he might do, I stepped close and briefly laid my head on his chest. A sigh heaved from him as he eased away. We swirled around the room in silence for the remainder of the dance, then he brought me back to my drink.

For the rest of the feast, I set aside the concerns over our future together and danced, ate, and drank until the guests began to leave.

The candle maker sat patiently in the chair he'd occupied all night, waiting for his wax. With the dwindling crowd, the chair beside him opened. I sat with a sigh.

"A feast well done, Benella," he said. "Much like the ones I remember."

"Thank you. Would you like me to help gather the wax?"

He shook his head and nodded toward Edmund. He already had a bucket and a thin, flat piece of metal for scraping. He blew out the pillar near the fire and started to scrape the candle and puddled wax away from the surface.

"The young baker already offered his assistance and a ride home. He's a good man. Too bad he married your sister."

"Sir," I said with censure.

He only chuckled.

"I said what we both thought. And it's the truth. I saw the way your sisters sought you out tonight, and how you avoided them. It's odd they're both missing now, hmm? I wonder what troubles they will cause you next."

"I dearly hope none," I said with a sigh.

He laughed again.

"I better help clear away the remaining food," I said, standing. "May I send any home with you?"

"I wouldn't be opposed to a pastry or two if there are any left."

I nodded and went to the table where Kara was combining everything onto trays and stacking the empty ones. I sent Retta over with two pastries for the candle maker, then picked up a stack of trays.

"You shouldn't be doing that," Kara said when she saw.

"Nonsense. If not this, then what?"

"Lord Ruhall is saying good-bye to guests. Perhaps you should join him?"

"I'd prefer to do this so I can seek my bed sooner." Alec's announcement had changed my desire to say farewell. Many, like my sisters and the smiths, would only speak to me because of my upcoming social elevation, when in reality they resented me for it. Those who would see me no differently were few.

Kara didn't argue further, and I made my way to the kitchen without interruption. As the rest of the staff set the ballroom to rights, I remained in the kitchen to wash the trays once I put on an apron. Edmund came in carrying his trays.

When I saw him, I paused washing to thank him.

"I had several people ask who made the pastries. I hope this helps business."

"I'm sure it will. Do you want Bryn to come help?" he asked, eyeing the trays Tam had just carried in and set on the table before leaving again.

"No. I'm sure once the ballroom is clean, Kara and Egrit will ban me from the kitchen."

"Oh, yes. Congratulations, Benella. You did look the picture of a Lady tonight."

"Thank you, Edmund."

He left, and after a few minutes, I heard the wagon rumble away from the door. No doubt to go to the front for his wife and the candle maker.

As I'd predicted, Egrit and Kara came to shoo me from the kitchen. Exhausted, I headed for my old room. After all, there no longer seemed any point to sleeping on the floor. And the bed in the Lady's room was so very comfortable.

I carefully hung my dress and buttoned myself into one of Alec's shirts that I'd collected. Then, I blew out my candle and settled into bed.

In the dark, I heard a faint rhythmic sound. Footsteps. They continued for a long while. Pacing. Eventually, the hushed noise stopped. I waited, thinking Alec would join me, but the door didn't open. I sat up and saw the faint light from under his door.

Curious, I left the warmth of my bed and approached his room. Pressing my ear to the door, I heard a slight rustling that let me know he wasn't yet sleeping. I nibbled my bottom lip and debated what to do. Then I heard him sigh. The hitch in it had me gently easing the door open.

He sat on the edge of his bed with his elbows on his knees and his head in his hands. He still wore his shirt and pants, but the jacket lay draped over his chair. His defeated pose struck a tender chord, and I approached him in silence.

He didn't move when I stood before him. I reached out to gently smooth his hair. His head jerked up, startling me. His tormented gaze held me. Then he reached out, gently gripped my waist, and pulled me to stand between his parted knees. He sighed shakily and set his forehead to my chest.

I stood there with my hands at my sides, looking down at his dark head. Finally, I gave into my impulse and reached up. My fingers brushed through his hair slowly as I tried to soothe whatever plagued him.

His hands tightened around my waist a moment before he lay back, pulling me with him. Sprawled on top of him, I stared down at him with wide eyes and a rising sense of panic. Did the announcement of our intent to wed mean...

He gently eased me to his side, his hand tenderly smoothing back the stray strands of hair from my face.

"Sleep, Benella."

Realizing I wasn't in danger, I sighed and curled beside him, content to stay as I was.

* * * *

The next morning, I woke in my own bed and quickly dressed. The sun already lit the sky. Though I had no care to see Blye off, I wanted to thank Ila once more. However, when I knocked on Ila's door, her room was already empty. I hurried downstairs and met Mr. Crow coming from the kitchen.

"Did Ila leave?"

"Yes, Miss. Swiftly is driving her and the other Miss Hovtel back to the Water with the carriage."

A swell of relief and regret washed over me. That Blye had left without a word did not bother me.

"Your sister, Bryn, is waiting to speak with you in the kitchen," he said.

I had no desire to speak to her, yet curiosity won. She should be with Edmund; she'd seemed so delighted with his company last night.

"Very well," I said and went off to the kitchen. The warm room welcomed me as did Kara's smile.

"I have a plate waiting for you," she said, glancing at the table where Bryn sat.

"Thank you, Kara. Are you managing comfortably this morning?"

"Yes. The men are working in the second apple orchard instead of hunting this week."

"Good," I said with a nod. With only cooking duties, Kara could handle the kitchen duties well without Bryn. I turned to address my sister.

"Bryn. I thought you and Edmund meant to spend some time together," I said, moving toward the table to claim my breakfast.

"I thought we could take a walk," she said, standing.

I paused and eyed my plate for a moment. That she wanted to speak with me made me more curious than hungry. That she wanted to do so where no one could hear worried me.

"Of course," I said, moving toward the kitchen door.

Kara stared after us as we left.

Bryn set a moderate pace down the drive and remained quiet until we'd progressed a good distance from the manor.

"Congratulations on your engagement," she said. "When do you plan to wed?"

"By winter solstice."

"So quickly. Is there a reason to hurry?" She glanced at my

stomach. "Perhaps the baker was successful?"

I shuddered at the unwanted memory.

"No. He was not." In the distance, I saw the gate.

"Lord Ruhall, then?"

"No. Why are you asking these questions?" I said, studying her.

"I'd only thought it would be nice to have a sister likewise with child. Someone to share the aches and fears of pregnancy." She sounded sincere.

"I'm sure I won't be long behind you once I'm wed." I tried not to think what that meant. My mind wasn't ready to grasp what would occur in less than two months.

She set her hand on her stomach.

"The babe moves now. Flutters that make me smile. Thank you for allowing me a week with Edmund. Waking early to walk to the estate and departing after dinner leaves us little time together. I've missed him."

"I'm sure Edmund misses you just as much. I hope business improves so you won't need to work at the estate."

She nodded as we neared the gates.

"And if it doesn't?" she asked.

I remained quiet, certain she would reveal the point of this walk soon.

"The people here are more tightfisted than before," she said. "Soon, we won't have the coin we need to buy flour because customers insist on bartering for bread. Yet Edmund continues to trade."

My lips thinned as I recalled how many times she had sent me to the baker to try to trade.

"His solution is that I keep toiling in your kitchen. He knows that won't work once the babe comes. What happens when we run out of coin? His father plans to remarry so we can't go back," she said as we walked through the gates.

I had a moment's unease leaving the safety of the estate, but remained silent.

"Edmund keeps telling me we need to give it time and refuses to discuss other options. When I press him, he only becomes upset with me."

Empathizing with Edmund's strained patience, I continued to walk and wait for her to arrive at her point. We cleared the dense trees that surrounded the estate and moved through the outer woods along the road.

"You can imagine my relief when Lord Ruhall announced your

engagement last night."

My insides chilled. She meant to use me again. But how?

"Blye had hoped it would be her; but as long as he chose one of my sisters, I don't mind."

"How does our marriage ease your mind?"

"As you've said, you'll be with child soon enough, and with our mother gone, you will need my help with the birth. Certainly, you'll want me closer once your time comes. And, Edmund's talents are wasted in the village. I've heard many estates in the South pay handsomely for a private baker. Working for Lord Ruhall would be his dream come true."

Edmund's dream? I doubted that.

"With such a large, vacant manor, we could even have our own suite of rooms. I don't expect you to pay Edmund the annual forty gold he would earn in the South. Thirty-five would do well."

She meant to live at the manor and have Lord Ruhall pay Edmund an exorbitant amount of money the estate couldn't afford. And why? Because she was worried the business at the bakery wouldn't pick up. I could understand her concern to a point and might have been moved to grant a reasonable request. But not this.

"No."

She stopped walking and turned toward me. We stood just on the edge of the tree line. In the distance, I could see the village.

"What do you mean no? It's a fair wage."

"Does Edmund know you are discussing this with me?"

She grimaced and a flush colored her cheeks.

"I thought not. Go home, Bryn. Spend time with Edmund. Show him you love him, and stop scheming."

"I should stop scheming? You had better look at yourself. According to what Mrs. Wimbly said, you've been playing the Lady since you arrived there. Your plan to ingratiate yourself may seem to have worked for now, but Lord Ruhall will see through you eventually and know you're no better than the rest of us. I wish it would have been Blye. She's not nearly as selfish."

My mouth popped open as she whirled and stomped away from me.

"Selfish," I said, following her. "I went to the very baker who tried to rape me because you asked it. I've walked the estate and set traps for meat, so you could hoard the coin that Father gave you to purchase food. I've been called a whore, though we both know it's not me who deserves the title." Her face flushed scarlet. "And still, I spoke up on your behalf when you needed employment. I've done much and more for you, Bryn. What have you ever done for me?"

I stopped following and stared after her as she hurried away from me. We'd almost reached the village. From the shadow of the smithy, I saw movement. Bryn didn't notice it as she passed but then Bryn didn't notice much unless it benefited her.

Splane stepped further into the light and watched Bryn walk by. I backed into the shadows of the trees, then pivoted on my heel. Where was Tennen?

Eleven

A healthy dose of self-preservation had me picking up my skirts and running. Tennen's words from the night before rang in my ears, and I cursed myself for a fool. I should have asked Tam to follow me. Better yet, I should have stopped at the gate and told Bryn I wouldn't walk further.

Busy with my self-recrimination, I wasn't prepared for Tennen when he stepped from behind a tree. I ran right into his extended arm, and the impact sent me flying backward. I landed so hard, it knocked the breath from me; and my lungs refused to inhale.

My mouth opened and closed like a fish out of water as he dragged me by the arm further into the trees. My vision danced from lack of air, and my heart pounded fiercely in my chest. I finally managed a weak inhale just as he dropped my arm.

Tennen fell upon me, his expression twisted with hate. The impact robbed me of my hard won breath, and I weakly struggled to get out from under him. He caught my hands and held them tight within one of his.

"I heard what you said to Bryn. I think it will be my babe that grows in your belly. Just like with your sister's."

His other hand started pulling at my skirt. As it hitched higher, baring my legs to the air, I mouthed my denial. I had no air to speak it. Thrashing beneath him caused his grip to tighten painfully on my wrists. Heedlessly, I tugged harder, trying to free them.

He leaned on me to pin me with his weight, then set his mouth near my ear.

"I'm not like the baker. I won't fail. You'll bleed on my shaft." He laughed. "If you haven't already bled on someone else's."

I panted with fear.

His grasping hand found my bared thigh and gripped it tight. He pulled it to the side to settle his hips firmly between my legs. His coarse pants abraded my tender skin. When he let go of my thigh, he pulled back just enough to fumble with his pants. His harsh breaths filled my ear as I continued to buck and tried to free my hands. Twice our hips connected, and I felt the bulge of his desire. Nausea and terror filled me.

Desperate, I turned my head, looking for something, anything, to help me. No branch lay nearby. No beast, either. I wailed, a keening sound thick with my despair, before the sight of his ear cut the sound short. I opened my mouth, bared my teeth, and darted forward. Clamping down on his ear, I held tight as he grunted then yelled.

He stopped fumbling with his pants and forgot my hands in his desperation to pull me from his ear. The moment my hands were free, I released my hold and shoved at him with all my might.

He flew from me, drifting up and away. I blinked, confused by my strength and disoriented in my fear and desperation. But, I wasn't the cause of his removal.

Alec stood behind Tennen, lifting him from me by the back of his shirt. Tam hurried to my side and said something I didn't hear. I stared as Tennen flailed for a moment then found his feet. A disconnected part of me registered Tam discreetly lowering my skirt. Mostly, Alec's rage-twisted face held my attention.

Before Tennen could stand, Alec changed his hold to the front of Tennen's shirt and drove his fist into Tennen's stomach. Tennen's drawn moan of pain didn't stop Alec, though. His next punch broke Tennen's nose.

Tam gently assisted me to a sitting position, which helped clear my head.

"Lord Ruhall," Tam said. "You'll kill the boy."

Alec didn't seem to hear as he drew back once more.

"Alec."

I didn't know why I spoke his name, but he stopped and turned his head to look at me.

"I want to go home."

It wasn't until I said it that I realized just how desperately I wanted not to return to the manor, but to Alec. The one who'd always made me feel safe whether beast or man. Tears welled in my eyes, and a soft sob escaped me.

Alec thrust Tennen to the ground and came to my side. He squatted beside me and gently smoothed my hair from my face. In his gaze, I saw the love and worry he held for me.

He carefully lifted me into his arms then set out toward the estate.

I didn't look over his shoulder at Tam, who had Tennen by the arm. Instead, I rested my cheek against Alec's chest and closed my eyes.

When we neared the estate, he started issuing commands.

"Take Tennen to the Head. Get Egrit. Benella needs her help to wash and change."

He mounted the stairs as he spoke, and I was certain he left Tam and Mr. Crow scurrying in his wake.

We'd barely entered my room when Egrit arrived. Alec carefully set me on my feet. I trembled but stood on my own. My mind was blank as I watched him walk out the door.

Egrit didn't speak as she helped me from my dress. I shook too badly to do it on my own. When I stood in my underthings, she wet a cloth and washed my face, arms, and hands. Then she knelt and wiped the backs of my calves. It was the part of me that had touched the ground when Tennen had yanked up my skirt. I trembled harder.

"Did he...?"

I shook my head and closed my eyes. He hadn't, but I could still feel the press of his hips against mine. Tears started anew.

When no dirt remained, Egret pulled a nightgown from my wardrobe and helped me into it.

Once she got me in bed and under my thick covers, she left. The door remained closed for no more than a moment before it opened again. Alec strode across the room and sat on the bed beside me. He pulled me into his arms and just held me as I continued to cry.

I was so angry. At Bryn. At Blye. At Tennen. At the whole Coalre family, really. And, at Rose. How was the North any better than it had been before the enchantment?

Alec's hand ran over my hair again and again. I knew he meant to soothe me. And, he did. Eventually, the tears stopped, and my hitched breathing slowed.

Safe, I slept.

Dreams plagued me. In them, I ran through the trees from a monster toward the beast, neither one gaining or receding. My heart raced until gentle hands and words pulled me from my terror-filled world.

"You're safe. I'm here with you." Alec stroked my hair and held me close. The dream faded, and I fell into a peaceful sleep.

I woke sweat-dampened and alone. Frowning, I looked around the room for Alec. The sun had passed its zenith, and a tray waited beside the bed. Sitting up slowly, I winced at my sore wrists and aching legs. I swallowed hard and refused to think about why I was sore. Instead, I eased from the bed, ignored the tray, and put on the remaining clean dress that waited in my wardrobe. The one I'd worn was gone.

With a steadying breath, I left the room and walked the familiar hall. Each step anchored me. I belonged here, with Alec. Not because I thought myself better than anyone else, but because I wanted to make the North a better place. A safer place. My home.

When I reached the stairs, I heard raised voices.

"—harmless prank."

"Prank?" Alec's shout echoed through the halls. I hurried toward the sound. It came from the entry. "He attacked her, and this wasn't the first time."

Alec was speaking of Tennen.

"He's always liked the girl."

I recognized the smith's voice and started to descend the steps.

"He only went too far trying to get her attention. I'll sit him down and speak to him," Tennen's father said.

"It's too late for paternal talks," Alec said just before Mr. Coalre came into view.

When Mr. Coalre saw me, he flushed. Alec turned and met me at the bottom of the steps. Behind him, Mr. Coalre took two steps toward us.

"Benella, Tennen isn't a criminal. Do the right thing."

His words struck me like a blow, and my steps slowed. The right thing? What did he think was right? To let Tennen go? Of course Mr. Coalre would think that. After all, he had gotten away with so much. My thoughts collided as Alec scowled over his shoulder at the man.

"Yes," I said half to myself, "I will do the right thing." I focused on Mr. Coalre.

"Go, get Sara."

Alec's shocked gaze flew to meet mine.

"Alec, we need to go to the Water and speak with the Head."

Mr. Coalre didn't even thank me before he rushed out the door.

Alec held out a hand as I reached the third step. I wrapped my fingers around his.

"Why, Benella? He deserves to be punished for what he did."

Alec looked angry and concerned. It was only right. He'd saved me from Tennen so many times.

"He does," I agreed. "But there are truths you do not know."

"Then tell me."

"Patience," I said softly, alighting from the last step. I wrapped my arms around his waist and held him close. He embraced me in return.

Behind me, I heard footfalls on the stairs.

"She is well, Mr. Hovtel," Alec said without releasing me. "She wants to go to the Water and speak to the Head on Tennen's behalf."

I didn't disagree.

* * * *

"Eat," Alec said, handing me a meat pie before we cleared the gate.

My stomach twisted with nerves, but I took the food and nibbled on it. We continued a distance in silence while Alec watched me closely.

"What are you thinking?" he said softly.

"That I'd rather not go to the Water."

"We can turn around."

"No," I said with a shake of my head. "We must go." I needed to make the North safer in order to have a future here.

Too soon, we stopped before the home of the Head. Alec opened the door, stepped out, and turned to offer me a hand. As I descended, the door behind Alec opened. I recognized Mr. Pactel, the Head, immediately. Alec kept my hand on his arm as he turned to greet the man.

"Welcome, Lord Ruhall. It's good to finally meet you in person. A pity it's under such poor circumstances." He turned to me.

"Miss Hovtel," he said. Nothing more.

But really, what could one say to a woman twice almost raped? Any attempt at condolence would sound inane. However, I found it interesting that he came to greet Alec personally.

"Sir," I said in acknowledgement of his greeting.

We followed Mr. Pactel inside where he led the way to his study.

Sara and her husband already waited within. Pale Sara sat in a chair, her hands demurely folded in her lap. She didn't look up when we entered but kept her gaze on her hands.

"I admit to skepticism when Mr. Coalre told me you meant to speak on his son's behalf," Mr. Pactel said as we took our seats.

"I would prefer to continue this conversation without Mr. Coalre or Lord Ruhall," I said. Mr. Coalre objected loudly; and Alec frowned at me, not in anger but speculation.

"Please," I said softly, meeting Alec's gaze. He nodded and stood. Mr. Coalre had no choice but to follow Alec out the door. Mr. Pactel eyed me expectantly but I didn't address him. I turned to Sara.

"Silence brought me unfounded hatred from the men in your family. Silence brought me abuse at the hands of Tennen and then Mr. Medunge. I only kept silent because I thought I protected you. Now, I fear what silence will bring me next if I continue to keep company with it."

She lifted her gaze and met mine. Tears ran down her cheeks.

"I won't speak for Tennen," I said to her. "I have much to say against him. He is malicious and views women with contempt, much like his father.

"I asked you here to give you a choice, Sara. A choice to save yourself and your other son. Splane hasn't yet fully adopted his father's or Tennen's attitude."

Pain reflected in her gaze as she understood what I meant to do.

"I won't keep silent any longer."

I turned to Mr. Pactel and started at the beginning of my tale. I spared no detail of what I'd witnessed so many months ago or of the torment Tennen unleashed upon me with Splane's help. Mr. Pactel listened to each encounter with a stoic expression that cracked only once. He frowned as I recalled Edmund's mention of Mr. Coalre's visit to establish the same deal with the new baker as he'd had with the old.

When I finished, Sara turned to me.

"I didn't know. I am so sorry."

Mr. Pactel made a sound of disbelief and leaned forward in his chair.

"Miss Hovtel said you were there when the prior baker attempted to rape her. Were your eyes closed?" he asked sharply. "For if they were open, how could you not know?"

She paled further at his words but didn't take her gaze from me.

"I didn't know Tennen and Splane chased you and hurt you. I didn't know Tennen waited in the house for you." She faced Mr. Pactel. "I didn't know why we needed to go to the baker that morning. I thought it was for me. For more bread. It broke my heart that my son meant to send me. When I saw Benella, I was first so relieved it wasn't me." She turned to me, her expression full of remorse and apology. "Then you started to fight. I wanted to step forward but...Patrick stopped me. I was so afraid."

"I believe you," I said. Fear of her husband had stolen her courage to stand up for herself. How could she ever stand up for me? I didn't blame her for her inaction; I pitied her.

"You would have me see her as innocent?" Mr. Pactel asked me.

His words brought back what Rose had once told me...that I would call the guilty innocent. I'd thought she'd meant Alec, but now I understood. My silence had protected Mr. Medunge, Mr. Coalre, and Tennen.

"Coerced and controlled by her husband, she kept her silence, just as I kept mine. I believe we are both innocent of any crime. Our guilt lies in our fear and compassion. Consider that as you judge those who are guilty of much greater crimes."

Mr. Pactel sat silent for a long while, studying Sara.

"Your husband will be sentenced to work in the mines for one year for his crimes against you. With my ruling, he forfeits his rights to any material wealth. Your son, Tennen, will work five years and also forfeit any material wealth. What is theirs is yours as recompense.

"You can choose to remain in this room as I sentence your husband or you can leave."

She stood. Trembling, she straightened her shoulders.

"Before the Head, I sever my marriage to Patrick Coalre." Then, she turned and walked out the door.

Through the open door, Mr. Pactel asked that the guard fetch Mr. Coalre and Lord Ruhall.

I stood.

"I would prefer to leave for the sentencing."

He nodded and led me through a side door into a very small sitting room.

"I will have Lord Ruhall join you as soon as I've spoken with him."

Minutes after he closed the door, I heard the murmur of low voices. Then, the smith began to yell and curse. The sounds of a struggle reached me before the room went very quiet. It remained so for a long while. The abruptness of the door opening to my left brought me to my feet. Alec paused in the doorway as he caught the fear and panic in my eyes. After a moment, he stepped in and continued toward me.

"We can leave now," he said softly.

I studied his face. The slight downturn of his mouth and the thin line of his lips held me in place.

"You're angry."

He sighed and gently took my hand in his.

"You should have told me."

"It wasn't my truth to tell."

"It was. Because you were the one to suffer the most. I would have protected you and brought the smith and his son to the Head's attention sooner. Instead, I paid the pair to pick apples." He didn't mask his disgust.

"I needed to give them a chance to choose to reform like Rose did for you."

"You are not Rose. You are fragile, easily hurt."

The bruises on my wrist told the truth of his words. Why had I suffered through the abuse I had? Was my lesson to learn not to trust or give second chances? I thought not and held firm to my belief that we were meant to make mistakes and learn from them. Perhaps I only needed to learn to be more wary of who to trust and who might deserve second chances.

With his hand warming my back, he guided me from the room.

Tam hopped into the driver's seat as soon as we emerged into the late afternoon light. Alec helped me into the carriage. Once we settled into our seats, he called to Tam. The carriage lurched forward.

"When Kara told me you went for a walk, I became worried. Rightfully so, it seems. Why did you leave without someone?" Alec asked gently once we crossed the bridge.

A half snort escaped me, and I looked out the window.

"I did leave with someone. I left with Bryn. She had asked me to walk with her." I shook my head. "I was foolish to go. We upset each other, and she left me near where you found me."

"What upset you?"

"Her selfishness," I said, meeting his gaze. "She told me she was glad we were marrying. Then proceeded to outline how you could hire Edmund, pay him an enormous annual wage, and allow them a suite of rooms at the manor. When I said no, she accused me of being selfish and that Blye would have been better suited as your wife."

He remained silent, studying my face, then looked out the window for a time. The tense clench of his jaw showed his emotion.

"Tam," he called.

"Sir."

"Take us to the bakery in Konrall."

A jolt of concern struck me.

"Edmund had no knowledge of our conversation."

"I guessed as much," he said.

"What do you plan to do?"

"Tell Edmund what his wife has caused."

I sighed and nodded. Keeping silent served no purpose.

When the carriage stopped before the bakery, I took a steadying breath. Alec disembarked first, then reached to help me descend. Down the road, Splane carried items from the smithy to the wagon, filling it with all manner of tools and metal.

"What will they do?" I asked quietly.

"Sell what they can and start anew elsewhere," he said, glancing in the direction of the smithy.

Tam hopped down from the driver's seat and took the horses by the lead.

"I'm going to see if there's something we can use."

Alec nodded and led me inside. He kept my hand on his arm, and I was glad for the support. I didn't want to face Bryn.

"Welcome, Lord Ruhall," Bryn said with an eager smile. She didn't glance at me.

"Bryn, Tennen attacked your sister after you left her this morning," Alec said without preamble.

Her gaze flicked to me before returning to Alec. She remained silent, watching him expectantly. Edmund appeared from the kitchen.

"Good afternoon," he said pleasantly. His welcoming smile faltered when he saw Alec's displeased expression. "Can I help you?"

Alec repeated his statement, and Edmund's eyes flew to me.

"Were you injured? Would you like to sit?"

"Thank you, Edmund. I'm fine, now. Alec came upon us before I suffered anything serious." Alec's fingers twitched over mine, and I gave his arm a gentle squeeze.

"We came because I hold your wife responsible," Alec said with a good deal of anger.

Bryn's mouth dropped open, and her face paled.

"After Benella told Bryn that she would not hire you and allow her sister and you to live at the manor, Bryn grew angry and left Benella alone on the road."

"I've walked that road twice a day for weeks without incident," Bryn said in quick defense.

"But Tennen didn't hold a grudge against you," Alec said, lowering his eyes to her belly. A small gasp escaped her, and her eyes began to water. "You knew he disliked Benella, and I suspect you also knew he'd attacked her before. Long before your family moved to the Water."

Alec turned to Edmund.

"My feelings toward your wife do not extend to you. I believe Bryn has manipulated you as much as she has Benella. No man should suffer a manipulative wife who carries another man's child."

Bryn flinched and paled as she understood what Alec was suggesting. With panic, she looked toward Edmund. Edmund's cheeks flushed, and he wouldn't look at her.

"But that choice is yours alone," Alec said.

"No," Bryn said wretchedly, finally finding her voice. She rushed the few steps to Edmund's side and clung to his arm. "Don't sever our marriage. I only spoke to her for you. You work so hard. You deserve so much more than this."

I looked away from the display.

"This?" Edmund said. "I'm proud to be a baker. I am a damn good one. If you're not proud of that, if you don't want to build a future with me, here, in this bakery, if you don't want to work beside me and share the success earned by our own labors, you should marry another."

His footsteps marked his retreat. I looked up and saw Bryn standing there, shaken. She stared at the door to the kitchen, not even noting us.

"Decide, Bryn," I said quietly. "Who do you want to be? A loved wife or a lonely woman always wanting more than she has?"

Her gaze turned to me, and I saw the flash of anger there. Then her shoulders slumped, and the emotion disappeared. Like Edmund, she turned away from us and fled into the dreaded sitting room off the store.

* * * *

I sat in the library, pretending to read the book I held. Neither Father nor Alec disturbed my contemplations under this pretext. Today's events needed consideration. Not Tennen's attack or the Coalre family's departure or even Bryn's numerous hurtful rejections. No, the events that held my mind revolved around Alec, who currently paced quietly in his study.

How he'd reacted when he'd found Tennen on me, the enraged expression on his face, the way he'd struck Tennen...that was the beastly way he would have acted while enchanted, the way I'd wanted him to act when he'd found the baker atop me. He'd never changed. Not really. And I had refused to see that for so long. He had held my heart as the beast; and though I'd tried to deny it, he held my heart still. He wasn't perfect, but I'd never wanted perfect like my sisters had. I'd wanted real. I wanted someone who could love me as I was and who I could love as he was.

The crackle of the fire almost drowned out the distant sound of Alec's footfalls as he paced.

How many times had I hurt him with my denial? The lonely beast, punished for fifty years, was still there despite the clothes and title. And he hadn't lied when he'd said he needed me. I'd thought he just meant my body or perhaps even my assistance. But it wasn't any one thing he needed from me; he needed all of me. My love. My company. My compassion. My cool head. Living with Alec wouldn't be easy, but I already knew that. It would be an adventure filled with love and consideration. I had been a fool to wait so long to accept what he offered me. I wouldn't wait a moment longer. Our life together would start now.

I softly closed the book and stood. Father looked up at me, and I gave him a reassuring smile as I started toward the study. Alec caught sight of me and stopped his pacing. He waited patiently with worry furrowing his brow until I stood before him.

I reached up and gently ran my finger along the crease.

"Why are you worried?"

His gaze searched mine, then he took my hand in both of his. He traced the mottled bruise circling my wrist. The gentle touch and the anguish in his gaze made my stomach twist. He closed his eyes and pressed his lips to my palm. I rested my other hand against his cheek, trying to comfort him. He held me like that for so long, I thought he wouldn't speak of his concern.

"I worry that I've done you a greater wrong than those sentenced today," he said, opening his eyes. "Last night, when we danced and I saw your conflict, I wanted to grant you your wish to go your own way, but I couldn't. I'm too selfish to let you go. I want you as my wife; yet, you fear what that entails. A selfless man might offer to give you time, might promise not to touch you after we speak our vows. I'm not a selfless man. My need for you might be what finally drives you away. And I can't stand the thought of losing you."

My heart constricted then grew for the man before me. The hold on my hand loosened with his admission. He worried he'd trapped me into a marriage I didn't want. I thought of Bryn and Edmund and soothed my fingers along his cheek.

"I have fears," I agreed softly, "but I do not fear you."

He exhaled, warming my palm.

"I need you to need me as badly as I need you," he said.

I had no words to soothe or reassure him; I wanted reassurance myself. He'd made his plans clear. As soon as we spoke the vows, he would make me his wife. The thought made my stomach clench and my pulse leap as my hands fell to my sides. The experience with the baker and Tennen had been rough and disgusting. Yet, before either had hurt me, Alec had shown me there might be another side to the act. Fear warred with remembered passion. I wanted to trust him, but the idea of what he wanted to do to me was terrifying.

He seemed to sense my uncertainty because he closed his eyes with a grimace.

Seeing him so upset broke through some of my fear. Alec held my heart. He had since the first day he'd held me while I slept. I needed him, and he needed me just as much.

I struggled to calm my breathing and rose up on my toes to lean into him.

"I have fears," I said softly, repeating my words, "but I do not fear you."

He opened his eyes and studied me. With deliberate slowness, he lifted his hand to my cheek, stroking my skin with a gentle finger.

"I can feel you shaking," he said softly.

His pained gaze held mine.

"I don't know how to ease your mind, Benella."

I didn't know if he could.

"Every time I see you, I want to..."

He released my hand and ever so slowly lowered his head. My breath caught, and I grew hot and cold in waves.

"One kiss. Say yes."

My heart stammered, and I trembled as he hovered inches from my lips. His breath fanned my face.

"Yes."

His hands rose, capturing my head and delving in my hair. I licked my lips. His gaze dropped to my mouth and the pained expression he wore became more strained.

"So beautiful," he said softly.

He pressed his lips to the corner of my mouth, a chaste kiss. Then he slowly nibbled his way along my jaw. My skin heated, and I exhaled on a sigh. I tilted my head to give him access to my neck. A shiver ran through me when his lips found the tender place just below my ear.

"When we are husband and wife, I won't attack you. I'll love you," he whispered.

I shivered again. He pulled back to study me. Lifting his hand, he ran a thumb along my bottom lip. Then, he leaned in once more.

Warm and firm, his mouth brushed against mine; and his hands drifted to my arms. He held me for a moment then pulled me to his chest. The angle of the kiss changed, and his tongue stroked my bottom lip. I shivered and lifted my hands to set them upon his jacket.

His mouth left mine; and only then, did I realize I'd closed my eyes. When I opened them, I found him studying me with concern. Had he thought I meant to push him away? I smiled slightly and leaned forward, lifting my lips.

He groaned faintly and met me. His tongue traced the curve of my lower lip before his mouth opened and nibbled at my lip. I made a small noise. He took advantage of my parted lips and dipped his tongue inside, touching mine. My heart leapt at the sensation, and I opened further. His hands tightened on my arms before one slid down to the base of my spine. He pressed me firmly against him. I felt the evidence of his desire, and a sliver of fear shivered through me. But, I pushed it aside and focused on the kiss and the memories of the things we'd done before. His mouth on my breast. His tongue between my legs. A heat grew within me, and I pressed myself against him.

He broke away from the kiss and stared at me.

Dazedly, I returned his regard. My lips tingled. My pulse raced. Kissing Alec was more thrilling than I had imagined possible. I hoped the rest would be as well.

"I think I'll retire for the evening," I said softly.

He nodded jerkily.

Father was already gone from the library when I stepped from the office. As I walked to my room, I wondered what the night would bring. My stomach tightened with coiled nerves as I undressed. After I lay in bed, it took a long while for sleep to claim me.

The feel of his lips on the back of my neck and his arm around my waist roused me from a dream.

However, when he only settled behind me, I drifted back to sleep.

* * * *

I woke the next morning with no recollection of Alec coming to me. I glanced at the empty place beside me, but it looked untouched. Puzzled, I dressed for the day and went to his room. The bed lay undisturbed. Perhaps only remade?

After a long search, I found Alec near the barn. He and Tam were loading baskets into the wagon. I watched the fabric of Alec's shirt stretch over his well-muscled back with each move. The kiss from the night before rose to my mind, and I blushed. He caught sight of me while my face was still red and paused in his labor.

"Good morning," I said.

His gaze swept over me. Concern deeply etched his face.

"Good morning."

"If you wait a moment, I'll fetch a wrap and join you."

Alec set the basket he held into the wagon then approached me.

"It would be better," he said softly, "if you stayed here." He gently brushed a loose strand of hair from my face. "We'll return before dinner."

He turned away and climbed into the wagon with Tam. Tam clucked to the horses, and they rumbled off. Frowning, I watched them disappear around the manor. Why did he think staying here better for me than picking apples?

Still puzzled, I went inside to see what I could do to assist Egrit and

Mrs. Palant. Both assured me they didn't require help and suggested I read in the library. Withholding a sigh, I went to the kitchen. Since Bryn was with Edmund, surely Kara would need assistance. However, she gave the same answer and sent me off with a biscuit and egg for breakfast.

My disappointment only lasted a moment. I didn't much care for cleaning and cooking, anyway. Hurrying to my room, I changed into my long forgotten pants and shirt and grabbed my bag from the bottom of the wardrobe. It felt odd, yet pleasant, to fit the strap across my shoulder and feel the bag rest at my hip. Recalling the last time I'd gone without word, I went to the library to find my father.

"I'm off to explore the east side of the estate," I said from the door, already turning to walk away.

"Wouldn't you rather read in here?"

His words, so similar to everyone else's, stopped me.

"No. I've too much energy for that. I'll see you at dinner." I waved and left before he could say more.

I walked toward the grove of picked apple trees, then beyond. The vegetation between the trees grew thick and slowed my progress. I found several berry bushes, long shed of their fruits, and noted their location for next year. Walking through the trees didn't distract me as I'd hoped it would. My mind kept turning toward Alec.

The remembered feel of his lips on my neck warmed me. Preoccupied with my idle thoughts, I jumped badly when Rose stepped out in front of me.

Thinking for a brief moment she was Tennen, alarm widened my eyes and robbed me of breath, and my hand flew to my chest.

"Benella," Rose said quickly, "it's only me." Worry filled her gaze as she wrapped her arms about me. "What have we done to you?" she said softly, holding me tight.

Her tone and comforting touch reminded me too much of Aryana. Angry, I pulled away.

"Why are you here?"

She released me and stepped back to study me.

"To check on you." Her gaze flicked over me, settling briefly on my wrists. "Two are gone and two remain. I worry for you."

"What two remain?" I asked, a cold terror filling my stomach.

I heard my name and turned toward the distant call to cock my head and listen. It sounded like Alec. I glanced at Rose but found myself alone.

With her last words echoing in my ears, I quickly started toward the direction of the call.

Twelve

I called back to Alec, and a few minutes later, heard the snapping of twigs as he forced his way through the bramble. When he finally appeared, he was red-faced and disheveled. Twigs and leaves decorated his hair, and his sleeve had a tear. I'd never been so glad to see him. However, the way he rushed to my side concerned me.

"What happened?" I asked.

"Why aren't you reading?" His angry, demanding tone surprised me.

"I wasn't in the mood to read." I waved at the woods around us. "It's too beautiful a day to spend indoors. Soon the leaves will fall and the snow will come. I'll spend enough time indoors then."

"Benella, you need to rest."

"Is that why you came rushing through the woods? You think I need rest?"

He ran his hand through his hair, seemingly frustrated; and it touched me that he worried so about me. I stepped close. He stilled and looked down at me as I laid my hands on his chest.

"Go pick your apples. I will keep myself busy."

"I'd prefer you return to the estate."

His surly expression made me smile.

"Why? I'm perfectly safe out here." Doubt made the words bitter. Who were the two that remained?

"Benella, yesterday..."

And, with that, I understood why no one needed my help.

"Yesterday was yesterday," I said. "I refuse to dwell on it. Learn from it, yes, but not dwell. Tennen and the baker are gone, and I'm safe enough within the estate. Stop worrying so much and go pick your apples."

He reached up to gently run his knuckles along my jaw.

"Do you know how many times I've thought I lost you?" He didn't wait for my answer. "As a beast, each time you came to me and left again, I thought it would be the last I saw you. Then, you agreed to stay. But only on the condition I allow you to leave the estate once every seven days. Again, I thought each time would be the last. Then, when Rose gave you that dress," he said the word with anger, "I thought some man would woo you to him.

"But you returned. You always returned. Yet, I couldn't trust your devotion was real. Was it for me, or only to spare your father? Then you gave me the answer to free myself, to become a man who might win your heart. But instead of finding you in your bed that morning after the curse was broken, you were gone. And when I finally found you, abused and fighting for your freedom, you wanted nothing to do with me. You left."

I understood then that leaving the manor so soon after Tennen's last attack had scared him. I stepped closer.

"Shh. It's done. They're gone, and I returned then and will not leave now. Instead of the past, let's focus on the future. When do we want to wed?" I asked, hoping to distract him from his worry.

His gaze searched mine.

"Do you wish to wed me, Benella?"

His uncertainty tugged at my heart.

"Yes. I do." I took his hand in mine and gently tugged him toward the path he'd made. "So, how soon would you like to wed?"

"How much time do you need to plan the wedding feast?" he asked.

Looking over my shoulder, I made a quick face at him then turned back to the path.

"We've already welcomed those closest to the estate, so I see no need to do so again by winter solstice. And I would rather not invite your peers—much too expensive. The idea of a private wedding followed by a dinner with the staff is more appealing. If you agree."

He remained quiet for a long while.

"Are you certain that is what you wish?"

I stopped to face him.

"Only if you wish it as well."

"Someone once told me a woman's wedding should be a pageant of beauty and extravagance."

"Displays of extravagance for the sake of extravagance are wasteful. And a wedding can be beautiful without a crowd."

He stepped close to me and cupped my face.

"I want whatever will make you happy." His lips brushed mine in a gentle, brief kiss before he stepped back once more.

In the distance, I heard another voice calling both our names. Alec looked off in that direction.

"Swiftly was searching near the apple grove. Come."

He led the way to the grove, let Swiftly know I was fine, then escorted me to the house. When he tried to steer me toward the library, I groaned.

"Why do you keep insisting that I read?"

"I thought you liked reading."

"I do. But if you recall, I'm not fond of being ordered about. Why does everyone want me to read so badly?"

He stopped walking and turned toward me. Worry etched his features, but his appearance distracted me from it. His hair and clothes were still a mess.

"You should go change and clean up. I'll find something to occupy myself."

He hesitated.

"Have you eaten yet today?" he asked.

"Yes. An egg and a biscuit."

"I believe Kara is making pheasant soup and bread. The bread was in the oven when we left to find you."

My mouth watered at the idea of fresh bread.

"I'll check to see if it's done," I said, already turning.

"I'll join you. There's no point in changing when I plan to pick more apples yet today."

We walked to the kitchen together. I suspected his reluctance to change had more to do with keeping an eye on me than concern over dirtying another shirt.

When I stepped into the kitchen, I saw everyone already at the table. My steps faltered when I met Otta's gaze.

I'd thought when Otta had exposed herself as Rose the night of the feast that Otta wouldn't return. Her presence as Rose in the woods had firmed the belief that I wouldn't see Otta again. Yet, there she was.

"Are you all right?" Alec asked, reaching around to steady me.

I plastered a smile on my face and met his gaze. Determination and worry kept me from glancing in Otta's direction again as I nodded.

"I have a tray ready," Kara said from the butcher's block, pulling Alec's attention from me.

"Thank you," he said. "I'll carry it."

I turned and left the kitchen without waiting for him. My heart was pounding. Should I tell him? I'd kept Sara's secret and learned my lesson. Yet, Rose wasn't doing anything to hurt me. Nor had she caused any problems since the announcement. Telling Alec she was here would anger him; and undoubtedly, his temper would cause trouble.

Worrying my bottom lip, I hurried my steps to the library. Father sat behind his desk, reading yet another book. He looked up when I entered.

"Benella," he said, standing. He came and hugged me. "I'd hoped you and I might speak privately. You ran out too quickly this morning."

"I'm sorry about that, Father. Yes, we should speak," I said, thinking of Rose, "but Alec is just behind me with our meal."

"Afterward then?"

I agreed. Alec entered a moment later and set the tray on the table before the fire. Father sat in his chair and Alec next to me on the lounge.

"Without needing a celebratory feast, how soon can we wed?" I asked as he passed our plates to us.

He glanced at me, then Father, then cleared his throat.

"I will write Mr. Pactel today and inquire when he might be available. Would you prefer the ceremony in his home or here?"

"Here, please," I said before testing the soup. Hot and delicious, I took another quick bite.

"Is there a reason to rush?" my father asked, sounding nervous and strained at the same time.

"No," I said quickly with a glance at Alec. "There is no reason to wait either."

Father nodded and considered his soup. Something weighed his mind, but he remained silent. Alec picked up his soup and began to eat as Bryn's words came back to me.

"Father, I'm not pregnant."

Alec choked and sputtered on his soup. I patted his back absently while meeting my father's pained gaze.

"I swear. That is not the reason for a quick wedding. I don't care if others think that, but I don't want you to think it. I've settled my mind, so there is no reason to wait. I'll wed Alec but I want nothing to do with the pomp of Bryn's wedding. I want a simple dinner with those who mean the most to me. It takes little to plan for that."

I realized I still patted Alec, though he'd stopped making noise. Turning to him, I found his face flushed.

"Are you all right? I should have warned you, the soup is hot."

He shook his head, cleared his throat, and addressed my father.

"If you would prefer we wait—"

"No. Benella is right. She has never been the type of girl to fawn over a dress," here he smiled at me, "or waste time. A quick wedding suits her, and I have no objections."

"I will write the letter and send Swiftly with it today," Alec said.

Once we finished our soup, he went to his study to pen the letter, and I took the tray to the kitchen after a promise to return.

Kara was washing the bowls when I set the tray on the block.

"Would you like some help?" I asked.

"No. There's not much to do besides this. I already have a stew for dinner on the fire."

"Kara, Lord Ruhall and I were just discussing the wedding."

She immediately stopped washing and turned to me.

"Have you already decided how many guests?" Nervous excitement laced her words, and I smiled.

"Yes. Only those who live in this house. As I'm sure you've noticed, most people here have shunned me because of—"

"It shouldn't matter. You're marrying a lord. No one would say no."

"Exactly. They would only attend to be seen, to find favor or elevate their standing in the community. I've been used enough. I don't want that for my wedding day."

Understanding lit her gaze.

"Of course not. What did you have in mind?"

"The ceremony will be here with a dinner afterward. Everyone here can attend. I'm fond of roast if you think it manageable."

"A wedding roast," she said, nodding. I could see she was already planning. "When?"

"I'm not certain, yet. Lord Ruhall is sending a note to the Head as we speak. Soon though, I hope. I would prefer not to wait."

"I will let Mr. Crow know," she said. "Please tell me as soon as you've set the date."

I left her in the kitchen to plan and returned to the study. Alec was already gone and Father was waiting.

"I admit I was surprised when Lord Ruhall announced your engagement at the feast," Father said, as I sat beside him. "You'd given me the impression you were still opposed to the idea."

"At the time of his announcement, I was." His brows rose. "However, since then, I've realized several things. He truly does care for me. He doesn't always show it well, but it's there. I trust him completely, and I can't see myself with anyone else."

"Do you love him?"

"Yes, I do. It's frightening and makes me feel sick with worry at times; but it also warms me. When he's near, I feel safe and loved."

Father smiled and hugged me.

"Good," he said close to my ear. "I'm glad something pleasant is coming from everything that's happened."

"Something very pleasant," I said, pulling away. "But there is a reason to hurry this wedding."

"Oh?"

"Otta is Rose, Aryana, whoever. She's here, and she's watching."

His mouth dropped open.

"My hope is the sooner we're wed, the sooner she will leave."

"Have you told Alec?"

I shook my head.

"Can you imagine his temper and what he might do? I think it best to keep this to myself or he'll find himself re-enchanted."

Father nodded slowly.

"Then, we will see what the Head has to say."

* * * *

Swiftly returned by dinner with the Head's answer. Alec and I would marry in seven days. Alec called the staff together to make the announcement and to invite them to join us in celebrating our union. A few displayed shock. I wasn't sure what reaction Otta gave as I kept my gaze purposefully averted from hers.

Egrit's reaction, however, was hard to avoid. She rushed to me, her arms spread wide to wrap me in a breath defying hug. The excited squeal she let loose while she was pressed to my ear nearly deafened me.

"I'm so happy for you," she breathed before she let me go. She beamed at me, a wide and almost crazed smile, before Tam gently pulled her away.

Mr. Crow hushed the gathering and turned to me.

"Do you have any special instructions?"

I thought for a moment then shook my head.

He gave a slight nod and motioned for everyone to return to their duties. Alec wrapped his hand around mine and led me back to the library. Father was already gone for the evening.

"Will you read to me?" Alec asked, already moving to select a book.

I smiled and sat on the lounge, pretending that a swarm of butterflies hadn't invaded my insides. Alec brought me a book then moved to close the library door.

"Why are you closing the door?" I asked warily. He'd never closed it before.

He chuckled.

"Look at the book."

I glanced at it and found no title on the leather cover. Opening it, I discovered why. A fiery blush claimed my face as I stared at the sketched image of a naked woman in the arms of a man. My eyes devoured the caption, "The many ways to please a woman."

"I can't read this." I turned a few pages and found the amount of descriptive instruction equal to the images.

Alec sat beside me, and I jumped.

"And that is why you should read it," he said. "Your only experience with this has been unpleasant."

I opened my mouth to argue, and he silenced me with a finger over my lips.

"Because of your experiences, you're afraid of something that can be quite pleasant. I don't trust Bryn to instruct you as your mother might have, and I surmise your father would prefer to ignore the subject completely. I thought if you read this, you might not be so nervous on our wedding night."

He lowered his hand, and I glanced at the book once more with a frown.

"Not aloud, though," I said, looking up to silently plead with him.

He sighed and nodded.

"To yourself might be wise. But promise you'll come to me with questions."

"Yes. I swear."

I couldn't relax and read until he went to his study. Then, for the next hour, I found the answers to questions I hadn't known to ask and a few that Aryana had refused to answer. Before long, the room—and my face—grew too warm to continue. Closing the book gently, I stared into the flames and considered what I'd learned.

Alec thought I feared our wedding night. I didn't fear it because I knew he wasn't the baker or Tennen. Yet, I hadn't looked forward to it, either. The book had me reconsidering. The author expounded on the need to tease a woman's body before introducing one's manhood. The ridiculous term, even in my head, made me wince.

"Are you finished?"

Alec's voice startled me, and I squeaked and turned. He stood just behind me, looking down at me. I quickly stood, clutching the book.

"For tonight. I'd like to keep it, if that's all right."

He nodded and offered his arm.

"Shall we retire?"

I set my hand upon his arm and let him lead me from the room.

That night, he only waited until I slid beneath the covers to join me. He pulled me back against his chest and set his arm about my waist as he usually did.

"Thank you," he said softly.

"For what?"

"For staying. For agreeing to be my wife. For saving me from a life of depravity, deceit, and devastation."

But had I saved him? I couldn't be sure until we wed and Rose left us in peace.

*   *   *   *

I woke with my head on Alec's chest and my leg over his thighs. He wore a nightshirt and linen shorts. Regardless of his proper sleep attire, embarrassment would have flooded me, had it not been for the hand currently kneading my breast.

His touch was light yet, I still felt a thread of concern. Was he preparing me for more as the book had suggested?

I lifted my head to meet his gaze.

"Good morning," he whispered, continuing his gentle massage.

"Good morning. Shouldn't you be gone already?"

"There's too much to keep me here," he said.

Suddenly, he rolled so I was under him. Before I could panic, he ducked his head and closed his mouth over my nipple. I gasped in shock then pleasure as he suckled gently, sending waves of need rolling over me. Threading my fingers through his hair, I held him and tried to remember to breathe.

He lifted his head and grinned down at me.

"May I do that again tomorrow morning?"

That was all he wanted to do? I eagerly nodded.

"You can do it again now, if you'd like."

He chuckled.

"I think not. We'll be missed if we linger too long."

With disappointment, I watched him flip back the covers and leave the bed. He didn't turn back to look at me as he strode across the room and left me alone with my racing pulse.

I washed and dressed; and, by the time I finished, my pulse had returned to normal.

I opened the door to my room and found Alec waiting for me in the hall just as he had so long ago. His attendance touched something inside me and banished the remaining threads of doubt regarding our future together. I smiled at him and accepted his arm.

We spent the day together playing games in the library. Father joined us for a few of the games but mostly left us to our own amusement. Once Father retired after dinner, I again picked up the book and read until the room grew too warm. Alec escorted me to bed without comment.

Though he joined me and snuggled me predictably, my pulse still leapt at the memory of what had transpired that morning and what he'd promised would occur again. With a smile of anticipation, I closed my eyes.

He woke me with insistent kisses on my cheek, jaw, and neck. As soon as my eyes fluttered open, he kissed his way lower. My shirt already lay open for him, and I arched, reveling at the sensation of his exploring lips. His mouth closed over the same breast as the day before. The pleasant heat spread to my stomach and lower.

When he lifted his head, I gave him a sleepy smile.

"Good morning," he whispered.

"It is," I agreed.

He placed a kiss on the valley between my breasts then sat up. I wanted to pull him back down and beg him to continue for just a while longer. I considered doing just that, until he lifted a tray from beside the bed and turned to me.

"Please tell me Egrit did not bring that," I said with worry.

He laughed, his amused grin making him impossibly handsome.

"I went to the kitchen and brought this myself."

"In your nightshirt?"

He laughed loudly, and I clapped a hand over his mouth to muffle the sound. He licked my palm, pulled my hand away, and kissed my knuckles.

"Don't worry. I put on pants." He leaned back and picked up a piece of dried apple from the tray and fed it to me.

"Phillip mentioned we have a fair store of meat and lard but are low on everything else. Mrs. Wimbly did the purchasing when she was here, traveling to Konrall for flour and occasionally visiting the Water for produce. However, Mr. Crow wasn't sure if you wanted Kara to attempt it or if you wanted to make the purchases yourself during your next trip to the Water."

"I can make the purchases. Do we have apples to trade?"

"We do. Will you take Swiftly with you?"

"Of course."

* * * *

Swiftly pulled the wagon to a stop in the market district and hopped down from his seat. As he came around to help me from my perch, I took a fortifying breath and eyed the different merchant stores that offered produce. The last time I'd tried to trade hadn't gone well.

"Thank you," I said. "If you want to stay with the apples, I'll see if I can find someone willing to trade."

The first merchant greeted me with an air of indifference and said he would take a basket from me but only offered a few coppers.

"There are apples everywhere," he said. "It's harvest season. You won't find a better price."

I thanked him and tried several more merchants only to receive similar answers. With a frown, I returned to the wagon.

"They're not worth the trade. We would be better served to press the majority into tart cider as my father suggested." That meant I would need to part with some gold to buy the supplies I needed. Supplies we couldn't bring back with a wagon full of apples.

"Let's move the wagon to the trade street, Swiftly."

Doors opened before we even parked. Homes with children received the milk and cheese Kara had sent; however, the apples were so plentiful, we gave some to every house. Retta's mother didn't ask about her children, but she did thank us for the apples.

Back on the market street, I went to the merchants who had advertised the lowest prices and purchased sacks of vegetables and a small bag of sugar. While I waited by the wagon for Swiftly to carry the sacks, a familiar voice called my name.

I turned and saw Blye briskly walking my way. Her bright smile confused me, as did her exuberant hug.

"You look well," she said, her volume hurting my ear. She pulled back and smiled at me as she gave my arms a sisterly squeeze. Her gaze slid to the side then returned.

"How are the wedding plans? Have you and Lord Ruhall set a date?"

Movement around us slowed, and I realized her game. I averted my gaze to hide my anger and spotted Ila not far away. Her gaze met mine, and I found understanding there.

"Excuse me, Blye," I said, pulling from her false embrace. "I don't have much time here and need to speak with someone." I turned toward Ila.

Behind me, Blye twittered.

"I understand. I'll see you soon," she called.

Ila smiled in greeting as I joined her. Her hug felt true and welcoming.

"How are things with you?" I asked, withdrawing from her embrace. We started a slow walk toward the house of the Sisters.

"Well," she said with an excited grin. "Henick came to take me for a ride yesterday." Her eyes sparkled with excitement. It was the most animated I'd ever seen her.

"Ila, I'm so happy for you. He knows everything, then?"

She nodded. "Just as you said, he didn't care. Have you started to make plans for your wedding? Is your sister making your dress now that you'll be Lady Ruhall?"

I snorted in a very unlady like way.

"No, Blye will not make my dress, though I'm sure she'd like to. I'll wear the one you made me. Alec contacted the Head, and we'll marry in a week. I would like you to attend, Ila. It will be a very quiet ceremony," I said quickly, "so please don't mention it."

"I won't say a word. And I would be delighted to attend."

When we reached her house, she turned around and started the walk back to the wagon with me. Swiftly had everything loaded when she and I parted with a final hug.

"I will see you soon," she said with a wave. Her words made me smile.

*   *   *   *

The time until the wedding whittled away. Alec entertained me with walks, games, and fishing during the day. At night, I continued reading the book. The author's descriptions, and Alec's attentions when I woke, convinced me there could be more to the experience than I'd been exposed to. Though it reduced my hesitancy and my fears, nervous anticipation remained.

The day before my wedding dawned bright. I found myself on my back, my shirt spread open, and Alec's fingers tracing an idle path between my sternum and bellybutton.

"Good morning," he said with a secret smile that made my toes curl.

"Good morning."

Though he hadn't touched them, my breasts already ached because I knew what was to come. He didn't disappoint. He leaned over and set his mouth on me. I closed my eyes with a contented sigh. His fingers continued to trail my stomach, then down my legs. I knew what he was about and didn't mind. I trusted him and relaxed my legs.

Instead of trailing closer to where I ached, he pulled away from me altogether and stared down at me.

His face was flushed and full of want.

"One more day," he said, his voice husky, "then you're mine. Forever."

I nodded. "One more day." Saying it made my nerves jump but I didn't let it show.

"What would you like to do today?"

"If Kara doesn't mind, let's do something in the kitchen. We can do better than coddled eggs and egg tartlets."

He grinned and nodded.

"Dress," he said. "I'll meet you there."

I quickly obeyed and hurried to the kitchen, excited to spend another day with him. To my surprise, Bryn was at the block, kneading dough. When Alec had confronted her at the bakery, I hadn't given any thought to her returning to work in his kitchen.

She looked up at me, hurt painting her face.

"Were you going to tell me?" she asked.

I knew she meant the wedding.

"You've made it quite clear you want nothing to do with me as your sister, and I want nothing to do with you as Lady Ruhall."

Her gaze turned sad, and she nodded.

"I have. And I'm sorry for it. I hope one day that changes."

I inclined my head, neither agreeing nor disagreeing and left the kitchen. As much as I didn't want her there, I didn't have it in me to turn her away for Edmund's sake and her babe.

Alec met me in the hallway.

"Do you no longer wish to cook?"

"No. I was thinking we might talk to Father about fermenting apples."

Thus, we spent the day before our wedding pressing apples.

* * * *

Egrit woke me with a chipper good morning and a laugh when I sat up in a panic.

"Don't worry. I warned him I would wake you this morning."

I blushed crimson as she took my gown from the wardrobe and laid it out on the bed.

"Would you like a bath?"

I shook my head no. Sticky with the juice from far too many apples, I'd had no choice but to bathe the night before. My hair was oiled and dry.

"To relax?"

"Not now, but I might need one after dinner."

"Then, if you're ready, there is someone here to see you. She thought you might like company and offered to do your hair."

A smile lit my face.

"Ila?"

Egrit nodded.

I spent a pleasant morning closed in my room with Ila. She took her time braiding and weaving my hair and helped me into my dress.

"Do you have any questions about tonight?" she asked. "Are you nervous? Frightened? It would be understandable if you were."

"I am nervous but not afraid."

"Good," she said, stepping back to eye her work. "You are a beauty."

I laughed lightly.

"Thanks to your efforts. Thank you for staying with me, Ila."

She hugged me tightly. "I'm glad I'm here." When she pulled back, she wrapped my hand around her arm and led me from the room. My heart fluttered at the reality of what would soon take place. I would marry Alec.

Neither of us spoke as we walked down the hall toward the library. My nerves prevented it, and she seemed to understand.

All my trepidation evaporated when we turned the corner, and I spotted Alec pacing outside the library doors. He froze when he saw me. Beside me, Ila excused herself and went in.

Alec and I stared at each other for a moment before he exhaled slowly and strode toward me. He was dressed in dark pants and a matching jacket. A red bloom was tucked into the lapel, matching the threads in my gown.

When he reached me, his blue gaze swept over me.

"You are beautiful," he breathed. He reached for me, gently running his knuckles along my cheek.

"Will you stay? Will you be my wife?"

I turned my head to kiss his hand.

"I will stay. I will be your wife."

He pulled me close and set his lips on mine. The passion behind his kiss robbed me of thought.

A throat cleared and reluctantly Alec pulled back. I blinked at him and then glanced toward the doors. My father stood there, his amused smile causing me to grin in return.

"I wanted to hug you one last time as my daughter before you become Lady Ruhall," he said, approaching me.

Eagerly, I hugged him.

"I love you, Father."

"And I you." He held me tightly for a moment more before surrendering me to Alec.

Alec offered his arm as Father went inside. Holding him tightly, I let Alec walk me in.

The Head waited for us along with a small audience. I barely saw them or heard what the Head said. Time moved too quickly and soon Alec was speaking his vows to love and honor me in this life and the next. Nerves danced in my stomach as I realized my turn had come. Taking a calming breath, I spoke my vows to do the same.

Cheers erupted around us, and Alec pulled me in for another kiss. Another throat clearing and good-natured laughter forced us apart so he could lead me to the dining room.

Someone had set the length of the table. Alec took the seat at the head with me at his right and Father at his left. Everyone joined us and that was when I noticed my sisters. Bryn quietly sat beside Father. She didn't look at me. Instead, she struck up a quiet conversation with Father.

Blye almost sat beside me, but Egrit stopped her.

"One seat over, Miss Hovtel."

Ila took the seat beside me, and I sighed in relief.

Mr. Crow, Kara, and Egrit brought the food out. As I'd asked, they had kept it simple. We served ourselves and passed the portions to the next person. Conversation flowed around the table, and it was a relaxing meal...until Ila excused herself for a moment.

Blye took that as an opportunity to speak to me.

"Now that you're Lady Ruhall, you'll need new dresses. I could stay here and work on them."

The horror of the idea certainly had to have shown on my face because the conversation around the table quieted. I looked away and caught Otta glaring at Blye. I wanted to smile at her.

"No," Alec said. "You will not make her dresses, and you aren't welcome to stay here any longer than it takes for you to visit with your father."

Blye's face flushed scarlet, but she said nothing further. Ila returned and eyed the quiet table as she resumed her seat.

She leaned toward me and softly asked if everything was all right.

"Yes," I said, taking a bite of roast.

"It's been brought to my attention," Alec said to Ila, "that Benella is in need of a few more dresses in her role as a Lady. The dress she wears now is beautiful, and I would like to see her have a few more of that quality."

I frowned at Alec, not for his snub of my sister, but for asking for additional extravagant dresses.

"This might be a bit more formal than I will need for every day," I said diplomatically.

Ila laughed and patted my hand.

"Have no worry. I know what kind of dress you like."

She did. I smiled at her and turned to Alec.

"I still prefer my pants," I whispered.

He choked a bit on his food and shook his head at me. As we finished, Bryn and Kara collected the empty plates and asked us to remain seated as they excused themselves. When they returned, they carried a large cake.

"Edmund and I made it for you. A gift to celebrate how sweet life can be. If you let it," she said quietly.

My eyes watered. I wasn't ready to trust her to be my sister, but her gift, her words, and her new consideration of Father gave me hope.

* * * *

A tub of water waited in my room when I finally excused myself from the table. I sent a silent word of thanks to Egrit and stripped off my gown.

The manor was settling in for a quiet evening, and I knew what that meant for me. Nerves coiled in my stomach. By giving me the book, Alec had hoped to ease my fear of the unknown. Though I appreciated his thoughtfulness, the author's side notes about easing the pain of the first time hadn't reassured me. I would have preferred to remain ignorant of that part.

With a shaking hand, I hung the dress in the wardrobe then padded to the water. Steam curled from the surface. I'd no sooner slipped into the water when the connecting doors opened. I jumped slightly and turned to watch Alec enter. His gaze locked onto mine as he slowly closed the door behind him.

"Will you douse me with water if I watch you?" Though the words were playfully said, his expression remained serious.

"No, husband, I won't." I attempted a smile while trying to calm my stomach.

He didn't linger by the door but came to the tub and knelt beside it, watching me as he rolled his sleeves from his corded forearms.

"Are you afraid?" he asked.

"Are you?"

"Very. I'm afraid you'll run or worse, stay and hate me afterward."

Hearing his fears helped ease a few of mine.

"I won't hate you, Alec."

He looked down and dipped a finger in the water. My pulse leapt because I knew he could see me clearly. Yet, he didn't reach for me. Instead, he exhaled slowly.

"You didn't answer. Are you afraid?"

"No, not afraid. Very nervous." I lifted my hand from the water and held it out so he could see my tremble.

He glanced at my hand, and his expression took on a pained appearance. I reached for his hand and held it.

"Nerves have never stopped me before," I said softly.

He met my gaze, and his lips curved in the barest of smiles.

"And for that, I am grateful."

He stood, keeping hold of my hand. When he gave a gentle tug, I knew he wanted me to rise. My heart beat harder as I rose. His gaze drifted down my torso then back up again.

"Wife. A lifetime will not be long enough."

The warm bath water lapped at my calves as his fingers remained locked around mine. He swallowed hard several times and released my hand. His heated gaze lifted to meet mine as he reached out to trace a finger along the underside of my breast. It took a large amount of effort to keep my breathing steady.

"Will you promise to tell me if you become frightened?"

His thumb brushed over my nipple, and I shivered.

"Yes. I promise."

He dipped his head and kissed my shoulder.

"Do you promise not to run?"

His lips skimmed my skin from collarbone to the top of my breast. I brought my hands up and dug my fingers in his hair. A small noise escaped me as his breath washed over my nipple.

"Benella. Do you swear?"

"I swear."

His mouth closed over me. The strong pull sent a tingle to my stomach and further still to the point between my legs. Too quickly, the insistent tug stopped. His lips moved from my nipple, nuzzling me and spreading kisses from one breast to the next before he lifted his head. My hands fell loosely to my sides. His eyes glinted with fervor as he studied me closely, a hungry beast once more.

He wrapped his hand around mine and helped me step from the tub.

"Sit on the bed, Benella."

My pulse thundered, and my knees felt weak as I turned to do as he asked.

Sitting, I looked up at him as he unbuttoned his shirt. The bare expanse of his chest claimed my attention as he shrugged the garment off. I exhaled slowly. He knelt before me, and I clenched my hands in my lap to hide the shaking. He reached for them and smoothed a thumb over my knuckles. Our gazes remained locked as he leaned forward and placed a kiss on my knee.

My breath hitched as I recalled the last time he'd kissed me there. He lifted his head again.

"Will you give me everything?"

"Yes."

His hold on my hands shifted to my legs. His fingers traced my skin from knee to ankle as he kissed higher up my leg.

"Lay back."

With a blush, I lay back on the bed and opened myself to him. He made a low sound and fitted his torso between my legs.

The first touch of his tongue made me gasp. My fingers fisted in the covers, and I arched, trying to press myself against him. He set a hand on my stomach to hold me in place as his tongue circled my sensitive nub. A small noise escaped me.

"My beauty," he said as he teased me. "My heart."

His free hand stroked the inside of my leg, knee to thigh, then teased the hair between my legs. His tongue distracted me from his intention until his finger probed my opening. I tensed, expecting a painful thrust, but none came. He continued to tease me with his tongue while he idly explored with his fingers.

After a few moments, I relaxed and lost myself to the sensations of his mouth on me. A familiar need began to build, and I groaned with want. He closed his mouth over my nub and began to suckle. I gasped and twisted my fingers in his hair. He sucked hard and flicked his tongue at the same time he slowly slid a finger into me. The invasion didn't take away from the tension coiling tighter and tighter inside me. He eased his finger out then back in, and my legs began to tense. My release was close.

His mouth and hand left me. Dazedly, I opened my eyes. He stood between my legs as he stripped away his pants. Before I had time to worry, he leaned over me and bent his head to my breast. His hot mouth tugged on my nipple as he ran a hand between my legs.

Something pressed insistently against my opening. He switched to torment my other breast, distracting me from thought, then kissed a trail up to my collarbone. He claimed my lips for a searing kiss before pulling away to look down on me. With both hands braced on the bed, one on each side of me, his heated gaze met mine.

It took a moment to realize the pressure had remained between my legs.

"I love you," he said as he slowly pressed forward.

A sudden sharp pain had me bracing my hands against his bare chest. He stopped moving and began raining kisses upon my brow.

"Wait," he said. "Please, wait. It is a moment of pain for a lifetime of pleasure. I swear."

I heard the fear in his voice and held myself still. After a moment, the pain faded.

Tilting my head back, I found his face so close to mine. His jaw was tense and sweat dotted his skin.

"It's better now," I said.

He kissed me hard.

"No, but it soon will be."

He reached between us and set his thumb on my sensitive spot. He circled it twice then started to move his hips. I drifted in the pleasure of his touch, reveling in the coiling tension, while I gasped and reached for the release I knew would come.

With a cry, I found it. He thrust into me several more times before he groaned and stilled. His sweaty chest pressed against me. Between us, he twitched within me.

"Tell me you don't hate me."

"I don't hate you. I love you."

He kissed me soundly.

* * * *

A noise woke me in the middle of the night. When I opened my eyes, I found Rose beside the bed and sat up with a gasp. Panic flooded me while Alec remained undisturbed in his slumber.

"What are you doing here?" I asked.

"I'm here to thank you, Benella," she said, surprising and confusing me. "And to say good-bye. What I set out to do has been done. Alec has found purpose and love. I only hope that someday you'll forgive me for the lies and manipulations I used to bring you two together."

"You're leaving?" I didn't trust that I'd understood her correctly.

She smiled at me.

"Yes. As I promised. I was only waiting for you to see the truth. A truth I saw within you so long ago when your family first came to this area. The possibility of love—for him."

"What do you mean when we first came here? I didn't meet you until we moved to the Water."

She studied me for a moment before answering.

"I've watched over the North for a long time. I knew of you as soon as you entered its boundaries. I've watched you since you were young, observed how you overcame each trial life gave you. You are intelligent, determined, courageous, and kind. And I knew once I sent you to the beast, you would find a way to free him. Yet, I worried for you. Your strength was also your weakness. You were too kind. Too willing to sacrifice yourself for those you cared for. I helped you as much as I could while still keeping both of you unaware. Alec had so much to learn; you had so much to teach him.

"Hold fast to your love for one another, and this life will not disappoint you. You will balance each other well."

She turned to go.

"Wait," I said, believing she really meant it. Though I still resented the way I'd been used, I also realized, without her manipulations, I wouldn't have met Alec.

She stopped and looked back at me.

I slipped from the bed, unconcerned with my nakedness and crossed the room.

"I already forgive you. Thank you for sending me here, for bringing me him."

Rose surprised me by sniffling.

"I wanted to spare you but not as much as I wanted you to truly find happiness." She hugged me tightly.

"You don't need to leave."

"I do," she whispered in my ear, "but I will return for the birth of your babes."

She pulled away and left the room. I returned to bed, and Alec pulled me close.

"She's gone?" he asked, his hand settling over my stomach.

"For now," I said.

Epilogue

A breeze played with my hair as I sat on the bench in the orchard. Tam glanced at me and gave a nervous smile. I smiled back, trying to reassure him. From somewhere behind us, a sweet soprano rang out in a song about union and love.

Alec offered his arm and helped me stand. I absently rubbed a hand over the bump of the babe's foot, currently lodged just below my ribs, while turning to face the back with the rest of those assembled. Egrit walked the path between the apple trees. She wore a green dress Ila had made for her. Delicately embroidered leaves adorned the skirt, and a wreath of real leaves adorned Egrit's hair. I glanced at Tam wondering if he saw the wood nymph I remembered. Based on the love in his gaze, I decided he saw the nymph and the woman as well.

Egrit gave me a radiant smile as she passed us on her way to Tam. As soon as the two clasped hands, the short ceremony began. After the Head announced the union between them, I heard Tam breathe "finally" right before pulling Egrit into his arms for a passionate kiss.

Alec wrapped his arm around me and pulled me tight to his side.

"I know just how he feels," he whispered in my ear. "I remember well the moment I realized you were finally mine."

I smiled and turned toward him. He was ready with a kiss.

"None of that now," Father said from beside me. "This is about Egrit and Tam."

I laughed and pulled back to see Tam reluctantly doing the same. The pair waved to the well-wishers and invited everyone to join them inside for dancing and a feast. Most of Konrall was there, and hosting the wedding was our gift to the bride and groom.

The children on the bench behind us cheered. I turned to grin at Retta, Lettie, Mrs. Palant and her little ones, and the new children who'd joined us over the passing months. Like before, Mrs. Palant kept the young ones busy with light chores in the evening, but mostly they were with us for their education and care. My smile grew bigger as I thought how Father had even started teaching with Mr. Roost, dividing the class to make it more manageable.

As soon as Tam and Egrit passed us, we stood and followed the newly wedded couple. As we passed by the Kinlyn clan, who were all seated on a bench near the back, I grinned at Ila who sat next to her husband, Henick. He'd found his rainbow in her.

The walk inside took longer than it should have because of my waddle. My back started to ache, but I kept any sign of discomfort from my face. Regardless, Alec glanced at me continually. He knew.

"Don't even consider it," I warned him.

"If I carried you—"

"You'd draw attention to us. This is about Egrit and Tam."

He made a slight growling noise, which made me grin.

"Beast," I whispered.

"Beauty," he said, bending to kiss my cheek.

I snorted.

"Only you would think an apple with legs beautiful."

He threw his head back and laughed. Then, despite my warning, he scooped me up in his arms.

"You are hardly an apple, madam." He stepped aside so the guests could pass us.

There were no censuring looks, only knowing grins. When Bryn spotted me, she moved to the side to stand with us.

"Is everything well?" she asked.

Since our wedding, Bryn had changed considerably. She'd started visiting Father regularly and stopped worrying about her social standing. Instead, she'd focused on her marriage. It was easy to see she and Edmund were truly happy now as Edmund carried little Benard, who babbled and watched the leaves above us.

"Everything is well. The walk taxes my back," I said, assuring her.

Once her selfish nature had disappeared, I'd welcomed her visits as well. Alec hadn't been as quick to forgive. It was only her genuine concern for the babe and me that had brought him around.

"And she was too slow," Alec said with a teasing smile.

"She'll slow down more," Edmund said. "Like a loaf of bread. When the rising slows, it's done."

Bryn made a sound between a laugh and a groan.

"You would compare pregnancy to a loaf of bread?" She shook her head and laughed when he grinned at her.

The last of the guests filed past us, and Edmund moved to follow.

"I'll take little Benard in and see if we can't give Kara a hand in the kitchen."

While Bryn gave her son and husband a quick kiss, I nudged Alec.

"Put me down."

"Not until we're inside. You wouldn't want to tire yourself before we even have a chance to dance, would you?"

I shook my head and looped my arm around his shoulders as he started to walk behind Edmund. Bryn kept us company.

"I received a letter from Blye yesterday," she said.

"Oh? Has she found a suitable shop, yet?"

"Yes, she'd found one since her last letter, but I don't think she'll be there long. Her mistress doesn't care for the extravagance of Blye's creations," she said with a smile. Recalling Blye's gown for the feast, I had no doubt Blye's mistress had valid concerns.

"She mentioned she wrote Father, too," Bryn said.

I nodded, having read the letter as well.

"Nothing as detailed as you received. Just that she was doing well and sends her love to all of us. How far south is she now?"

"Almost to Towdown."

"I'm sure that's been her destination all along," Alec said.

We broke through the trees to the breathtaking view of the manor. The vines and vegetation were gone, replaced by a fine lawn under Tam's care. People milled about the front entrance, congratulating Egrit and Tam.

"I agree," I said to Alec's observation. Blye wouldn't be happy until she was making gowns for the rich and elite of Towdown, the center of trade. No, she wouldn't even be happy then. She'd want to become one of them.

For a moment, I felt pity for Blye. Her search for material wealth and social standing wouldn't bring her happiness. Happiness wasn't so easily obtained. It took kindness and some true sacrifice, neither concept truly understood by my sister.

I sighed and ran my fingers through the hair at the nape of Alec's neck. He glanced at me, a look so full of longing and love that my pulse fluttered. His expression turned knowing as I flushed and gave him a small, secret smile.

"Bryn, I think Benella is feeling a bit worn. I'll take her to her room to rest for a few minutes before we join the feast."

Bryn laughed and waved us ahead as Alec's stride lengthened.

"I'll make excuses for both of you. Don't take too long."

"No, not too long," he said, pressing a kiss to my cheek. "Just a lifetime."

Authors Note

I hope you enjoyed the conclusion of the Beastly Tales!

Did you know I also write young adult romance under Melissa Haag? Keep reading for more information about Touch and Hope(less).

Your support keeps me writing, so please consider letting others know about this story by leaving a review on Goodreads or any of the retailer sites where this title is available.

Happy reading!

Melissa

HOPE(LESS)

A riveting sweet romance by Melissa Haag

It's lonely being different, but Gabby's adapted. Really. Until she meets werewolf Clay.

Clay is everything she doesn't want. Unkempt and quiet, he watches her too closely. And yet, if he's everything she doesn't want, why does she need him so much?

Discover werewolves and young women with unexplained abilities in Hope(less).

Touch
A young adult romance by Melissa Haag

Home before sunset.
Sleep before dark.
Never go outside at night.

According to the family curse, Tessa needs to find "the right boy" before her next birthday or she'll be living by those rules forever. It should be easy. After all, with a touch, she can see her future with a boy...a future where he dies young. She would do anything to get rid of her curse, except follow in her ancestors' footsteps.

Then, she meets Morik. He's a demon and the reason behind the visions and the rules. He long ago brokered a deal with Tessa's ancestors, and he's come to collect.

Tessa has a choice to make. Stand before Morik as her ancestors failed to do or continue to hide from what waits in the dark. Her time to decide is running out.

CPSIA information can be obtained
at www.ICGtesting.com
Printed in the USA
FSOW01n2014210716
23011FS